LOVE IN THE BARGAIN

ALSO BY KASEY STOCKTON

Women of Worth Series

Love for the Spinster

Love at the House Party

Love in the Wager

Love in the Ballroom

Ladies of Devon Series

The Jewels of Halstead Manor

The Lady of Larkspur Vale

The Widow of Falbrooke Court

The Recluse of Wolfeton House

The Smuggler of Camden Court

Stand Alone Regency Romance

His Amiable Bride

A Duke for Lady Eve

All is Mary and Bright

A Forgiving Heart

An Agreeable Alliance

Scottish Historical Romance

Journey to Bongary Spring

Through the Fairy Tree

Love in the Bargain

WOMEN OF *Worth* BOOK ONE

Kasey Stockton

GOLDEN OWL
PRESS

This is a work of fiction. Names, characters, places, and incidents either are the product of the author's imagination or are used fictitiously. Any resemblance to actual persons, living or dead, events, or locales is entirely coincidental.

Copyright © 2019 by Kasey Stockton
Cover design by Once Upon a Cover

First print edition: May 2019
All rights reserved. No part of this book may be reproduced or used in any manner without written permission of the copyright owner except for the use of quotations for the purpose of a book review.

For Jon, my eternal hero.

PROLOGUE

MISS SMYTHE'S SCHOOL FOR GIRLS,
ENGLAND 1810

"If we do this, there is no turning back."

I held my breath as Freya sipped from the ancient silver goblet, her grimace a testament of the distasteful concoction within. She wiped her mouth with the back of her hand and passed me the cup, her twelve-year-old face full of equal parts reverence and disgust.

"You don't have to do this," she whispered.

"Yes you do, Elsie," Rosalynn countered with equal gravity.

I swallowed the lump in my throat. Tears pricked the corners of my eyes, and I nodded once. I had not made this decision lightly.

Cupping the goblet in both of my pale hands, I lifted it to my lips and let the lumpy fluid slide into my mouth. I clamped my lips shut as I sputtered involuntarily. The leftover stew from tonight's dinner mixed with who-knows-what Rosalynn found in the kitchens had a distinctly tart aftertaste, and stew should not be tart.

Shuddering, I swallowed the glob of Promise Juice and set the goblet on the wooden floor in the center of our circle. Rosalynn gripped my hand in hers, giving my other hand a pointed look. Obediently, I clasped Freya's and we all bowed our heads.

Rosalynn began. "With this Promise Juice…"

"With this Promise Juice," Freya and I recited.

"We make a pact…"

"We make a pact."

"That the Sisterhood of Deserving Females shall never let a man determine our worth."

I peeked at Freya out of one eye. She squeezed her eyes closed when I got a jab in the knee by Rosalynn's elbow.

"That the Sisterhood of Deserving Females shall never let a man determine our worth," I repeated, trying to sound confident.

Rosalynn's voice became strong, authoritative. "Nor will we give up our power through matrimony. We will keep our dignity by honoring ourselves foremost. We hereby declare to sustain one another through the perils of society and the ideals that are pressed upon us by our mothers. These things we swear, breaking the bond of the Sisterhood of Deserving Females upon penalty of *death*!"

My fingers ached from Rosalynn's firm grip. I squeezed Freya's hand once supportively, took a deep breath and began the remainder of the oath.

When we completed the vow, we raised our heads. Freya would not look me in the eye, but Rosalynn was in her element. Her rich brown eyes glowed in the candlelight with empowerment and strength.

Our hands dropped to the wooden floor. I felt less changed

than I had anticipated. But alas, I had made a promise that would impact the rest of my life, for the good. I hoped.

"Now," Rosalynn said in her distinctly knowledgeable tone. "Nothing will come between us. We are forever united."

"Except when we leave tomorrow for the summer term," Freya countered with a teary smile. "I will miss you both so much."

"It is only a month," I reminded her, thoughtlessly.

Rosalynn pouted, her energized face turning sullen. "For you two, it is only a month. Then you get to be together while I am stuck in the wild, withdrawn from polite society and forced to endure the company of The Tyrants."

The Tyrants; her nickname for her brothers.

"Summer will pass, and we will be back here at school together before you know it."

A loud thump sounded in the stairwell and we all stilled. "Quick," I whispered, "the candles!"

Turning in unison, we each blew out the candles behind us while heavy footsteps ascended the attic stairs. Mr. Peele's head came through the doorway, his shiny forehead reflecting light from his candle. Leaping to my feet, my foot collided with the forgotten goblet on the floor in my haste. I watched in horror as a spray of the Promise Juice doused Mr. Peele's torso, arm, and lantern.

He let out a yelp and stumbled forward, falling before me on the rough wooden planks.

"Run!" I yelled, jumping over his legs.

I raced down the stairs, hoping the footsteps following behind me were from Freya and Rosalynn's feet, and not those of our school caretaker.

I turned at the landing and raced for my bedroom. Jumping into my bed and pulling up the blankets, I held my breath in a futile attempt to slow my breathing. Two other doors down the corridor closed swiftly and silence ensued.

The thin blanket moved in rhythm with my rapid breathing. I winced when I heard Cecily, my roommate, turn over in her bed and groan. She did not, however, wake up. Minutes later I screwed my eyes shut when the doorknob twisted quietly. I forced myself to relax and my mouth to droop, silently counting slowly in time with my deep, even breaths.

Wincing when the lantern light roamed over my face, I moaned groggily and turned away from it. I hoped my acting was believable, and I cheered internally when I heard Cecily moan softly, the rustle of blankets when she turned over as well.

Time seemed to drag while they searched all of the student bedrooms. It was probably mere minutes later that I heard the headmistress sigh in frustrated defeat while she walked away with Mr. Peele, unable to positively identify the curfew breakers.

I relaxed into the feather mattress and sighed. Perhaps I did feel lighter. I was forever changed, and it had to be for the better.

CHAPTER 1

LONDON, 1816

"For the love of all things holy, you are *not* to tell your Aunt Georgina that we are back in Berkeley Street for the Season," Mother said, fixing her husband with a fierce look.

Father forked a sausage on his plate and shoved it into his mouth, watching her and refusing to respond.

"David, I shall not reside here another moment if that woman—"

"If she what? Calls on us?" Father asked, tossing me a wink before spearing another sausage. "You'll tuck tail and run home?"

I took a bite of the toast on my plate. He had perhaps gone too far this time.

"Mr. Cox," she said acerbically.

Mother only used Father's surname when she was particularly displeased.

"I shall not endure that woman's theatrics for an entire

Season. I refuse! We are trying to bring Elsie out. How are we to find her a husband if your Aunt Georgina scares them all away?"

"Mother," I cut in, swallowing frustration. We must have had this conversation fifty times, at least. "I promised you I would attend the Season. I did not agree to marriage. You know how I feel about that institution."

"That institution brought you into this world, young lady, and I would prefer it if you did not spout nonsense at my breakfast table."

I glanced at my father, but he was busy analyzing the coddled egg on his plate, his bushy eyebrows pulled together. No help at all.

Not that I needed it. I pushed back from the table and rose. "I am expected at Freya's. Her mother is taking us to choose gowns for the Gibsons' ball."

Mother popped a strawberry in her mouth, all the while glaring at Father.

I suppressed a sigh. "I shall be home in time for dinner. Do we have any engagements this evening?"

"No," Mother said around another strawberry, her glare unrelenting.

"Very well, then." I left the breakfast room behind with its multitude of feelings, certain I would never understand the greater intricacies of the marriage relationship. Besides, whatever was the matter with Aunt Georgina anyway? Yes, she was a tad eccentric, but surely she would not force her company upon us.

My parents had been attending the Season each year for longer than I'd been alive. Aunt Georgina had had plenty of opportunities to pester them before now. Yet, in my entire life, I had only met her twice. There was little evidence she was going to suddenly change her desire for a relationship.

I dressed quickly for my outing with Freya and left the house with Molly, my maid. We walked the ten minutes between my

London home and Freya's, and I dismissed Molly the moment I stepped inside the Hurst's townhouse. It was, perhaps, too early to call on an acquaintance by proper etiquette standards, but Freya and I did not bother upholding proper etiquette with one another. I was led into the parlor where Freya and Rosalynn already sat, their heads bent together over something on their laps.

"What is it?" I asked, crossing the room and installing myself on the sofa beside Rosalynn.

"Isn't it magnificent?" Freya lifted the parchment to show me a watercolor portrait of a dog.

It was a rather charming dog and expertly painted. One ear stuck straight up while the other flopped down and a little pink tongue dangled out the side of its mouth.

"She should be named Clementine," I said decisively.

"Yes, I like it," Rosalynn agreed. "I found this in a quaint little shop on Bond Street yesterday and it almost makes me wish to acquire a dog of my own. But alas, I feel I cannot be bothered managing such a creature. So I will simply look at this one instead." Grinning unrepentantly, she put away the painting.

"We cannot leave for the shop yet," Freya said. "Mother is still abed." She tucked a lock of curly, copper hair behind her ear. "I tried to convince her that we could choose our own gowns, but she wouldn't relent." She lifted her dainty shoulder in a shrug. Her hair was mostly pulled up, away from her face in loose waves piled into the semblance of a bun. Her soft features were perpetually turned up, evidence of her cheerful nature.

"*Mothers.*" Rosalynn shook her head, disgusted.

I wanted to scoff—good naturedly, of course. I was proud of myself for smiling instead. "Have The Tyrants come to Town yet?"

"Cameron has." Which I knew already. He had escorted Rosalynn to London only last week. "The rest of my family is traveling down together later. I believe they are set to arrive the day after the Gibsons' ball."

"Then why are you attending?" I asked, with some confusion. Rosalynn was not only morally opposed to men, she also despised formal dancing. On *principle*, if nothing else.

Her lip curled. "Because Cameron *wants* to attend. And he will tell my mother if I fail to do so."

Freya and I exchanged glances. It was apparent we did not have all the information. The way Rosalynn stood and began pacing the Aubusson carpet proved further how much she did not want to fill us in.

But no matter. She would tell us when she was ready.

"Do you think I should choose a nice blue silk to offset my hair?" I asked Freya, fingering my honey colored locks. "I am convinced *you* need to find a green similar to the gown you wore to the school holiday formal—"

"Elsie, you do know that we are limited in our color options, do you not?" Freya's concern was sweet.

Of course I knew debutantes wore pale colors. Mother had not failed to remind me multiple times before agreeing to this outing. I was simply trying to bring Rosalynn out of her pacing and into the conversation.

"Of all the ridiculous—" Rosalynn threw her arms in the air and groaned. She resumed her pacing, mumbling something incoherent under her breath.

Nearly there, but not quite. I asked, innocently, "Can we not wear *any* colors though?"

"Only pale colors," Rosalynn cut in, never breaking stride. "It is supposed to symbolize our *purity*."

"You sound disgusted." Freya said this as though it was an uncommon occurrence. It was not. At least, not where Rosalynn was concerned.

"Are you not?" Rosalynn countered, hands on her hips. "You should be. Why are we bending to such ancient rules?"

I smiled wryly. "I believe it is what some would call tradition."

"Tradition is dull," she muttered.

"Regardless, it is tradition," I said.

"So is marriage, but we are not going to bend that far."

Silence fell upon the room. We each knew the importance of maintaining our childhood vow, the toll that men took on their wives' well-being. Our own fathers had reiterated this to us time and again. One did not grow up with the fathers we each had and look upon the concept of marriage with favor.

A clock chimed in the corridor, breaking the tension, and Rosalynn slumped into a chair.

"What is it?" Freya prodded gently.

Rosalynn took a gulp of air and raised her face to the ceiling. "Mother has decided to take away my inheritance, pending marriage."

We gasped in unison. Rosalynn's inheritance was the very thing that triggered the origin of our Sisterhood of Deserving Females, that made ours a feasible goal. But it wasn't only Rosalynn's. Freya and I were both to be independently wealthy in the future. I had no siblings, and my father's estate was not entailed, so eventually all he owned would be passed down to me. Freya received an inheritance from her maternal grandmother when she was six years old in the form of an estate. She had never before visited the thriving country house, but the reports she found in her father's study were promising, indeed.

"What are you going to do?" I asked.

Rosalynn locked her eyes on me. "I do not know yet. I must live the facade until I work that out, I suppose."

The wheels in her mind were plainly turning. She had a plan, though I could not fathom what it would be. With three older brothers, one of them a future duke, her inheritance took the form of a trust placed in her name years ago. She was not to receive property or the like, but sufficient money to live out her life in comfort. We had all assumed we would end up together one day, living happily under one roof like we once did in school. Only this time, we would be in charge of ourselves.

"It will all work out." It had to. She could move in with me if needs be.

Freya asked, "But how?"

"I don't know," Rosalynn answered, determination lining her brow. "But I agree with Elsie. Somehow, it will all work out."

The mood was heavy when Freya's butler came in to announce that Mrs. Hurst was finally prepared to leave.

Freya pasted on a wide smile. "Shall we drown our woes in beautiful new gowns?"

Rosalynn stood, wiping her hands down her dress to remove invisible lint. Even in distress, she was the most dignified person I knew. Perhaps that was what came of being a daughter to a duke. "Yes, let's."

Freya shot me a worried smile when we followed Rosalynn outside, and I tried to reassure her with a grin.

All was not lost, yet.

Mrs. Hurst bustled about the shop directing each of us in our choice of style, fabric, and embellishments. She was a self-proclaimed expert at matching a woman with her ideal gown, and I had to admit that so far, I had been satisfied with her input.

Watching from one end of the shop while Mrs. Hurst showed Freya a few fashion plates she thought would suit her, I considered how the excursion would have gone differently with my own mother in tow.

It was not an altogether horrid image, but an experience I would perhaps receive less enjoyment in. My mother, though an expert of many things, much like Mrs. Hurst, could not abide being proven wrong. She would dig her heels in and fight me on any opinion for the sheer opportunity of obtaining a victory. Considering that she did not have the option of winning any match against my father, I could see why she chose to exert her authority over me. I did not blame her, entirely, but I did not enjoy it either.

"Freya and Mrs. Hurst are quite the team," Rosalynn said *sotto voce*. "My mother would have merely swept in, directed a few shop girls to measure us, chosen fabrics, then hurried home to await the delivered parcels at her leisure."

"She is of a status where that is possible," I reminded Rosalynn. "Not many people would begrudgingly serve a duchess."

Rosalynn merely glanced away. "It is not really worth the title, though, is it?"

"What is not worth the title?"

"Putting up with my father."

I chose not to respond. I'd heard many stories about the ruthless dictator who ran the Nichols' household. He was not physically abusive, but he was a duke and thus undisputed in all things. His commands were to be followed, regardless of how unreasonable or senseless they seemed, and he frequently ostracized his wife and children.

Rosalynn's mother played the dignified, graceful duchess to perfection. But according to her daughter, she was alone almost always, her pride and geographical distance keeping her from enjoying much of a social life.

Though Freya and I had visited each other's homes numerous times during school holidays, neither of us had ever been invited to Rosalynn's Northumberland estate.

Mrs. Hurst bustled toward us, beaming. "I think that is everything, girls. Shall we be off then? Gloves next, I should think."

Rosalynn leaned in to whisper as we followed Freya and her mother from the shop. "Is she always this cheerful?"

While Rosalynn had visited our homes on occasion, I had the benefit of spending more time with the Hursts. "Yes," I said simply. Mr. Hurst was often away on business and Mrs. Hurst ran the home with effortless cheer. Freya mentioned once that her mother was significantly happier apart from her father, but I chose not to disclose that now. Although it was telling, perhaps, that Mr. Hurst had not yet joined his family in London.

"False," Rosalynn said with a single nod. "No one in a marriage such as theirs is incessantly happy."

But not everyone is secretly unhappy, either, I defended silently. Perhaps in Rosalynn's own discord, she wished to see discomfort in others, too. In doing so, she would not feel as alone. We climbed into the carriage and I reached over and squeezed her hand. She shot startled brown eyes at me and I smiled, hoping to melt a little of the ice she used to guard herself.

While she slipped her hand away, she gave me a playful smirk. I would count that as a win.

CHAPTER 2

Nearly a week following the shopping excursion with Mrs. Hurst, I raced up the stairs of our townhouse to change for dinner. The look on our butler, Billington's face was evidence enough that Mother was furious with me, and I was bound for another tongue lashing.

I had spent the afternoon at Freya's home with Rosalynn retrimming bonnets when I realized it was nearly time for dinner. I had rushed home, ignoring the knot of dread that grew when I recalled the conversation I'd had with my mother before I left home that morning, when she'd berated me for spending more time away from home than in it over the past week.

The Gibsons' ball was fast approaching, she had said, and I had yet to refresh my dancing instruction or finish replenishing my wardrobe. The ball was the unofficial start of the Season, and our social schedule was bound to be unceasing from there on out. I had assured her I would return well before dinner, but time had simply gotten away from me.

Molly assisted me out of my dress and into an evening gown for dinner faster than a horse might race around a track. I sat hard on the vanity chair and watched as her fingers deftly pulled my pins out and retwisted my hair into a loose bun at the nape of my neck while I yanked on my gloves.

"Thank you, Molly. You are a gem."

I raced downstairs and through the corridor only to come to an abrupt halt at the drawing room door. No one had told me that we were to have visitors.

Mother's tinkling laugh was joined by a heartier male tone—a tone that most certainly did not belong to my father.

Peeking through the doorway I caught sight of my mother on the settee near the fire, another woman sitting beside her and a man opposite, leaning against the fireplace with his arms casually folded across his chest. He was about my father's age, if not older, and his booming laugh overpowered the women's.

Opposite them, I caught sight of my father speaking to a younger man in the corner of the room. The man listened earnestly to whatever Father was telling him, but spared me a small glance when I stepped inside. He turned his attention back to my father before I could so much as smile.

The dismissal was not quite what I was used to, but I did not mind. It was something of a relief to avoid the inevitable rejection I would have to deliver.

"Elspeth, darling, come here," Mother said.

I obeyed, though I hated being called by my full name. It belonged to an aged spinster who held conversations with her cats, not a debutante.

"I would like to introduce Mr. Fenway and his wife, Mrs. Fenway."

I curtseyed to the strangers while my mother continued. "And this is my daughter, Miss Elspeth Cox. She is coming out this Season."

"Splendid!" Mr. Fenway said, his round face giving way to more jovial laughter. It was apparent that he was a jolly and good-natured fellow. His thin wife a calming sort, opposite in every visible way.

"How nice, dear," she said quietly. "Have you enjoyed many balls yet?"

"Not yet." I sat on the chair beside hers. "I am to attend the Gibsons' ball next week."

"Lovely."

Billington stood at the door and announced dinner. I rose and ran my hands down my gown, smoothing the rumpled fabric. When I glanced up, the young man who had been speaking to my father was by my side.

"Miss Cox," Mrs. Fenway said proudly, "allow me to present my son, Mr. Harry Fenway."

I curtseyed under his scrutiny. Apparently, I had been too quick to dismiss him earlier. He was making up for his previous lack thoroughly.

"May I escort you into dinner?" he asked, his voice low and silky. He did not inherit his father's corpulence, but he certainly received his deep voice.

Nodding, I took his arm and we followed our parents in to dinner.

I wracked my brain for some connection to the name Fenway, but I had never before heard it in my life. Not that I often listened to my parents discussing their friends, but I had thought I was acquainted with most everyone they knew. Evidently, I was wrong.

Dinner was an intricate menu that veered significantly from our regular cuisine. It was apparent that Cook had been given ample time to plan and prepare. Was I the only member of the house unaware of the Fenway's invitation to dine? It would seem so, and given the younger Mr. Fenway's sidelong glances, it was clear the invitation had included more than just a meal.

"How do you know my father?" I asked Mr. Fenway.

"I don't," he answered. He stabbed a potato and popped it in his mouth. "My parents do, though I cannot say how."

Cannot say how? "Is it very covert?"

"No," he said, shrugging. "I simply do not know."

Returning my attention to my plate, I pushed boiled potatoes around with my fork, while the young Mr. Fenway polished off his meal at an alarming rate. If he continued to eat at that pace, he would surely catch up to his father in no time. I swallowed the rude remark and filled my mouth with food instead.

"Elsie is quite accomplished at the pianoforte," Mother said at the other end of the table. "She can draw sufficiently, of course, and arrange flowers to perfection."

My ears burned. What was the meaning of this boastful display?

"Does she ride?" the elder Mr. Fenway asked, his brows pulled together intently.

Father scoffed. "Of course. And her archery is impeccable."

Mr. Fenway nodded appreciatively. The younger Mr. Fenway turned to me. "It seems you have acceptable accomplishments."

"Do you, as well?" I retaliated.

He tucked his chin, shock momentarily widening his eyes. "Of course. Why would you question it?"

Why, indeed?

"If I am to be examined for skill and acceptability, shouldn't you be inspected also?"

He looked affronted. "I am a gentleman."

"Precisely," I said under my breath.

The women were excused to the drawing room, and Mrs. Fenway asked to hear me play the pianoforte, to which I gladly obliged. Even when Mr. Harry Fenway joined us some time later and came to stand behind me, dutifully turning the pages of my sheet music, I continued to play, unrelenting, until it was time for the Fenway family to take their leave.

My arms ached from the continuous playing, my fingers growing sore, but I did not mind. It was far better than making mindless conversation all evening with a pompous, arrogant man.

"Elspeth, could you not even *try* to speak to the young man?" Mother asked when the door closed behind our visitors.

"Whatever for?" I turned on the seat, and her livid face pulled me up short, her cheeks rounded, mouth taut.

Mother's voice was as icy as her expression. "How do you expect to find a husband when you refuse to carry on a simple conversation with a nice young man? You will not hide behind that pianoforte for the entire Season. I will not allow it."

I glanced at my father, but he was retreating to the sofa. He did not involve himself in these conversations anyway. Not unless he wanted to end them.

"You know how I feel about marriage, Mother. This is not news."

She took on a harassed, exasperated expression. "Your feelings on the matter are unrealistic and ridiculous!"

"Unrealistic to live out my life peacefully in the manner that I wish?" I asked calmly, trying to balance her anger with level-headed composure. "Ridiculous to think I could possibly be happy without a man to obey? Why must I marry to be happy, Mother? Where is that law written?"

Her cheeks went ruddy, and her lips clamped together, vibrating in anger. But instead of a scathing retort, she turned toward my father. "Mr. Cox, do something."

"What am I to do?" He scoffed. "I can't very well force her to speak. And that Fenway was a pompous toad. He thought himself far above his station to be sure."

I thought for certain Mother's face would explode. "Far above his...? *Ugh!*" She stormed from the room, leaving us in silence.

"I did try to converse with him at dinner, Father," I said, placating.

"Like speaking to a parrot," he mused. "He was too busy thinking of himself to listen."

Father could be surprisingly astute at times.

I stood to leave, and he stayed me with his hand. With tired eyes, he ran his hand over his face, sighing like the weight of the world sat upon his shoulders. "Elsie, your mother only wants what is best for you."

Nodding, I waited for more; for him to say he wanted what was best for me too. But he remained silent. He gave me a crinkly smile and I bid him goodnight, choosing not to examine the uncharacteristic gentleness he had shown.

I'd never been particularly close to my father. I knew he loved me in the sense that he was my parent and wasn't that what they did? Love their children? At least, I assumed so. Growing up, I was always with my governess or away at school, and when I was home briefly on holiday visits, he was usually busy with his estate business or off in town with my mother. Though he was not a direct influence for much of my life, my father still held a constant place between my mother and me, even when he was not present. I knew as surely as the sun rose that he had the final word. He was in command.

Molly helped me undress and into bed, and I found myself staring at the darkened ceiling. Was there a man out there that respected women? *Really* respected them?

When Rosalynn had come up with the concept for the Sisterhood of Deserving Females, I had understood it to mean that I mattered, just as much as a boy. We were all human, after all, why shouldn't that be the case? Growing up under the thumb of my father, watching him treat Mother with little respect, had further solidified my resolve to remain my own master.

Like Mr. Fenway's shock at dinner tonight when I questioned his accomplishments, no male of my acquaintance would bat an eye if I were to simper and acquiesce and publicly announce I was less intelligent because I was female.

But I knew better. And I was not about to go down without a fight.

CHAPTER 3

The morning of the Gibsons' ball dawned cloudy and gray. The walk I had planned with Freya and Rosalynn in the park was either going to be postponed or redirected, and I was utterly disappointed. We had intended to stop in at Gunter's and try an ice.

"Mrs. Cox is waiting in her sitting room. She requested your presence when you're dressed," Molly said, helping me into my pale blue walking gown.

"Do you know what it is about?" Mother was never awake before me. Concern balled in my stomach. This could not be good.

Molly shrugged.

I took my time in dressing and meandered toward Mother's sitting room with growing dread. The pleased look on her face when I discovered her nestled on her chaise longue with a blanket over her knees and a breakfast tray beside her only worried me further. It had been a week since the Fenway family came to dinner, and Mother had been uncharacteristically quiet since then. Her happiness now did not bode well for me.

"Sit, Elsie."

I obeyed, lowering myself on the stiff velvet chair opposite her.

"I am not going to mince words. I have devised a proposition, and your father has agreed to it."

The roaring fire behind me warmed my back to an uncomfortable degree. I clasped my hands in my lap and swallowed. "What is this about?"

"You." She picked up her teacup and took a long sip, watching me over the rim with thoughtful eyes. Setting it back on the tray, she speared me with a look. "I wish to strike a bargain. If you will agree to put in every effort this Season, and I mean *every* effort, and still come out of it without a single thread of interest in a man, then your father and I will transfer your dowry to you and you may do with it what you wish."

I stopped breathing. Could I have heard her correctly? "Define 'every effort,'" I said cautiously, clasping my fingers so hard they ached. Hope edged into my heart, and I pushed it back, keeping it at bay until I was certain it was worth it.

She picked up a strawberry and chewed it slowly. Her eyes closed fractionally and she very much resembled a feline on the hunt. "You must attend every event; accept every dance that is asked of you. You may not decline callers, requests for outings in the park or to the museums, and you must have a pleasant demeanor. I will not have you accept an invitation to dance or ride with a gentleman, only to be surly with the sole purpose of putting him off."

Leaning toward me, she lowered her voice to add severity to her final words. "And while you and your friends have made a silly little pact to avoid marriage and men and all things natural, you cannot enter into this agreement without promising that you will open your mind and your heart to the possibility that Miss Hurst and Lady Rosalynn could, possibly, be wrong about matrimony."

My breath shallowed, but I tried not to show my mother just

how tremendously her statement hit me in the gut. She offered me the very thing I hoped and wished for, on the condition that I question my very basic beliefs.

How could I agree to that honestly? If I complied to Mother's outline, then I would be breaking the pact I had made six years prior.

But without it, where would I be?

"And if I don't agree?" I hated how small my voice sounded. I wanted to sound strong, but instead, my words rang hesitant and insecure.

"Then we have no agreement, and I cannot guarantee anything."

"What do you mean by anything?" I asked.

She adjusted her blanket over her knees, her mouth fixed in a thin smile. "Exactly that. Your father's estate is not entailed. While that has created the possibility for him to pass it on to you at some point in the future, it also means he may do whatever else he wishes with it. He can leave it to anyone. Or sell it, for that matter."

The threat could not be clearer. If I did not comply, I would be destitute.

Standing, I looked at my mother's triumphant face. My stomach swirled and distaste climbed up my throat. "How long do I have to decide?"

"Until tonight. You must tell me before the Gibsons' ball."

Nodding once, I turned and raced for the door.

"Elsie?" Mother called.

I glanced over my shoulder, disgusted by her posture, arranged like a lioness reveling in her authority.

"Do consider this carefully. Once you have made up your mind there will be no turning back."

Billington ordered the carriage for me, and I took Molly along to Rosalynn's house at once.

Freya could perhaps be more sympathetic to my dilemma,

but she would never fully understand the predicament my mother placed me in. Mrs. Hurst was not the sort of mother that incited irritation or petty disagreement. She and Freya had a decent relationship. Rosalynn, on the other hand, knew meddling, irritating mothers very well.

"Good day, Miss Cox." Potter, Rosalynn's butler, welcomed me into the foyer with a familiar smile. "I believe Lady Rosalynn is in the music room. Allow me to direct you."

"Thank you, Potter." I followed the aging butler, though I knew where to go.

We moved up a flight of stairs and turned down the corridor when one of The Tyrants came toward us. His dark head bent, he focused on straightening his cuff, his posture that of a man who knew his place in Society quite well, and relished in it.

"Send for my curricle," Lord Cameron demanded of Potter as he passed us, his voice deep and biting.

I startled, the effect of his demand grating on me more than usual that morning. Why did men need to be so autocratic? It would be easier not to detest them if they weren't perpetually domineering.

"Very good, sir," Potter said.

"Lord Cameron," I called, unable to stop myself.

He halted, glancing over his shoulder, and his eyebrows raised in surprise. Had he not noticed me walking behind the butler? He was so like Rosalynn, with the same dark coloring and deep, powerful eyes that made me wish to shrink away. The Nichols family was entirely too intelligent for their own good. Most of the time.

"It is raining outside," I explained. "You just commanded for your curricle to be harnessed, so I was unsure if you were aware, but I thought it prudent to pass along the information."

"Yes, thank you, Miss Cox." He glanced from me to the butler and back, an annoyed expression working its way onto his handsome face. "I suppose I'll take the carriage then, Potter."

"Very good, sir," Potter said from behind me.

"Good day, Miss Cox." Lord Cameron bowed, watching me in a curious way. His gaze snagged on me and held for a moment. I inclined my head and turned back for the music room, nearly bumping into Potter. He deftly moved along and announced me to Rosalynn moments later.

"Are we not to meet at the park?" she asked as I let myself fall onto her sofa.

A smile worked its way onto my lips. "Does no one in your house look outside in the mornings?"

She glanced up and took in the windows, surprised, apparently, to find them streaming with rain. "Oh," was all she said.

I stared at the window, watching the water make rivulets and streams, racing each other with starts and stops. How was I supposed to explain my predicament to Rosalynn? She would understand, wouldn't she? For all of her strong ideals, she had a thorough comprehension of Society, growing up as a lady of quality and daughter of a duke. Of the three of us, Freya, Rosalynn, and myself, Rosalynn certainly held the highest rank by a landslide.

Yes, she would certainly understand.

"My mother has given me an ultimatum."

Rosalynn immediately set her sheet music on her lap and turned toward me on the sofa. "What about?"

"Marriage."

Rosalynn stilled. She appeared to take one deep breath and measure her words. "She cannot force you. It is your basic human right to accept or deny a marriage."

"That is not the issue." I found my nerves beginning to dance. I simply needed to explain it all at once, get it out into the open. And I needed to not fear my friend's reaction, for, though I acted unsure with my mother, I had already made my decision.

The challenge then, was breaking the news to Rosalynn and keeping our friendship intact.

I took a deep breath. "She has agreed that if I do not have even a single thread of interest in a man by the end of the Season, then she and my father will turn over my dowry and I may do with it whatever I wish."

Rosalynn gasped, her hands coming together in front of her. "This is splendid, Elsie. It solves both of our dilemmas!"

"I have not explained it all to you, yet."

"Go on, then," she said. Her excitement was evident, her eyes glittering.

"I have to put in every effort this Season." I numbered off on my fingers as I spoke. "I must accept every dance, caller, carriage ride, walk in the park, and escort to the museums and gardens. And I must do so pleasantly, without any nefarious motives."

She nodded in understanding. "You cannot be disagreeable in the hopes that men will naturally leave you be."

"Precisely."

"But that is not so bad." She shrugged, offering a consoling smile. "When you consider the length of the Season, it is only a few months that you must agree to court and be courted, and then freedom is yours. And you are not even of age! Oh, how did you find yourself so fortunate?"

Fortunate? She would not think so when she heard the rest of it.

"That is not all," I continued hesitantly.

Rosalynn gave me a look as though she could not fathom what might make this plan distasteful. I knew how she felt, but I could see that she was uncomprehending. I worried that her ideals would make her unbending as well.

"She brought up our Sisterhood of Deserving Females pact," I said carefully.

The words sat heavily in the room, and Rosalynn's demeanor turned wary.

I clasped my fingers in my lap and continued. "I can only enter into the agreement on the condition that while I have made a pact with you and Freya, I will also consider the prospect that we were wrong to do so and that I might open my mind to the possibilities."

"What possibilities?"

I lifted a shoulder. "Love?"

Rosalynn's eyes grew wide. "Your mother said this?"

"Not in those particular words, but yes." She had said I needed to open my mind and my heart. What else could she have meant?

She scoffed. "I thought my mother's threat to pull my inheritance if I did not marry was severe. But she never required me to fall in love."

"I'm not required to fall in love, only to admit that it is possible."

"For what purpose? Why is love even something to consider? It is not as though your parents…"

I glanced away. She did not need to finish her sentence. I made no secret of my parent's ill-suited marriage. They tolerated one another well enough, but theirs was an arranged marriage, and they had never pretended otherwise.

"She cannot force you to believe anything," Rosalynn said firmly.

"Of course not, but I cannot in good conscience agree to this plan unless I am willing to consider the option that we were wrong. We have asked our mothers to consider for years that we are sturdy in our belief that we are intelligent women of worth —that we do not need a man to lead and govern us. Is this not her way of doing the same thing in reverse?"

"But we aren't wrong," Rosalynn said, her brown eyes wide. "The moment we marry we give up every single paltry right we have. Anything we own instantly becomes the property of our husband. We must obey our husbands to the degree that, essentially, we become their property. If we stay unwed, we retain what little rights we have." She shook her head, her eyes glowing with intensity. "But that is not the point, Elsie. I do not believe men are inherently bad. The point is that we retain our dignity and the power to govern ourselves. We maintain our independence."

"I know all of this, Rosie," I said gently. "I knew what I was agreeing to when we made that pact as knobby little girls. And this is a way for me to find peace in it. If I agree to her demands, then I satisfy my mother's wishes, as well as my own. I'll be able to come out the other side of this with my own independence. Not a house I won't inherit until my healthy father dies, in who knows how many years, but money to live off of now."

"Then do it," she said simply.

"I think I might."

We looked at one another as a small chasm grew between us. I wanted so deeply for her to understand. But by making this agreement, I was essentially breaking our pact.

"And when you come out the other end of this, happily unwed and with a large income, we can find a lovely little cottage somewhere and plant a beautiful garden full of tomatoes and roses and live peacefully."

"That sounds lovely." I smiled. She was attempting to fill the gap I put between us, and I loved her for it.

"This is all for the best, perhaps." Rosalynn sighed. "Instead of going through Season after Season hoping our parents finally come to terms with our ideals, we'll only have to suffer through once."

"Precisely. Now, how do we explain this to Freya?"

She tilted her face away from me, and I knew she was thinking, her eyes squinting fractionally. "Perhaps we keep it to the bare bones of the agreement. Otherwise, we may complicate things too much. Freya is not resilient. The stipulation that you cannot say no may distress her."

"I cannot like deceiving her, though." It was true that Freya might not understand, but it should be up to her to determine her own feelings on the matter.

"We will not lie. But we shan't cause her unnecessary stress, either."

I had time. Nothing need be decided now. My body was tired, the strain from the morning taking a toll on me. "Care to play a duet?"

Rosalynn grinned. She held up the sheet music she had been holding in her lap ever since I sat on her sofa. "I thought you'd never ask."

CHAPTER 4

Mother's victorious smile was bound to send me over the edge. The carriage rocked us slowly toward the Gibsons' ball, and I caught her grin periodically with light from lanterns swinging outside our window. I tensed further each time. It was impossible not to feel as though I had just signed my life away. But the opposite was true—this would unlock my future.

Mounting the steps to the ballroom, Mother leaned in to whisper. "You may not decline a *single* dance."

I could have laughed. Did she really think I would find enough partners to dance every dance at my first ball? I knew no one beyond Mr. Fenway and Rosalynn's brother, Lord Cameron. Though I was unsure if I could even claim an acquaintance with Lord Cameron in the general public when I had only been around him a handful of times in the quiet of his own home.

"I am aware of the conditions of our agreement," I reminded her.

Father walked behind us, and we stood in line to greet our hosts. Flickering candlelight from enormous chandeliers spread from the ballroom and a country dance was beginning. Couples lined the center of the room, a border of spectators eyeing the dancers and discussing them from behind their fans.

Rosalynn stood on the other side of the room beside her brother. Their dark heads were bent together in conversation, their resemblance strong.

Mother grasped my arm when I turned to go. "You will remain by my side, Elspeth," she said through gritted teeth. "I have introductions to make."

Suspicion slithered down my spine. It mounted and grew as Mother led me toward a well-dressed man in a vivid purple waistcoat and striped bottle green jacket. A watch chain dangled from his pocket, and he looked down his sloping nose at my simple white ball gown with rosettes embroidered along the neck and hemline. Did this Town beau think me dowdy? He certainly didn't look awed.

"Mrs. Cox, you look absolutely dazzling this evening," he drawled.

"Oh, Lord Fischer," Mother simpered. I wanted to be sick. I glanced over my shoulder, but Father was left behind, speaking with other men. He wasn't even bothered by Mother's fingers grasping Lord Fischer's coat.

The dandy seemed to mind, however. His pointed look was enough to remove her pudgy claws.

Awkwardly, Mother transferred her grip from his arm to mine. "Allow me to introduce my daughter, Miss Elspeth Cox."

I curtseyed. His shoes were even more flashy than the waistcoat. I was unaware shoes could be purchased in a golden yellow leather.

"Pleased, I'm sure."

"Elsie has come to London for her first Season," Mother said. "She was so worried she would be forced to stand and watch the dancing all evening, but I know that cannot be the case. I was only telling her this morning how honorable and valiant the men of the drawing rooms are."

A flush spread over my cheeks. She was begging him for a dance—and being dishonest about it besides.

"I hope you are proved correct, ma'am," he said obediently, turning to me. "May I take the next dance, Miss Cox?"

Bowing my head to hide my shame, I nodded, playing the bashful debutante in the hopes that he would escape until our set began. Relief momentarily visited but was quickly chased away by the arrival of another young man that Mother chose to solicit for a dance.

Thirty minutes later, I had never been more mortified in my entire life. My schedule was full except for the two waltzes that mother had dashed away—you don't want to be seen as *fast*, Elsie—and I was standing opposite Lord Fischer while we waited for the minuet to begin. His eyelids drooped, slowly running up and down my person. Clearly, he was unimpressed.

I tried to see myself through his lens. My white gown, faintly rouged cheeks and intricately designed hair made me appear overly done up. I looked like every other marriage-hungry debutante in the room—nothing set me apart. I supposed I would be unimpressed too.

Not that I had been *trying* to impress him, or any man. But it was my first foray into London Society, and I wanted to make something of a good impression on the general population. Wasn't that all anyone wanted at the base of their motives? To be accepted, if not esteemed?

I could still want to be held in good opinion *without* desiring a husband.

Lord Fischer and I came together for small spurts of time, but the majority of the dance was spent moving down the line or to another partner and back. When the set ended, I was returned to Mother's side momentarily before my next partner arrived to whisk me away again.

It was more than an hour before I earned a break by way of a waltz, and I took the opportunity to search out Rosalynn and

Freya. I found them near the table holding refreshment and took hold of each of their arms. They glanced up in unison.

"Deliver me from this wretched fate."

"Whatever is going on?" Freya asked, cupping my shoulder. "You have not sat out a single dance. I didn't think you even knew that many gentlemen."

"My mother does." My shoulders drooped with exhaustion. This was only my first ball of a Season that would last three more months. How ever was I going to endure?

Rosalynn stepped in. "Mrs. Cox made her a deal. If she completes the Season without interest in a man then she can take her dowry now and live independently."

Freya's eyes could not have possibly grown wider than they did at that moment. "But you are only eighteen."

I released their arms and leaned back against the wall. "I *know*. Many women don't find husbands until their second or third Season. I am choosing not to analyze this gift too closely and appreciate it as it is."

"You haven't a partner now, though?"

"I am not allowed to waltz," I explained. "The only rule my mother made tonight that I agree with."

Freya's gaze followed the dancers floating in time with the smooth music. "Neither am I," she said wistfully.

Rosalynn's posture straightened. She gazed at Freya's uncomprehending face. "You *want* to though, don't you?"

Freya's cheeks bloomed with color and she straightened, turning away from the dance floor. "Of course not. I was only admiring the way the gowns moved along the floor."

Rosalynn's eyebrow raised in judgment. She looked stunning, her cheeks lightly glowing and her dark hair curled and plaited in a regal design. Freya's bright red hair was similarly arranged, but she had the unfortunate skin tone that seemed to wash out against a canvas of white. Even Mrs. Hurst's expert advice could do nothing for Freya's bleached face.

"I must return to my mother." I sighed, sorry for myself. "Mr. Fenway is next. I vow I will lay abed all morning tomorrow and still my feet are bound to ache."

"No." Rosalynn shot her arm out and stopped me. "We must meet tomorrow and reconsider your dilemma."

"I have to go on calls with my Mama," Freya said apologetically.

"Come to my house then," Rosalynn said. "Add the Duchess of Clifton to your list of calls to make. She arrived this morning with the rest of The Tyrants."

"Why did they not come to the ball this evening?" I asked.

"Tarquin and Geoff went to their club. Mother needed to rest from the journey. I have no idea what my father is up to."

"Your house it is," I agreed. "Now wish me luck."

Mr. Fenway found me minutes later and led me into a quadrille. His sweaty palms and leering smile gave me a shiver of disgust.

"Your first ball is turning into quite the success."

"Thank you, sir."

"I did not guess when we came to dine that I was getting a leg up from the rest of the *ton*."

His cat-like grin was unnerving. His fingers pressed into my flesh and instinct told me to turn and run. I glanced up and caught Mother's smug smirk, my mind racing back to the conversation that morning and the very binding terms of our agreement.

I was caught; I could not flee the dance floor. Neither could I give this man any reason to think I was uninterested in his verbal advances.

Alarm crept on like a slow-moving wave, engulfing me all at once in utter dread. For the first time, the unfavorable possibilities of my agreement presented themselves. By consistently saying 'yes,' not only would I be making my interest known to *any* man that requested it, but I would not be able to put them off, even when I was repulsed.

Mr. Fenway's predatory gaze stuck to me like honey, making my skin crawl.

What had I gotten myself into?

CHAPTER 5

A broken leg. That would do it. A broken leg would inhibit dancing, rides to the park, and comfortable at-home visits. It would void the agreement and give me a full year to come up with an alternative.

I sat at my dressing table and brushed my honey-colored hair, focusing intently on my determined brow in the reflection. The morning light came through the window and rested on my arms, warming them thoroughly.

Only, how was I going to execute the plan to break my leg? Such an accident could potentially inhibit my walking in some way for the remainder of my life. That certainly wasn't ideal.

No, a broken leg was out. I would need to come up with something different.

Illness?

But how would I obtain an illness short of visiting a hospital? Even then, there was no guarantee I would contract a safe illness and not a terminal disease.

That was it. I had no other choice. I simply had to run off to the continent with a band of gypsies.

Setting the hairbrush down with a thump, I dropped my head in my hands and groaned.

Molly finished putting away my night clothes and came up behind me to fix my hair. I looked at her through the mirror. Would it be feasible to escape through the servants' entrance? Perhaps I could find a position as a maid or governess in a well respected London home. Eventually I might save enough money to live contentedly for the rest of my life.

I looked at Molly, her fingers deftly weaving my hair into something presentable. That wouldn't do either. If it were possible to save enough to retire and live comfortably on a service job, there wouldn't be anyone left in service. Not to mention the difficulty of obtaining a job without a single reference to my name.

The answer was before me, I merely did not want to accept it. Mother had offered me the money I needed to set up comfortably in a cottage somewhere in a small country town or an apartment here in London. I only needed to last the Season.

I stifled another groan. But the Season was going to be so much work! I hadn't anticipated before agreeing to the bargain just how tiring a ball could be, nor how many men would request to call on me afterward.

Glancing at the clock, I calculated how much time I had to get out of the house before Mother awoke. It was my only chance of getting to Rosalynn's before she could waylay me. Last night I told each man who asked to call that I would be delighted to receive them. I had done my part.

No one mentioned I had to remain home at all times on the chance that they would indeed call.

I glanced at Molly in the mirror. "I am running late. Will you get my bonnet and tell Billington that I need the carriage straight away?"

"Yes, miss."

"Good." I turned on my seat and looked my maid square in

the face. "And Molly, I needn't say that I am in quite the hurry to get away...undetected, right?"

"Right, miss."

Nodding once in dismissal, I turned back to the vanity and looked at my ordinary face. If Mother had not taken the initiative to beg for dance after dance, how would my first ball have turned out? I might have been able to sit aside and gossip with my friends, enjoying the dances like they had. I certainly would not have had so many dances without Mother's aid.

I needed to be on my way to Rosalynn's home fast. She was a balancing voice of reason and would do nothing but remind me that I had made the right choice. The only choice, in this situation.

"You simply must get out of the bargain. There's nothing else for it."

Rosalynn slammed the newspaper on the table in front of her sofa and leaned back against the cushions.

"But I cannot," I wailed. "I have no other course of action available to me!"

"Read this, and you shall change your mind."

There was only one issue with Rosalynn's reasoning: I did not have it in my power to change my mind. My mother had very distinctly said there was no turning back.

Warily, I picked up the newspaper. It was opened to an article circled in ink.

DEBUTANTE TAKES TON BY STORM, read the caption. I glanced at Rosalynn, and she lifted her eyebrows in response.

When I sat unmoving a few moments more, she grabbed the paper from my hands and cleared her throat.

"Miss 'C' made her first appearance at a ball hosted by the distinguished 'G' family. She twirled from man to man, dancing every dance, sitting out none but the two waltzes. One would assume that was a show to preserve her purity. Has no one informed Mrs. 'C' that the waltz has been positively accepted in London circles for the last two years? Perhaps she was too busy gathering partners for her daughter to realize her dated notions were unfashionable. Nevertheless, Miss 'C' has made a splash, and I predict that she is the one to watch."

"The one to watch?" I all but yelled, my heart racing. "What an absolute heap of—"

"Ahem." Rosalynn cleared her throat and widened her eyes.

A prickle of chagrin ran down my neck when I turned my head to find Lord Cameron leaning in the doorway, his arms crossed casually over his chest and an amused smile on his lips. His dark hair was carelessly arranged, contrary to the rest of his immaculate appearance. My pride stung. It was distressing to be caught losing my head by a man who always appeared composed.

"A heap of what, exactly, Miss Cox?" he asked, sauntering into the room and dropping into the chair opposite our sofa. My back straightened instinctively, and I looked to Rosalynn for direction.

"No one invited you to join our conversation, Cam. You are being positively rude right now, and I fear that if you don't leave right away you shall scare away my friend."

"Miss Cox isn't frightened of me," he responded cooly, his gaze coming to rest lazily on my face. My rebellious cheeks heated right away, and I met his stare with what little pride I could claim.

"Of course not," I lied. Well, perhaps it wasn't a lie entirely. I wasn't frightened of Lord Cameron. Intimidated, maybe. But not frightened.

"See? Now let me see that newspaper." He snatched it from the table before either of us could protest, and his eyebrows drew together steadily while he read. "Is this all?" he asked, dropping it on the table.

"Is that all?" Rosalynn scoffed. "Elsie has been described as an out of fashion country bumpkin with a meddling mother! To say the least, this will draw attention to her from every eligible male in London. This is absolutely dreadful."

For the first time ever, I saw Lord Cameron display confusion. "I must be lost," he said. "Why would that be so horrible?"

"Because she cannot refuse—"

"It isn't," I cut in. But not quickly enough, apparently. Rosalynn apparently piqued his interest.

He focused on me with an intensity that I felt to my toes. "What can you not refuse?"

My lips clamped together. Rosalynn must have felt the same inclination, for she remained silent as well. This was one secret I was bent on keeping.

Lord Cameron looked from his sister to me and back again, small lines forming between his eyebrows. "What have you to hide?"

"Nothing," we said in unison.

"Besides," I added with uncertainty, "my name was not actually used. They blanked out everything but the first letter. Surely no one will know it is me of whom the author speaks."

"Try again," Lord Cameron said. "They leave out names to protect themselves, but everyone usually knows to whom they refer. There was a decent sized group of debutantes at the ball last night, but only one of them danced every dance." He leveled me with a look. "Except the waltzes, of course. We wouldn't want anyone to deem you fast, would we?"

Rosalynn glared. "Quit, Cam."

"What is so ridiculous about sitting out the waltz?" I asked.

"It is an antiquated notion, nothing more," he dismissed, waving his arm languidly. Amusement glittered in his eyes. "Do not fear. No one will think you fast, Miss Cox, they will be too busy thinking you old fashioned."

That stung. I wasn't sure which was worse.

"You may leave now," Rosalynn said icily.

He rose, dipping his shoulders in a bow before strolling from the room.

"Is he correct?" I asked the moment the door closed behind him.

Rosalynn looked uneasy.

"Be honest with me, please," I pleaded. "I would much rather be prepared."

She sighed. "Yes, he is correct. Only the stuffy old matrons look down on waltzing, and refusing to dance it will set you apart. It could make you appear old fashioned. But that is not such a horrible thing!" she rallied. "You do not actually want to attract a husband, so if your mother is allowing you to refuse waltzing, then I would count that as a win and take advantage of it while you can."

"True," I conceded. "I spent all morning devising ways to get out of this bargain, but I came up with nothing reasonable. She must have known before she got me to agree that I would be going against my very ideals. The very essence of this agreement takes all of my power away."

Rosalynn turned sympathetic eyes on me. "I know, it is unfair. But at the end of this you shall have everything we've ever dreamed of!"

I slumped back on the sofa. "If I survive, you mean."

"Oh pish, you'll thrive. You might even enjoy yourself if you can turn it into a game."

A loud voice boomed in the corridor and Rosalynn stiffened immediately. We were quiet, listening to the deep voice call orders to the butler, and then speak to Lord Cameron, though it was hard to decipher what was said through the closed door. By unspoken agreement, we waited until the sounds faded to silence.

"Geoff is turning into him," she whispered.

I didn't need to ask her to clarify. She referenced her eldest brother, Lord Stallsbury; he'd been, as of late, mimicking their brute of a father more and more. I reached across the sofa cushion and picked up her hand, squeezing it in support.

Freya and I had ample reason for wanting our own independence. As women who would lose every single one of our meager rights and power over our substantial inheritances the moment we wed, we were valid in wanting to maintain a small semblance of our pride and the ability to self-govern. But neither of us had the past or the experiences that Rosalynn did. Neither of us hid from our fathers in damp closets or spent hours in the cool woods of northern England to avoid incessant shouting. We couldn't truly grasp the depth of why Rosalynn so desperately vowed to never, ever marry.

"I must get flowers in this house immediately!" a shrill voice rang through the corridor. "What has Rosalynn been doing with her time this past fortnight? It is positively dusty in here."

We exchanged glances, and I squeezed her hand once more before letting it go. The duchess walked past the closed music room door directing a maid to make sure every table had fresh flowers on it before noon.

"Perhaps we really could flee to the continent with a band of gypsies," I offered.

Rosalynn looked at me strangely.

I shrugged. "One of my escape ideas."

"You can't escape yet," a male voice said from the doorway. I startled, for I had not heard the door open. "Mother expects you in the drawing room in five minutes."

I turned to see Lord Tarquin, Rosalynn's middle brother, dip his head in acknowledgment before turning to go.

"How has it been having all of them under one roof again?" I asked.

"How do you think?" she countered. "Tyrannical, naturally."

I stifled a laugh. It was difficult to imagine her grown brothers locking her in the school room or sending her on errands for imaginary items in the forest. While they had taken advantage of her naivety as a child, she was much too intelligent to fall for their pranks now.

I followed Rosalynn to the drawing room. Her mother tolerated my presence for the first hour of visits, but my welcome was well worn out by the time Freya and her mother arrived.

"Wasn't last night just grand?" Freya asked dreamily, squeezing onto the settee between Rosalynn and me.

"Not for all of us," Rosalynn said diplomatically.

Freya dipped her head, abashed. "Oh, right. Sorry, Elsie."

"Don't be. If my biggest troubles are that I was asked to dance too many times, then I vow it could be far worse."

"Perhaps, but I wouldn't jinx myself," Freya said with a giggle.

"Have you seen the paper?" Rosalynn asked her.

"Yes, and Mama was glad it wasn't I who was called out. She is going to allow me to waltz at Almack's."

"I didn't consider your mother, Elsie," Rosalynn said suddenly. "Does she read the papers?"

My stomach dropped. "When she wants to keep abreast of the gossip, yes."

"Oh, drat."

"Perhaps I should go home and try to confiscate them before she can read the report. Maybe I'll accidentally drop them into the fire."

"If you wait a few minutes, we can take you home," Freya offered, smoothing a stray curl away from her face.

I nodded. I had sent Molly home when I arrived, so I would

have to wait at least thirty minutes while a message could be dispatched home requesting the carriage back.

"There were so many beautiful gowns last night," Freya said. "I did not realize that we could all look so different when we are forced to wear the same light colors."

Rosalynn lifted her eyebrows. "Wait until Almack's. The dress code is even more severe."

"Will we see you at the card party tomorrow?" Freya asked.

"I'm not sure," I said.

Rosalynn said, "You probably will. I know we were invited."

Mrs. Hurst stood, and Freya and I followed suit. "Until then."

CHAPTER 6

The front door had barely closed behind me when Mother stormed out of the drawing room at the top of the stairs, her face mottled with rage and her hands gripping the banister tightly.

"You are to come up here now," she said with measured tones.

"Yes, Mother." I knew this was coming. It had been four days since the first ball, and I had made a game of finding ways to make myself absent during the daytime. I'd kept busy—hiding in Rosalynn's drawing room, taking an outing to Hyde Park with Freya and her mama, shopping with Rosalynn and the duchess. And then, today, a trip to the Royal Menagerie with Freya and Rosalynn.

I mounted the steps and entered the drawing room prepared to receive admonishment. My father lounged on the couch, his legs stretched, ankles crossed. Oh dear. I tensed. This was worse than I'd thought. It took something truly significant to pull Father from his study.

Silence sat thick between us, but I was not about to break decorum and speak first. Mother watched me with no small amount of dissatisfaction. I stood as though awaiting trial—my father the magistrate, my mother the gleeful spectator.

Much of my life fell into this pattern; it was entirely familiar.

Father coughed, his fingers interlaced over his ample belly. "It has come to my attention that you are avoiding your mother."

I kept my mouth closed, years of these trials only taught me that to be silent and acquiesce was the best stratagem. It mattered little if the accusations were dramatized or exaggerated. Arguing only made the punishment worse.

"You have embarrassed her by not being home to receive your callers. It is not she who looks to wed this Season, Elspeth, and it is not she who needs to be here pleasantly awaiting your visitors."

It was not me, either, but heaven forbid he remembered the one thing I told him about myself. Specifically, the decision I made six years prior to never marry. That belief had only solidified the older I'd become, and the longer I'd lived with my father's commanding presence.

Clearing his throat, he continued, "You are not to set foot out of this house in the next fortnight without the express permission of your mother. Do I make myself clear?"

"Abundantly, sir."

He glanced at me sharply. "I can easily make that a month."

"No, sir. I only meant that I fully comprehend the extent of my crimes and I promise to dutifully commit myself to Mother's side until she is fully satisfied."

Why had I said that? The words had spilled from my mouth without my consent, and I knew I would regret them. Mother grinned smugly.

"Dress for dinner, Elspeth," she snapped. "We are dining out tonight."

"Yes, Mother."

By the time I reached my bedchamber Molly had an evening

gown laid out and a strand of pearls with matching ear bobs resting on the dressing table.

"Do you know where I am to dine?" I asked her. The servants knew more than I did most of the time.

"Lord McGregor's, I believe."

I stepped into the white gown with a sheer overlay of faint silver and lace-capped sleeves. "Should I know that name?"

Molly shrugged. "He's an earl from up north somewhere. Didn't hear anything more than that."

The carriage ride was mostly silent, interspersed with Mother's little etiquette reminders. One would believe I hadn't spent years trained up by a governess, and then later at Miss Smythe's school, based on what Mother felt compelled to tell me. Did she really think I would forget to curtsy?

As we entered the earl's stately home, Mother leaned forward and whispered, "You may not deny them, Elspeth. Do not forget."

I didn't bother gracing her with a response. She took perverse joy in reminding me of my misery.

The dinner party was larger than I expected, and Lord McGregor considerably younger. He had brilliant red hair and a square jaw. The interest in his eyes was evident when Father introduced me, which was altogether terrifying.

It was with great relief that he turned away and spoke to another debutante, freeing me to glance about the assembly.

Catching Rosalynn's eyes across the room, my shoulders immediately relaxed. I had an ally. Mother was conversing with another society matron, so I took my chance to escape.

I was not leaving the room, nor was I escaping any men. Surely it was safe to assume I was not breaking any rules.

"I am so glad to see you," I said, sidling up to Rosalynn.

"Is Freya here?" she asked.

"Not that I've seen. The only redhead in here is the earl."

Rosalynn shook her head, her dark eyes sweeping the room. "It is so strange to think of him as the earl."

My eyebrows pulled together. "You know him?"

"Oh yes, our estates practically border one another."

"How long ago did his father pass away?" I asked.

"About a year and a half ago, but Jack went into a dark place after his father's death. He is only recently coming out into society again."

I knew the name. "*This* is Jack?"

She looked surprised, swinging her gaze back to me. "Of course it is."

I could not help but laugh, her confusion amusing. In all the years I'd heard stories about Jack—he was so close to her brothers that Rosalynn had always lumped him in with The Tyrants—never once had she mentioned that he was heir to an earldom. Being the daughter of a duke, though, it was probably inconsequential to Rosalynn. She outranked him.

What an odd thought.

"I cannot picture this man covering you with red paint in your sleep," I said, "or tricking you into jumping in the lake because he told you your cat had swum out and gotten lost."

Her smile turned saucy, and she glanced at Lord McGregor. "I have enough stories to send Jack back to his castle in shame."

"But you wouldn't," I said factually.

She looked at me strangely. "Of course I wouldn't."

Dinner was announced. I found myself seated between Lord Cameron and Mr. Jessup, an elderly friend of my father's. I knew neither man beyond passing which meant it was bound to be a lengthy, tiresome meal.

"Have you come to a reasonable conclusion, Miss Cox?" Lord Cameron asked before diving into his soup.

My spoon stalled over my bowl. Had Rosalynn filled him in

on my predicament? I glanced at her across the table and a few chairs down, but she was deep in conversation and didn't look my way.

"I don't know what you are referring to, sir," I said plainly, sipping my soup. Ambiguity was my best course of action.

He shifted toward me, and I could feel the weight of his gaze. Glancing up, I caught the end of a sardonic look. Well then, he probably knew about my situation. I was going to have words with Rosalynn later, that was for certain.

Lord Cameron's handsome face was too attentive and his eyes too intelligent. I did not know if I could trust him, and that made me uneasy. But I trusted Rosalynn, and if she informed Lord Cameron of my situation, then she must have had good reason to do so.

"There's not much I can do," I finally said in resignation, returning my attention to my soup. "I need to wait it out and endure the Season. It cannot be so terrible."

"So says the woman who has never before endured a Season."

"Have you any advice for me?"

He smiled, half of his mouth turning up more than the other. "Yes. Run away."

I couldn't help but return his smile then. "If you dislike it so fervently, then why do you choose to attend?" He had chosen to attend the Gibsons' ball last week; here he was again tonight, and I had seen him a handful of times in between. Lord Cameron was a grown man and not required to attend functions unless he wanted to. In fact, this was the first event since the rest of his family's arrival that I had seen Lord Stallsbury or Lord Tarquin outside of their own home, and they were likely only here because of their close relationship to Lord McGregor.

Lord Cameron shrugged. "I am a glutton for punishment, I suppose."

The conversation shifted in the room, and Mr. Jessup questioned me on my stay in London. When we moved on to discussing the weather, I had never been so happy to see the next course arrive and gladly focused my attention on cutting my meat into dainty bites.

"So you are no longer seeking an escape?" Lord Cameron questioned.

Would he not let it go? I turned the force of my exasperation on him. "Lord Cameron, why are you so interested in my pathetic situation?"

His chin tucked slightly, knocking a wayward lock over his forehead. "I am not interested."

He could have fooled me. We continued on in silence, my outburst ending the cordial conversation. Mother refused to let me be, however. Her gaze periodically strayed my direction, and the lump in my midsection grew. One particularly pointed glare catapulted me into speaking, though I knew not why I was bending to her will.

"I find that London is quite a bit stuffier than I had imagined it would be."

I stared at my plate, contemplating the foolishness of my comment, but I could plainly hear the amusement in Lord Cameron's tone when he responded. "You have not been to Town before?"

"No, I have." Why had I said that? London's ballrooms were stuffier than I had anticipated, but the weather had been chilly and even rainy on occasion. I must have searched my mind too long for an explanation.

"I find that the concentration of coal fires does have an adverse effect on the air," Lord Cameron put in diplomatically.

For some odd, unexplainable reason, his response had me swallowing a giggle. My fork remained mid-air as I tried to push down the mirth, but it would not do. Making the mistake of glancing at Lord Cameron, I read the amusement glittering in his dark eyes and let out a very unladylike laugh—exactly the sort of thing Miss Smythe taught me never to do in polite company.

My one consolation for the indelicate sound and the subsequent silence in the dining room was that for one minuscule moment, Lord Cameron had released a laugh that mimicked my own. He was able to cover his more readily than I was, however, and multiple looks of astonishment were directed solely at me.

Lord McGregor, saint that he apparently was, began speaking to his neighbor again as if nothing untoward had occurred, and the rest of the table followed suit.

Lord Cameron wiped his mouth and leaned closer to me, saying with an entirely straight face, "And how do you feel about the crowds, Miss Cox?"

"I choose not to comment, sir."

"Oh come, you cannot back down now."

"Watch me," I said, glaring playfully at him from the corner of my eye.

I was going to do my utmost to act with decorum for the rest of the evening, to the extent that Mother would not have it in her power to berate me further. Now, if only Lord Cameron would quit giving me amusing glances.

CHAPTER 7

No. No, no, no!
I threw the newspaper onto the floor and stood, pacing to the sitting room window and back. Then I paced again.

Oh dear, what was I going to do?

The door opened and Mother walked in, regally seating herself on a chair and calling to the maid to bring some tea. She appeared calm and collected. Had she possibly missed the article? I glanced to where I threw the newspaper on the floor. Perhaps I could kick it beneath the sofa without her noticing. My toe inched forward.

"Come sit. You're bound to wear holes in my carpet," she demanded. "We need to discuss how we are going to handle this situation."

I pulled my foot back. Evidently, she was already aware.

"Your father doesn't know, and he doesn't need to. We have vouchers for Almack's tonight and will know better how the article has affected us then. I want you to direct your maid to pay special attention to your toilette. Not one single hair can be out of place. I expect you to ooze ladylike decorum." She speared me with a look. "Do I make myself clear?"

"Yes." Though how I was meant to ooze decorum was outside my realm of comprehension.

She nodded once, the matter settled. The maid brought in the tea service and we drank in silence, waiting for callers—if any—to show up. The clock on the mantle ticked a steady beat, punctuated periodically by passing carriages outside.

Mother broke the silence. "I have changed my mind about the waltzing."

I supposed it was nice while it lasted. "You'd like me to waltz?" I clarified.

"You shall not reject anyone who may ask. Though I doubt anyone will," she added quietly.

I swallowed my umbrage at her remark. The article wasn't that bad. Did she think I was going to shift from many suitors to none because one gossip article announced that I had 'guffawed at Lord M's table like a caged bird in need of some exercise?'

I cringed. Very well, it truly was that bad.

What made it infinitely worse was having zero callers arrive, for Mother was sure to think I had scared them all away deliberately.

"Well," she said, as she stood. "Get your shawl. We are going to the park."

"But it is positively freezing out today!"

Her cold expression brooked no argument. "And we need to be seen. I will not sit here and idly wait while your chances slip away because of one poorly written article. We need to do some socializing."

I groaned. "Can't that be accomplished at Almack's?"

She glared again and I stood without complaint. "Give me a moment to find my bonnet."

We had the lucky coincidence of arriving at the park in time with Mrs. Hapworth, and Mother walked a distance with her while I trailed behind with Cecily Hapworth, who I had not seen since rooming with her at Miss Smythe's School for Girls.

Though we had never been friends.

"Are you enjoying your Season?" I asked her.

"Exceedingly, yes," she answered. Her fair hair was pulled back and hidden beneath her bonnet, but her simple beauty was hard to mask. "It all feels overwhelming at times, though. I can never remember the right names and who belongs to whom."

"If you discover a trick for that, please share it with me. I suffer from the same difficulties."

Miss Hapworth shot me a pitying look and my spine straightened instinctively. "It must be terrible to be discussed in the papers."

At least I was being discussed. I swallowed my retort and smiled at her instead. "I'm managing. I believe the gossips will grow bored with me and move onto someone else shortly. That is the nature of these things."

"I envy your positive outlook," she said. "I would absolutely die if those things had been said about me."

Sudden memories assaulted me from our days together in school. Cecily was never easy to be close to, regardless of my efforts. Though, her pride was likely to blame. She'd had her own set of rumors to deal with at the time.

It was fortuitous that Mother called me along and we bid farewell to the Hapworths. I had been biting my tongue too hard to sustain a prolonged conversation.

"Obnoxious woman," Mother muttered. That time my smile was genuine.

Her sudden gasp pulled my attention, and I glanced up sharply to find a deep green barouche pull up beside our walking path, an older woman with a familiar grim smile eyeing us closely.

"There's nothing for it," Mother said under her breath. "We'll have to greet her."

The carriage came to a stop when Mother walked toward it. Recognition dawned, and I smiled at the older woman. Aunt Georgina.

"My, you have grown considerably," she said, eyeing me through her quizzing glass. "Pretty little thing, to be sure. But that determined upper lip will cause you some trouble, my dear."

"Good day, Aunt Georgina," I said pleasantly. "You look well."

"Of course I do," she replied comfortably. "The sun does wonders for my complexion."

I hadn't noticed before, but her white hair was unadorned. No bonnet or cap sat upon her head, though her neck was lavishly wrapped in a long fur mantle.

"You have not come to visit." The accusation was firmly directed at my mother. I was impressed that she did not shrink under Aunt Georgina's shrewd eyes.

"We have been busy with Elspeth's come out."

"Yes, I've read all about that," she replied coolly.

The women glared at one another.

Drawn to step in and bridge the gap, I said, "Might we call on you, Aunt Georgina?"

She pulled her eyes away from my mother and settled them on me. Silence descended on us while she appeared to make up her mind. "Very well. I have a thing or two to share with you. Good day."

And with that, she was off.

Mother turned for home immediately, huffing out muttered irritations. I scurried to keep up, contemplating what sort of interesting things Aunt Georgina had to share.

CHAPTER 8

Almack's was every bit as stiff and formal as I had been prepared to believe. The punch was sickly sweet, and I didn't bother with cake. Whispers and gestures followed me, and I had to work to keep the placid smile on my face.

Freya, on the other hand, enjoyed every moment of it. "Is this not just delightful?" she asked.

"I think I could find more enjoyment in a multitude of things," Rosalynn said drily.

I had to agree with Rosalynn.

My last partner was Mr. Howe, a portly gentleman I had danced with previously at the Gibsons' ball, and my poor foot had paid the price. He had come down so hard on my foot in the middle of the country dance that I could not continue on and had to be escorted away to a nearby bench. My toes continued to throb, and I tried not to worry about them while my friends kept me company. Mr. Howe had been kind enough to fetch me some punch and then ran from the room like a puppy with its tail between its legs.

I was quite certain he wasn't returning this evening.

"How is your foot?" Rosalynn asked.

"Is it possible to dance with broken toes?" I countered.

A deep voice spoke behind me. "Only if one wants to injure their toes further."

Lord McGregor stepped around our bench and smiled down at me, pity drawing his auburn eyebrows together. "I was seeking you out for a dance, Miss Cox, but I see it is not an opportune time."

"Perhaps if I am to sit out this dance then I will feel more the thing."

He smiled. "May I claim the next, then?"

Mother's face popped up in my mind, and I shoved it away. This was not a dance I would be sad to endure. I liked Lord McGregor's easy geniality. Well, unless my foot was still in pain.

"That would be lovely."

"In that case—" Lord McGregor turned to Rosalynn. "May I have the honor of this dance?"

She narrowed her eyes at him. "Very well."

Lord McGregor took Rosalynn's hand and placed it on his arm as he led her to the dance floor. He said something to her and she laughed, her entire face lighting up.

"Who is that?" Freya asked.

"That is Jack," I explained. "Or, I suppose he is Lord McGregor now."

Comprehension dawned on her face and Freya opened her mouth to speak when another man came and claimed her for the dance. She shot me a look that asked if I was going to be all right alone, and I nodded. The pain in my toes was slowly ebbing and while they still throbbed, I began to feel like perhaps they were not completely broken.

"I would ask you to dance," Lord Cameron said, coming to sit beside me, "but since they've struck up a waltz, I know you would have to decline."

I measured his sincerity but found it impossible to decipher.

Let him think what he would, for if I stated that I was now allowed to waltz then I would be asking for a dance, essentially. Which, after my first ball, was something I swore I would never do.

"It is just as well," I said instead, lifting my toes and testing them with a small stretch. "I have injured my foot."

He smiled softly, a hint of compassion in his gaze. "I noticed."

My eyebrows raised of their own accord.

"It was hard not to," he defended. "You chased poor Mr. Howe out of here."

"There was no chasing, only the breaking of bones and the subsequent request for rest."

"And are you resting sufficiently?" he questioned.

I shot him a look. "Well, I was."

Lord Cameron chuckled. "Touché."

"Where are your brothers this evening?" I asked.

"Somewhere else. They will never step foot in here again if they can help it."

"And you?"

"I cannot help it." He smiled. "I came with a friend."

I nodded sagely, as though I knew who the friend was. He wasn't forthcoming with the information, and I wondered if this friend was of the female persuasion. Not that it mattered to me if it was. Though the tightening in my stomach said otherwise.

"Any luck with your dilemma?" he asked.

"Which one?" I countered.

"Any of them, I suppose."

"Well, perhaps I ought to be grateful that I haven't been shunned this evening, despite my guffawing like a caged bird."

Lord Cameron winced.

"Yes, it truly was that bad." I shook my head slowly. "Can you believe someone would write that about a complete stranger? And who, I dare ask, is the informant? Rosalynn guessed a servant. I suppose that makes the most sense."

"They do hear everything," he agreed.

I tried not to pout, putting on a brave face. "I am ready for the topic to shift to another undeserving soul."

He eyed me carefully. "Why do you say undeserving?"

"Does anyone deserve to be discussed without a proper opportunity to defend themselves?"

He looked unconvinced, his eyebrows drawing together. "But the newspaper is only relaying facts."

"Facts? That is your justification? Lord Cameron, you surprise me." His handsome face and easy conversation had lulled me into a sense of comfort. But if he believed there was nothing wrong with the paper targeting me so directly, then perhaps he was not a man I wished to become friends with.

Rosalynn approached on Lord McGregor's arm, and I stood. My toes were sore. They likely would be the rest of the evening. But I could walk—particularly when it led away from this conversation.

"My dance?" Lord McGregor asked. I gave him my best smile, hoping the informants were somewhere watching now while I stepped out on the arm of the host from that awful dinner. If he did not hold me in contempt for my outburst at his table, the rest of the *ton* needn't either.

"My pleasure," I responded.

He led me to an open space and deposited me in the line of women before finding his place across from me. Tall and broad-shouldered, Lord McGregor had an easy way about him that naturally inspired trust. His wide smile was authentic, and his pale blue eyes glittered. And like a traitor, I found I liked the way he smiled at me.

"Lord McGregor, I must admit you are nothing like I imagined you."

The dance began and he moved away from me. It was some

time before he graced me with a response. "I am not sure what to make of that, Miss Cox."

"Only that I have known Rosalynn for quite some time. And girls that are confined together..."

The dance moved us apart once again. His interested gaze followed me closely as I moved through the steps of the dance and to my discomfort, I enjoyed the feeling.

"Girls that are confined?" he prompted.

"We share with one another."

"What do you share?"

I twirled away in a bubble of satisfaction. The warm glow in my chest growing, I caught his gaze and held it.

"Just stories," I replied, slightly out of breath. "Of red paint, and pretend drowning kittens, and bullfrogs in pinafores."

He let out a monstrous laugh that drew heads from every corner of the room. A small alarm went off in my mind warning me to scale back my grin, but I found I could not.

When the set was complete, he led me away and my mother pounced. She fawned over Lord McGregor's arm, pulling him toward my father so quickly I could not find a way to stop it. My cheeks bloomed and I released his other arm. But when they stepped away from me, I followed. I couldn't leave him to the wolves.

"Such grace, my lord. Absolutely floated across the dance floor," Mother was saying. "I vow, I've never seen a more beautiful dance in all my life."

This she said about a basic minuet.

"And I've scarce enjoyed myself more," Lord McGregor's low reply came, coupled with a conspiratorial glance my way.

"Close your jaw, Elspeth," Mother snapped.

I slammed my mouth shut obediently and smiled at the poor earl. He had no doubt been saying those things to appease my parents. Father was now asking him about the horses he kept in London. I wanted to run away and hide my face under a pillow.

Instead, I settled for smiling politely and nodding my head along to whatever they were speaking about.

"She would love to," Mother said, nodding vigorously.

Drat, I hadn't been paying attention. Lord McGregor watched me intently, while my parents were locked on him.

"Would you?" he asked.

What choice did I have? The original question was irrelevant. I was not allowed to say no. "Of course, my lord."

His answering smile made it worth it, whatever it was I had agreed to.

"Tomorrow?" he asked, this time directed at my parents.

"Yes, yes."

"Splendid." He picked up my hand and bestowed a kiss on the back of it. My breath caught in my throat. "Until then."

As he walked away, my gaze passed over the room and found the majority of eyes on me. A blush heated my cheeks. I had been named 'the one to watch' in the article, and evidently, Society was taking the advice seriously.

CHAPTER 9

"What do you enjoy doing in your spare time?"

Lord McGregor led the curricle deftly through traffic and into Hyde Park at the peak of the fashionable hour. Our carriage crawled at a snail's pace, affording us ample opportunity for conversation. I came to learn that I had agreed to a ride with him in the park today, which I was both relieved and excited to learn.

I considered what my mother would want me to answer, and what she would certainly wish for me to keep to myself. I settled on a healthy mixture of the two. "I enjoy playing the pianoforte, drawing, and archery," I said. "And when I have enough time, I thoroughly enjoy creating stories."

"Stories?" he asked, his auburn eyebrows pulling together. "Do you write books?"

"Yes and no. I write the stories sometimes, but with no intention of publishing them. I only enjoy the developing of the story, not the technical aspect of creating a book."

He seemed no more enlightened.

"For example, if given a free afternoon to fill how I wish, I would deposit myself on a park bench in a highly populated area and watch people. My mind begins spinning tales of their lives and before you know it, I have entire sagas playing out in my head about the family picnicking on the green."

"I see. Shall we give it a go? What do you know about that couple there?" he asked, pointing to a sour looking man in a barouche beside a frilly, excitable lady.

I turned to him abruptly. "I do not gossip sir, it is all a creation of my own mind. For my own pleasure."

His arm gestured in a large flourish. "Then create."

I eyed him from the side, gauging his sincerity. I did not feel as though he was mocking me, but I took my own little game and laid it bare for him to judge. Delicately clearing my throat, I began. "He is a small country squire."

"Is he really?"

"No, not really…oh, you are only teasing. All right, my lord, no more interruptions."

He nodded.

I continued. "He is a small country squire, and she was the local vicar's youngest daughter. After watching her grow older from a church pew and falling more and more in love with her from a distance, he chose to approach the vicar and request her hand in marriage." I settled into the bench, finding myself settling further into the story. "The vicar shocked our country squire by turning him down. At first, the squire was outraged. Who would provide a better life for the vicar's daughter than he? No one! But as time went on, he came to wonder more and more why he was rejected. Upon asking the vicar, he learned that the girl was high-spirited and her father simply thought they wouldn't suit.

"The country squire was outraged by this and demanded the lady's hand in marriage, to which she gracefully, and her father reluctantly, accepted. They had been married six months when the squire's bride asked to be brought to London for the Season. He agreed on the small hope that perhaps time in the metropolis would give his bride something to do and would, in turn, grant him some respite."

We both looked at the couple in question. The man sighed, his eyes drooping in boredom, and the woman jabbered on eagerly, pointing at various things and asking her companion questions.

Lord McGregor's shoulders shook subtly, and I glanced at him promptly to find him holding in a laugh. "You are something else, Miss Cox, if I can so boldly say. That is the most entertaining drive I have ever taken in Hyde Park."

"The pleasure is mine, my lord."

"Shall we go again?"

I looked around for another subject while our carriage came to a full stop.

"Miss Cox. Jack," Lord Cameron called from his own curricle, seated beside Rosalynn and facing us. He pulled his carriage to a stop beside ours. "What a lovely day we are having, are we not?"

"Quite," Lord McGregor said. "Though I'm afraid the weather was the least of my notice. I have been thoroughly entertained by Miss Cox. Lady Rosalynn, where have you been hiding such a gem all these years?"

"At Miss Smythe's school, naturally. I could not share her with the lot of you for fear she'd spoil." She sent me a saucy wink.

I returned a wry grin.

Lord McGregor clapped a hand over his chest. "Do not malign me so. You must let her make out my character for herself."

"I believe I have a general idea already," I said.

He turned his smile on me. "And do you like what you see thus far?"

"What cheek!" I backed away from him dramatically, but we were in a two-seated vehicle, and I hadn't much room as it was.

"She is not a timid flower, Jack," Rosalynn stated proudly.

Lord Cameron watched me with interest beside his sister. I wanted to know his opinion of me. Did he find me a timid flower, or did he see something more?

"No." Lord McGregor glanced down at me as though taking my measure for himself and stealing my attention. "Of that I am most certain."

As we pulled up to my house on Berkeley Street, I allowed Lord McGregor to help me down from the high seat.

"Thank you, sir. I enjoyed that ride immensely."

"As did I," he said gallantly. "Perhaps I may call on you at home soon?"

I caught my mother's eyes in the drawing room window before she let the curtain drop over her face. It swung a moment, dangling in the window like the bait I stood beside—Lord McGregor was going to become my mother's greatest accomplishment. Or at least, that is how she was likely imagining the situation.

My options were limited. I could not turn him away, and I could not change myself to make him despise me. But there was one thing I could do.

I stepped forward, allowing my hand to fall on his arm. Dragging my fingers lightly down his sleeve, I tilted my head to deliver a coy smile. "I would enjoy it above all things," I said, my voice low and sultry.

Widened blue eyes raked over me. He cleared his throat and stepped back slightly, disentangling himself from my grip. "Yes, well…I shall see you at the Waltons' ball? Yes?"

I nodded, but he was still backing away as though my fingers had been laced with poison.

"Lovely. Until then." He nodded a quick goodbye and hopped onto his curricle.

My stomach burned, shame swirling within me. I swallowed the bile rising in my throat and tried to find comfort in my success. He drove away, shooting me an uncomfortable smile over his shoulder, and I stood in front of my house, considering two things. The first, that I had most definitely come on too strong. The second, that it could be the very answer I had been searching for.

Glancing up to the window where my mother had previously stationed herself, I watched the curtain continue to sway and smiled to myself. I had done it. I was going to come out of this Season intact.

All I had to do was scare away the men by being the very woman I had described to Lord McGregor in my story earlier. I had to push them away with my excess of enthusiasm, as though my mind held no other goal than matrimony.

I would become my mother.

CHAPTER 10

This was it. This was the moment I was going to show them all. The musicians tuned their instruments for a waltz, and I had my sights set on Lord Fischer, standing only a few feet away. I had not shared a dance with him since that first ball, and he would be the perfect man to test my new strategy on. Coming on too strong had worked wonders on Lord McGregor, but how would it affect a different man? Particularly one who had never shown me any interest.

I sidled up beside Lord Fischer and let out a long, drawn-out sigh. His eyes caught mine briefly down his nose, he smiled politely, and then looked away again.

Dismissed. I suppressed an irritated scoff.

His clothing was no less fashionable today than it had been at that first ball, and he was no less foppish in his green and purple striped waistcoat and immaculate golden jacket.

Perhaps a different target would be better suited for this purpose. But no. I was already here. I swallowed my apprehension, stepped a little closer, and sighed again, drawing this one out even longer. "Oh, how I long to dance the waltz," I said dreamily.

Several moments went by before Lord Fischer faced me and held out his arm obligingly. I grinned triumphantly.

"Will you do me the honor, Miss Cox?"

"I would be delighted, my lord." I clasped his arm as he walked me out to the floor and I felt myself breaking through a barrier and joining the rest of society in something that before now I had only witnessed from afar. Despite my desire to waltz, and the need to test out my eagerness on an unwitting Lord Fischer, I was nervous. He lined me up in the outer circle of dancers, and we began the promenade. I suppressed the anxious swirling in my stomach and offered him a coy smile.

Before now, I had only ever done this dance with my dancing master. And he was a septuagenarian.

The feel of a man's strong arms leading me around the floor in the previously improper dance made me giddy and light-headed. I found my smile growing as we glided across the floor. I caught many surprised faces, which tempered my glee. Apparently, it had been common knowledge that I was the woman talked about in that first article.

I pasted my smile back on and enjoyed the heady experience that was waltzing.

As the song came to a close, Lord Fischer led me back toward my mother, but I subtly shifted his direction toward the refreshments. I was still delighted from the dance. It was chivalrous of him to step out with me when he probably would have avoided it if he could have.

No, not *probably*. Most definitely would have avoided it. Appearances mattered to the dandy, and I could not be someone he would choose to align himself with.

With no little chagrin, I turned toward him, grasping his arm. "Thank you, Lord Fischer. It was most kind of you, and I find I enjoyed the waltz every bit as much as I imagined I would."

"The pleasure was mine, Miss Cox," he said obligingly, dipping his head.

I was sure that was not true, and I let him escape just before my mother came upon us.

"Tell me everything," she commanded.

"I waltzed."

She let out a huff that bathed my face in garlic.

I noted my next partner nearby and stepped away from her. "And now I am due to dance with Lord Cameron. If you will excuse me, I am not letting a single opportunity slip away."

Mother's face was a mixture of irritation and delight, but she didn't stop me when Lord Cameron approached and led me away.

"You are enjoying yourself this evening," he said, tilting his head closer to me. His breath tickled my ear and sent a wave of shivers down my neck.

"Yes, I am," I agreed.

We took our places for the quadrille and his gaze was unyielding, his brown eyes fixed on me while we waited for the music to begin. "You are changed."

I mocked offense. "Are you implying that I have not previously enjoyed myself?"

"Yes, absolutely."

I had no rebuttal. Gratefully, the music began and did not give us an opportunity to finish the conversation. I was more than a little unnerved by Lord Cameron's accusation. Particularly because he had been somewhat correct. Oh, not entirely. I enjoyed dancing as a general rule. But until now I had found too much to be anxious about to consider taking any real pleasure in the dances. I had been too busy worrying about the bargain.

The set came to a close with limited conversation and an excess of scrutiny. "I find myself parched, sir. Would you be so kind as to escort me to your sister?" I asked kindly.

I was not about to try my little act on him. I knew without a doubt he would instantly see through it.

Rosalynn stood against the wall holding a glass of lemonade. I joined her and Lord Cameron left to procure me a glass of my own.

"You waltzed," she said, her eyes shining bright, her cheeks gently flushed from her own exertions. "Freya is out there now with Lord McGregor."

"You introduced them?" I asked.

"Of course." She looked at me sideways. "I only hope she does not question him on his past transgressions like my other friend might have done."

"It was a mere reference. I hardly said anything at all." I laughed. "He told you?"

"We do not have many secrets." She shrugged. "He is like a brother."

"Ah yes, one of The Tyrants."

"I believe," said Lord Cameron from behind me, "that I have outgrown that childish nickname."

Rosalynn grinned at me. "No, he certainly has not."

I accepted my glass of lemonade, drank it with unladylike swiftness, and placed the glass back in his hands. "I am late for a dance with Mr. Fenway. I can see him searching for me now." I looked at Rosalynn, who gave me a questioning gaze. "I will fill you in later." I grinned, and then I was off.

I'd found a way to endure the Season, for making a game of the men was unquestionably satisfying.

MISS C HAS WALTZED!
Indeed, Miss C has turned the tables on the Fashionable World, spurning antiquated ideals for the increasingly popular waltz. She was seen at Almack's last evening thoroughly enjoying the

modern dance in the arms of the distinguished Lord F . Might there be a new romance budding? Gentlemen, now is the time to stake your claims, or the lovely Miss C could soon be off the marriage market for good.

"This is the outside of enough!" Mother said, tossing the newspaper onto the floor beside the kitchen table.

Father wiped his mouth, speaking calmly as though he were appeasing a child. "Calm yourself, it cannot be as bad as that."

"Calm myself?" Mother seared him with a glare. Her chest rose and fell rapidly, her eyes bulging. "Mr. Cox, you must not understand. We were mocked for having values. Now we are mocked for attempting to modernize. Will these people never be pleased?"

"Perhaps," he said calmly, "we should cease trying to please the insignificant wretches behind the articles and pour our efforts into securing a decent match for Elspeth."

Mother paused, her jaw working back and forth while her brain concocted a new scheme. I swallowed.

"Perhaps I should lie low for a while," I cautiously ventured. "Surely they would find someone else to discuss if they had nothing to say about me."

"Not an option," Mother replied instantly. "With both Lord Fischer and Lord McGregor showing interest, it is the worst time to retreat. We need you seen now more than ever."

"But—"

"No," Father said forcefully. I slammed my mouth shut. "You will listen to your elders, Elspeth. We know better."

Resentment and annoyance built within me, begging my body to move and my tongue to fight. I wanted to shout, to defend my argument. Had they known better when they forbade me from dancing the waltz at the Gibsons' ball? Father returned to his meal, the matter closed. Reluctantly, I bit my tongue. Arguing was hardly worth the effort.

"Get dressed, Elsie," Mother said sharply. "We are going to correct this disaster."

I rose from the table, leaving behind my half-eaten breakfast.

The article certainly did not paint me in a very flattering light, but anyone who believed in a possible romance between Lord Fischer and me was positively blind.

I dressed slowly, not particularly eager to find out how Mother meant to correct this disaster.

"Molly," I asked while she fastened my dress, "would you happen to know who is informing on me to the newspaper?"

Her hands paused, and I found my breathing halt with them.

Was that indecision flickering in her eyes or mere nerves? "What do you mean, miss?"

"I just don't see who could be writing these things about me. While they are not altogether mean, they certainly aren't kind. And the more articles there are, the more concerned I find myself." I sighed, pouring my frustrations on an unwitting maid. "I only wanted to enjoy the Season. I don't even want a husband."

"Do you not, miss?" Molly finished fastening my gown, and I turned to face her. She hastily tried to mask her surprise.

"No, I do not. Is it really so odd that I would prefer to find a comfortable home somewhere where I can govern myself and never have to worry again about obeying someone else? Where I would be free."

Her eyes flashed. I had not considered until that moment how a servant might view my opinions. Ashamed, I swallowed a lump and straightened my shoulders. She may live a life of servitude, but she chose to work as a maid, and my higher status did not mean my feelings were less important.

"You have freedom," she said.

"Not entirely, no. I am not of age and must live by my father's word. He is my master. If I marry, my husband would become my master. As a woman, the only option I have, if I want to retain a semblance of independence, is to remain unwed. Becoming a spinster is my only choice."

Molly seemed to consider this. I didn't know why her opinion mattered to me. Perhaps I simply appreciated explaining myself to someone who was truly listening. Her ability to hear my story or validate my feelings did not diminish simply because I paid her to do my bidding.

"I don't know about those things. But I do know your mother wants you to look your best at all times," Molly said. I let her guide me to my dressing table and seat me on the tufted chair.

"Because I typically look like a disheveled pig?"

That pulled a small smile from Molly's lips. "I am only following orders," she said.

Yes, I thought, *I know how that feels.*

CHAPTER 11

Mother's face had never before looked as determined as it did riding in the carriage toward the Duke of Clifton's house that morning. "You will leave the talking to me," she said.

"Yes, Mother."

I pushed away my apprehension as we pulled in front of the stately building. Whatever mother's intention, Rosalynn was one of my closest friends. Surely she would understand.

Mother presented her card and minutes later the butler led us into the drawing room. Rosalynn raised her eyebrows slightly, and I grimaced. I wanted her to know this wasn't my idea. Of course, she should know me well enough to understand that all on her own. I hoped.

"It has been ages since I saw you last, your grace. And you look so lovely," Mother gushed.

"Thank you, Mrs. Cox." The duchess gestured for us to be seated. Her raven hair was pulled into an elegant knot and her gown flowed like one long strand of ribbon from her neck to the floor. "How is London treating you this Season?"

"Fabulously, your grace, as always," Mother simpered. I

wanted to hide beneath the pillow I was leaning against. I purposefully ignored Rosalynn's amused glance. "I could not be more pleased with Elsie's progress. She's caught the eye of many dignified young men. She'll have her pick between men of both title and fortune, if things continue this way."

"How lovely," the Duchess of Clifton said.

Mother continued. "I was just telling Lady Harriet the other day—you are familiar with her, yes? Her brother is the Earl of Ford—about Lord McGregor taking my Elsie on a drive to the park."

"Tea?" Rosalynn's mother lifted a teapot and began to pour.

"Two sugars, please. And the article from this morning"—she clicked her tongue—"I am just *overjoyed* Elsie is getting the attention she deserves. Nothing will be talked about this Season more than her, I vow."

"You've not heard then?"

The room was so quiet I heard a drip of tea fall from the suspended teapot and splash in the cup below it. Mother was not about to admit she did not know something, and the duchess was merrily guarding the gossip as if she held a freshly wrapped gift. Thus, I sacrificed for the cause.

"Please fill me in, your grace," I said. My mother sent me a glare and I quickly added, "I spend so much time *dancing* that I've hardly any time to hear the latest news."

Rosalynn's face was a picture of concealed mirth. I yearned to laugh but miraculously kept my face straight.

The duchess took a long, slow sip of her tea and set the cup gingerly on the table. "*The Green Door.*"

"Pardon?"

"It is a novel," she explained. "Rumor is circulating that the characters are real people. It has become something of a game to determine whose secrets the author has displayed for our entertainment."

"Oh, *that*." Mother laughed shrilly. "I know of *The Green Door*.

I have the book in my dressing room right now, I merely have not finished it yet."

She set her tea on the table and stood. "Come, Elsie, we have more friends to visit today. Lovely to see you, your grace. Thank you for the tea."

The duchess dipped her head in acknowledgment, a smile briefly tipping the corners of her mouth. She turned to me. "You shall be out of the spotlight soon, Miss Cox. Give this book another day or two to finish circulation, and I am certain no one will even remember your name ever graced the news."

Mother's entire face was tight when she ushered me back to the carriage, her lips pinched and cheeks rosy. I merely held on to hope that the duchess's words would come to fruition.

"To Hatchards," Mother said crisply to the footman helping us into the cab. "We must buy that book."

CHAPTER 12

"A parcel arrived for you, Miss Elsie," Billington said when we arrived home empty-handed. Mother humphed, dropping her shawl onto the butler's arms and stomping up to her dressing room.

I thanked Billington and took the bundle upstairs to my bedchamber. The note was in Rosalynn's hand, but I set it aside. I was fairly sure I knew what she had sent over. Untying the string, I peeled back the thick brown paper to reveal a leather-bound book with golden letters on the cover.

The Green Door.

Thank the heavens Rosalynn could see through Mother's paltry defenses and knew we did not have the book in our possession. She must have been aware *The Green Door* was sold out all over London for the time being, which was certainly going to aid in its exclusivity.

I opened up the first page and dove in.

The passage of time was evident in the darkening of my bedroom window and Molly coming in to light the lamps. I set the book down and stretched my arms high above my head, aware that I had wasted an entire day enthralled in the story of lords spurned and ladies deceived. It was captivating and entirely inappropriate, and Mother never would have allowed me to read it if she had gotten her hands on it first.

Thank you, Rosalynn.

Molly pulled a gown from the wardrobe and subtly helped me from my bed. I rubbed my tired eyes and yawned, allowing her to help me out of my day dress and into a…ball gown?

"Molly, you've chosen the wrong dress."

She gave me a small smile. "Heard it from the missus. Change of plans. You're going to a ball tonight."

I frowned. "Do you know where it is to be held? I've not heard of anything for this evening."

She shrugged. "Sorry, miss. I don't know."

Tucking the book under my pillow, I gave it one last longing glance before picking up my silver silk shawl and wrapping it around my shoulders. Mother was awaiting me in the foyer and made to leave when I joined her.

"Should we not wait for Father?"

"He is off at his club for the evening, so it is only us tonight."

"Where are we headed?" We descended the steps to the waiting carriage, the cool air patting my cheeks. The wind swallowed my question, and I asked her again once we were seated inside.

"Aunt Georgina has sent us an invitation for a soiree she is hosting this evening."

I glanced down at the simple rosettes embroidered on my gown. It was the same one I had worn to the Gibsons' ball. "But I am in a ball gown."

"Don't be daft. It is a ball."

How was I meant to know that? She had called it a soiree. It was not an enjoyable experience to consistently feel half-informed.

We approached a well-lit townhouse, complete with liveried

footmen lining the steps and music and laughter floating through the open windows. It was no Berkeley Street, but it was still a prominent neighborhood; a testament of Aunt Georgina's immense wealth.

"Be on your best behavior tonight," Mother said. As though I ever wasn't. "Yes, Mother."

There was no receiving line. Our names were announced, the majority of the people nearby turning to look. My cheeks grew warm from the attention, and I followed my mother with a meekness I did not know myself capable of. She spotted an acquaintance and walked directly toward the group of women she knew.

Though I recognized a few faces from other events, for the most part, I did not see many of my aunt's guests that I knew.

"Mrs. Cox, I did not think to see you here this evening," an older woman said as we approached, her beady eyes raking over mother's gown and then mine.

"Beatrice, did you not know Georgina Stuart is David Cox's aunt?" Mrs. Hapworth cut in, her long ostrich plume bobbing along with her head.

"I knew," the beady-eyed woman responded.

Mother smiled in a way that made me nervous. "Mrs. Johns, I recently learned of your son's return from Spain. How is he doing?"

The older woman's face went crimson. "He is home, recovering from his wounds."

"And your daughter, Mrs. Hapworth?"

"She is dancing now," the woman replied smugly. "With Lord McGregor."

My head spun to the dance floor, and I took in the attractive couple in the midst of a waltz. Lord McGregor smiled down at Cecily, leading her through the steps, and a small part of me did not like seeing them together. Strange, that. I watched him speak to her, his expression polite and engaged. Precisely how he had treated me.

But Cecily looked up at the earl with a pleased countenance that sent a fire through my chest, giving me the strongest urge to defend him against her. On further deduction, it was not jealousy I was feeling, but something of a more defensive nature.

I did not want the man for myself, but neither did I think Cecily deserving of him. He was a good man, and she was manipulative.

"They make a handsome couple, do they not, Miss Cox?"

"Hmm? Oh, yes," I said, my attention drawn back to the older women. "Quite lovely."

Before Mother could bring up the lone carriage ride Lord McGregor took me on to Hyde park recently, I hooked my arm around hers and said, "We really must greet my aunt, Mother, should we not?"

Her smile was tight. "Of course, Elsie."

I led her toward the back of the room where Aunt Georgina was holding court among a circle of older women. Her gown was a large arrangement of purple and gold, her ample girth covered in silk flowers and artfully placed bows. The violet feathers protruding from her elaborate coiffure were made all the brighter set against her stark white hair. Quirky style aside, it was clear Aunt Georgina was surprised by our appearance, and I strained to hide my embarrassment. It crossed my mind to wonder if Mother had brought me along to the party uninvited, but I refused to believe even she could sink that low.

"Elspeth, darling, I did not expect to see you tonight." Aunt Georgina stood and offered me her cheek. I obligingly kissed it.

Mother said, "It was kind of you to invite us this evening. Unfortunately, David had prior engagements but we could not pass up the opportunity to attend."

"I'm sure." Turning to me, my aunt gave me a very knowing smile. "Gratified as I am that you chose to attend one of my events, you don't need to sit by this old biddy all evening when you'd rather be dancing." She settled herself back into her chair and leaned forward, admonishing. "But tell me you will come by sometime this week? I've yet to get my visit out of you, darling."

My neck warmed. I had told her I would visit when we met her at the park and was long overdue on that promise. "Of course. I would love to."

"Splendid."

We turned to leave and she called, "Must you go, Mrs. Cox? I was looking forward to a quiet coze."

Mother stilled, pasting on a stiff smile. "Run along, Elspeth."

I looked at her with no little confusion. Run along? I was no child. Who was I meant to run along to? None of my friends were even here.

At that moment, Cecily came off the dance floor on Lord McGregor's arm, and I pivoted away. I would prefer not to be wrapped into a conversation with her if I could help it. Unfortunately, by not watching where I was going, I ran straight into another gentleman, only to lose my balance and nearly topple over. His arms shot out and steadied me, and I laughed to stem my awkwardness.

When I glanced up, I was stricken with the distinct impression that I had seen this man before, though I knew not where. His navy coat was nicely tailored and his smile wide, a familiar gleam in his eye as he took me in.

"Miss Cox," he said smoothly. "I am glad to run into you. Tell me, how have you been?"

I gingerly stepped away. "I am sorry, sir, do I know you?"

"You wound me," he said dramatically, slapping his hand against his well adorned chest. His neatly styled hair did not move as he dipped his head to speak to me. "Do you not recall the moment we met? I shall never forget it, I vow."

There was something so familiar about his face that I trusted the truth of his words. I simply could not place them. The answer was on the edge of my consciousness, close enough to know it was there, but still just out of reach, and it made me feel vulnerable.

"Shall we dance?" he asked, his smile wide and inviting. He had light brown hair and crinkles around his eyes that were evidence of his affinity for smiling.

Caution reminded me that I'd yet to learn his name. But I found it didn't bother me, and I placed my hand in his and allowed him to lead me into a cotillion.

The dance was a measure in patience. Each time I was within reach of my partner, I found myself wishing to know his name. I passed through another man's hands and my gaze continually traveled back to him. When the dance finally came to a close, he escorted me from the floor toward the back corner of the room. We were still in plain sight, but he helped me to sit on a bench out of the way.

"Major Gregory Heybourne at your service," he said with a flourish before sitting beside me.

Memories flooded me at once, and my mouth dropped open. I knew instantly who he was and where I had previously met him, and my face undoubtedly showed my shock.

He chuckled softly, a mischievous glint to his eye. "Have you been to Bath recently?"

"As a matter of fact, I have not been to Bath since I met you last. And you are so changed, sir. I never would have guessed…" Blood rushed to my cheeks, and I cast my eyes down. It was utterly mortifying to be in this position. No wonder he had chosen to conceal his identity until after we had danced. He knew I would have had a hard time accepting a dance from him if I'd known.

By my word, I never would have guessed that the tall, handsome man before me was the same gentleman I had danced with at the assembly hall in Bath when my parents had taken me on a short holiday two years before. I had been sixteen and caught up in my first public ball, when the kind Major Heybourne in his handsome regimentals had asked me to partner him. He had been at least twice as wide then as he was now, and his considerable girth made dancing a slightly difficult feat. It had turned dangerous when he tripped over my gown, propelling me into a group of ladies idly chatting nearby holding glasses of bright red punch.

I had doused all of them with their drinks, as well as myself, and twisted my ankle in the process, to the extent that I had to be taken home for the evening.

I was so mortified at the time that I stayed in my room at our inn until my parents were ready to travel home, refusing Major Heybourne when he came to the hotel to inquire after me.

"Have you been in Bath all this time?" I asked.

"No," he said, smiling. He did not appear to hold a grudge for the way I had cut him before, unable to face him in my shame. I had been young, however, and our acquaintance had only been of a few days in Bath. But I distinctly recalled Major Heybourne's consistent smiling, and his kind soul. "I was called back to fight Napoleon shortly after that incident. I had been on leave at the time, you'll recall."

"Yes," I nodded. "You look so changed," I couldn't help but say. Embarrassment immediately clutched my stomach. Why had I so brazenly commented on his change in weight? It hadn't caused me to appreciate his friendship any less at the time, and it didn't make me enjoy his company any more now. Though I had to admit his dancing was much improved. I suppose that was something to appreciate.

He laughed. "Lack of food on the Peninsula will do that to a man."

His jovial tone did not match his words. "That cannot have been easy."

"No, it wasn't easy," he agreed, his smile turning endearing.

"Elspeth!"

I jerked away from the shrill voice behind me. Mother stood there, her strained expression doing nothing to hide her discomfort.

I swallowed. "Mother, you remember Major Heybourne?"

Her face stilled. I could see her mind working to make the connection between the name she recognized and the changed man sitting before her. "Yes," she said finally. "From Bath, was it?"

I had yet to decide if it was positive that Mother recognized the Major when he stood and bowed becomingly, his bright smile winning him a smile in return. The episode in Bath had not been my best moment. I was glad we seemed to have put it behind us. At the time, I had wholeheartedly blamed the man before me. But in truth, it was a stumble; a simple mistake. It could happen to anyone, and I had long since let go of any resentment I had childishly clung to regarding Major Heybourne. I was gratified Mother seemed to have done the same.

"Are you staying in town?" Major Heybourne eyed me before turning back to Mother.

"We are in Berkeley Street."

"May I presume to call upon you at some point in the future?"

I glanced at Mother once and then back to the Major. It mattered not that she approved. I had only one answer I was permitted to give.

"I would like it above all things, sir." Not a complete exaggeration, if one was to consider the men that had asked me that same question so far. Major Heybourne certainly was among the highest on the list.

"How blessed I was to run into you, Miss Cox." Major Heybourne had a smile playing on his lips and I read the implication of his words.

Mother gave him a searching look. "Fortuitous, indeed."

CHAPTER 13

The ball was nearing its close when I spotted a familiar face sitting alone on the other side of the room. I caught her gaze and found I had no other recourse but to cross to where she sat. I approached with some trepidation, but it was unnecessary to worry about how I would be received. Or, so I told myself. "How are you, Cecily?"

Her hazel eyes searched my own, and I considered the possibility that I should have ignored her instead, as I had done earlier. But one does not share a room with another person for the entirety of our years at school and then give them the cut direct in the ballroom.

"I am well enough," she answered.

There was ample room on the bench, but I did not presume to sit beside her.

"Are you enjoying the Season?" I asked, beginning to regret my approach.

She nodded. "In part. I don't believe we'll be staying long, however. There are things that must be attended to at home, you see. I cannot be away for long."

I nodded. Though truthfully, I had no idea what she was referring to.

"Have you any more luck in remembering names?"

She eyed me. "I am improving, of course. With parties every evening it would be hard not to."

I waited a beat longer, then said, "I shall see you around, then."

"Perhaps," she said with a shrug, her attention floating back to the dancers.

I was dismissed, but it was no matter. I had never particularly liked Cecily, I only felt sorry for her undeserved reputation at school. If anyone should know that she spent each night in her own bed, it was I. But it mattered little what I said in defense, her reputation never recovered fully after the rumors involving her and the dancing master had made their destructive rounds.

Mother's beckoning gaze called me, and I met her at the door. Her face seemed to have aged in the span of the last few hours. Her eyes looked dull, her mouth drawn.

"Let's go home," she said weakly.

I picked up her hand and strung it through my arm, a rare surge of affection coursing through me. "Yes, Mama. Let's go home."

"This is perhaps the most entertaining thing I have ever read." I looked up from the leather-bound book in my hand and caught Molly's eye through my mirror. "I must find a way to present it to my mother."

"Shall I place it in her dressing room?"

"No." I sighed. "If I want her to know I've read it, then I must present it to her."

Molly continued placing pins in my hair, fixing me with a stare. "Why does she have to know you've read it?"

A smile played on my lips. It was not as though I'd never hidden novels from my parents. Of course I had. But the Duchess of Clifton's words rang in my ears. This was likely to be the most talked about thing in all of London's drawing rooms very soon. "It is bound to be brought up in conversations, and if Mother knows I read it then I needn't guard my tongue."

I carried the book down to the breakfast room, hesitantly peeking inside to ensure Father was not present.

To my astonishment, not only was he in the room, but he was sitting beside my mother. Their low voices and bent heads indicated the severity of the conversation. Hiding the book within the folds of my gown, I walked through the door.

The room went still. Mother's eye caught mine and she glanced at Father before straightening in her chair. I chose a seat across from her and sat down, shoving the book underneath my leg.

"Elspeth, you are awake."

I reached for the teapot and poured myself a cup, adding cream and stirring in one lump of sugar. "Good Morning, Mother. Father."

He grunted.

I could not stand to walk to the sideboard and fill a plate without revealing the book, and it was imperative I keep the book between my mother and me. It was not likely Father would disapprove entirely, but given his reaction the last time I presented a book to my mother in his presence, I was cautious. I had tried to convince her to read Mary Wollstonecraft's *Vindication of the Rights of Woman*.

It had not gone over well.

"Do we have any engagements today?"

"A dinner and musicale at the Hurst's home," Mother said.

My spirits soared. "Is that so? How lovely."

Father stood. "I shall return by this evening."

Mother gave him a firm look, their eyes locked in silent communication. He nodded once, imperceptibly, and then was gone.

What on earth was that about?

"We shall go to the modiste today," Mother said, buttering her muffin. "You need more gowns."

"Yes, Mother."

I was glad to be going to Freya's home that evening. Since Father had demanded I ask permission before leaving the house during the day, I had hardly seen Freya or Rosalynn, except for the balls and dinners we were all invited to. Which, luckily, was a good number of them.

I sipped my tea, determining the best way to explain how I got my hands on *The Green Door* when Mother stood to leave.

"Wait," I said. She turned toward me and I gulped, my hand fishing within my skirts for the book. "I thought you might want to read this. I borrowed it from a friend."

Honesty. That was simply the only way to go. She approached me, eying the book skeptically.

"*The Green Door*," she said aloud. Her eyebrows raised. "But where—"

"I read it in hours, Mother. It was fascinating. I vow Rosalynn's mother was correct about this book. My time in the spotlight is surely over."

She took the book from my hand and searched my face. Saying nothing, she turned and walked from the room. It was not kind to bring up the duchess's remarks, but it had been successful. Mother did not ask again from whom I received the book.

And if I had hit my mark, then she would spend the remainder of the day reading and I was free to do as I wished.

CHAPTER 14

The Hurst home was positively overflowing with flowers, assaulting my senses the moment I stepped through the front door. Freya had mentioned her mama's affinity for bouquets a time or two but never before had I seen it in action. The effect was stunning, regardless of the overpowering smell. Flowers of many varieties cascaded down the stairway and formed an arbor at the entrance to the music room, where they covered every available surface.

It was only a musicale—not even a ball. Clearly Mrs. Hurst did not do things by halves.

"Freya, this looks amazing," I said when I found her and Rosalynn standing beside the fireplace.

Rosalynn wrinkled her nose. "If only it smelled as nice as it looked."

"I'm immune to the scent," Freya said, delicately lifting one shoulder.

"I'm not sure if that is a blessing or a deprivation," Rosalynn said.

Freya looked thoughtful. "It's likely a healthy mixture of the two."

Lord McGregor approached, Lord Cameron by his side, both wearing dark coats and handsome countenances.

The earl turned to Freya. "May I inquire what is both a blessing and a deprivation?"

Rosalynn's lips tipped up when she answered Lord McGregor. "Freya has grown accustomed to the smell."

"Ah." The earl nodded in understanding. "It certainly is...floral."

"That's the best you could come up with?" Lord Cameron asked, one dark eyebrow raised in challenge.

Lord McGregor nodded decisively. "Yes."

Well, he was honest at least. I found him glancing between Freya and Rosalynn. Was he purposely not looking to me? I supposed I wouldn't blame him after I came on so strong following our ride in the park. He had probably appreciated that I was not seeking an attachment, at least in the beginning. He was an eligible earl. In marrying him, one would not have to wait for his father to die to gain a title. Which made Lord McGregor one of the best catches of the Season, to be sure. His following of doting debutantes was considerable, and I felt guilty for using him as an experiment.

Although, he had seemed interested at the time. Realistically, I had done him a favor.

"A ha'penny for your thoughts, Miss Cox?"

I pivoted toward Lord Cameron, startled to find his eyes fixed on me. "Pardon?"

He tilted his head, considering me. "Your nose was scrunched up, and lines have formed on your forehead. Those actions do not imply shallow thoughts."

I tried to guard my surprise at Lord Cameron's candor. "Why? For all you know, I was wondering whether there would be pudding with our dinner or not."

He did not look convinced, and it was a little frightening that he could so easily see through me. "Were you?"

"No."

"Honesty," he said, stepping closer, his mouth hitching into a half-smile. "Quite refreshing."

"To a degree," I countered, leaning back slightly. I was not about to inform him that I had been considering his friend's prospects.

"Elsie is astute," Rosalynn said, drawing my gaze from her brother's face to her own. "Do you care to venture a guess?"

"Regarding?"

"*The Green Door.*"

All eyes were on me, awaiting my answer. Was it socially acceptable to enjoy the book? Because I had, thoroughly. I took a leap and chose to go with honesty. "I loved it."

"Of course you loved it," Freya said. "We are not asking about the book in general, but the actual green door. Who do you think it belongs to?"

Oh, that. I had no idea. The green door allegedly led to a drawing room that revolved constantly with high society—and, subsequently, their scandals. Apparently, everyone in town had gone through the door at one point or another if the anonymous author were to be believed. "I have no earthly idea. Though I would love to find out."

"Wouldn't we all?" Freya asked dreamily.

"Not I," Lord McGregor said. "It makes no difference to me."

Rosalynn shot him a knowing smile. "Surely you've read the book, though."

He grinned. "Of course I have."

Dinner was announced and the sea of guests made their way to the dining room where I was surprised to find myself seated beside Lord Cameron once again.

"How fortunate I am," he said with great flair, helping me into my seat. I was beginning to see how Rosalynn considered him the charismatic brother.

"Bizarre is more apt."

"Not really," he said, "if you consider that we are both middle of the pack where our ranks are considered."

"I should think you far outrank me," I countered.

He gestured to the men in the room. "Not with two older brothers and a large gathering of titled men."

True. I slipped off my gloves and laid them in my lap.

His gaze prickled my skin, running over me like a cool breeze while we awaited the footmen. My shoulders shook with a slight shiver, and I tried to mask it.

"Would you care to enlighten me now?" he asked.

"If you enlighten me first," I said. "What should you like to know?" I did quite a bit of reading. I could probably talk his ear off about a number of subjects. And these dinners lasted hours—or so it felt. We had plenty of time.

Lord Cameron's face took on a contemplative expression. His dark eyes looked thoughtful, the muscle jumping in his jaw.

The first course was set before us, and I lifted my spoon.

"What is it you cannot do?" he asked with a measured calm. "What Rosalynn and you were discussing the morning in the music room."

My spoon stilled. Did he not know already? I searched my memory. "I was sure we discussed this very thing at the last dinner."

"I tried to," he said calmly. He was regulating his expression, his tone, as though he did not want to spook me. It did so anyway, and apprehension slid into my chest. "You seemed to think I already knew, and I was hoping you would reveal more in the course of the conversation. I was sorely disappointed."

"I am afraid you are going to remain that way."

Shock widened his eyes. "What secret could you and Rosalynn possibly have to guard so closely?"

My head reared back. "What is it with you gentlemen and your impertinent questions?"

"What does being a man have to do with anything?"

The poor man. He really, truly, did not know. "Nothing. You are superior, so what should I know anyway?"

His head tilted in that irritating, condescending manner. "Come now, Elsie, don't overreact."

A lock of his dark hair fell forward, and my hand itched to push it back, but I shook out the feeling, disgusted by my reaction. How could I feel attraction to a man who did not value my thoughts, who did not believe I could own a secret worth keeping?

"Heavens no, I should never. I'll just sit here quietly and eat my soup like a good girl." And ignore the fact that Lord Cameron used my Christian name without my consent, taking liberties wherever he pleased. Furthermore, I would forget how my heart had jumped in my chest when he'd said it.

His head nodded once, just slightly, in what was surely cautious agreement, and I had to grip my napkin in my lap to avoid reaching out and strangling him.

When he originally asked me to enlighten him, I should have begun a recitation of Mrs. Wollstonecraft's theories. It would have either bored him to tears or quieted him, either reaction eliciting silence which was thoroughly preferable to the insults I had just received.

My partner on the opposite side was a man I had never had much opportunity to get to know; but nor did I want to. Lord Cameron had soured my mood irrevocably and if I was to involve myself with any further conversation, I was bound to embarrass my partner or worse, embarrass my host. And the Hurst family was one I respected. I could not do that to Freya, or her mother with her multitude of innocent flowers.

Yes, even in the dining room. They were everywhere.

The remainder of dinner, I did not open my mouth but to eat. If either of my partners made a comment I simply smiled and nodded, to their evident relief. When Mrs. Hurst stood at the end of the meal and asked all of the ladies to accompany her to the music room while the men remained behind to enjoy their cigars, I did so with a curtsy, a polite smile, and a confident walk from the room, never looking back.

Lord Cameron was a rude swine. No, I forgot; he was a tyrant.

CHAPTER 15

"Elsie, you are seething." Rosalynn shot me a concerned look. My breaths were coming rapidly and I felt warmer than a fresh cup of tea.

I drew in a deep breath.

"What is it?" Freya asked softly.

"Men."

She exchanged glances with Rosalynn. They gently led me by the elbows to the chairs set up for the musicale and deposited me in one on the far right, taking their seats on either side of me. Mother was speaking to a group of women on the far side of the room and the other women were dispersed throughout it. We had the chairs to ourselves for the moment.

I gave Rosalynn a meaningful look. "Or perhaps I should more accurately say 'Tyrants.'"

She sighed. "I could have guessed. Cameron, I suppose?"

I nodded.

"He can be insufferable at times. Though I suppose we can hardly blame him. He doesn't know better."

"What am I missing?" Freya asked, glancing between us. "I don't fully comprehend."

Both sets of eyes sat on me expectantly. "He questioned me on my bargain with my mother. Though he did not know what he wished to learn, he was simply curious after overhearing us speak about it once. Things got out of hand afterward."

"He is the curious one," Rosalynn said nodding. "And I fear he does not let things go. Should we appease his interest so he can move on?"

"And have everyone learn that I cannot say the word 'no?' What kind of havoc would that wreak?"

Her brow furrowed. "I hadn't thought of that."

I had. I guarded this ridiculous bargain close to my heart like a cherished heirloom.

Our heads all turned toward the door when it opened to admit the masculine half of the party. Lord Cameron caught my eye, and I held his for a moment. I would not cower away from him, but neither would I play coy any longer. I was ashamed of myself for doing it at all in the first place. But in my defense, what other option had been available to me? Had I vented my emotions as I'd desired at the time, I would have created a scene. I was not interested in making another appearance in the paper anytime soon.

"What are you performing?" Freya asked excitedly. "I have prepared a Mozart piece, so I vow I will bore the men considerably."

"I am going to sing," Rosalynn said with nonchalance. She possessed an elegant voice and was often asked to sing at functions. There was no comparison.

"Do you need an accompaniment? I did not have sufficient time to prepare anything so I was hoping to avoid a performance."

Rosalynn gripped my arm. "That would be fantastic. I do hate to sing while seated."

As everyone took their seats, I was painfully aware of Lord

Cameron and Lord McGregor installing themselves directly behind us. My neck prickled in awareness and I did my best not to turn my head for the duration of the concert, except when Rosalynn leaned over to explain what she would be singing and the small variations she would make.

Freya played the pianoforte beautifully. After her performance, when it came time for Rosalynn's turn, I caught Mother's eye on the way to the front of the room, surprise etched on her face. At least it looked to be of the pleasant variation.

Rosalynn took her place in front of the instrument and I settled myself on the seat. After a beat of silence, we dove in, the room especially quiet in preparation for Rosalynn's angelic voice.

And she outdid herself. If I was not so sure of her natural love for singing and constant practice, I would believe she had taken additional lessons in preparation for this evening. Any practicing was undoubtedly a byproduct of her constant time spent in the music room of her home. Her oasis, she once termed it.

The audience broke into applause at the end of her final drawn-out note and I sat back a little on my bench, allowing the praise to flow and settle on Rosalynn's deserving shoulders. We took our seats shortly and I avoided Lord Cameron's gaze, fixing my own upon Lord McGregor, who was positively beaming. The earl must be an admirer of music.

Mrs. Hurst thanked all of the performers and invited her guests to stay for tea.

"Magnificent, Lady Rosalynn," Lord McGregor said from behind us. "As always."

She dipped her head coyly, but the smile on her lips was anything but.

"Oh drat," Freya said suddenly. "Mama needs me." She gave us a long-suffering look and crossed over our knees toward the corner of the room where the matrons were gathering and Mrs. Hurst was eyeing Freya significantly.

"Who paints the doors into their drawing rooms?" Rosalynn asked suddenly.

It took all of two seconds for me to realize she had gone back to discussing the book. Her mother was correct. It was going to sweep through society. My name could not possibly be bandied about the gossip columns come morning.

"Actually, a good many people do," Lord McGregor cut in.

She raised her eyebrow. "Have you taken to noticing doors in recent days?"

He smiled. "Perhaps I have. You may find you'll do the same."

I considered the door in the book and the wealthy matron who owned it. She lived alone, though she was surrounded by many people at all times. She was the hub of the social scene and never saw a lonely moment, if the author was to be believed, whoever it was. I did not personally know any woman who fit that description.

Rosalynn said, "I would like to know who the man is that escapes to France every six months to visit the other family he has secreted there."

"I should like to know who the woman is that laments her lack of children but secretly houses sixteen dogs in her tiny townhouse," I added.

Lord McGregor grinned. "I would be happy just to know who the lady is with a secret baby in the country and yet continues to come to London in hope of finding a husband."

We all looked to Lord Cameron. He blinked back at us.

"Well?" Rosalynn prodded.

He shrugged.

"You have not read it?" I asked.

He held my gaze. "No, I have."

We continued to regard him with interest. He was perhaps the most curious of our lot. How had he not joined in yet?

Rosalynn must have had the same thought. "Surely you don't think us daft. There is no way you aren't wondering to whom the book refers."

"I needn't wonder," he said, a self-satisfied smirk tilting his lips. "I already know."

CHAPTER 16

"The devil you do!" Rosalynn exclaimed, a bit too loudly.

Faces turned toward us from about the room and I shrunk in shame over her outburst. She had said a very unladylike word. Indeed, it was nearly disgraceful. Hopefully, the informant for the dratted gossip column hadn't overheard, or she would undoubtedly make lead news in the morning.

"Of course I do. It isn't so hard to figure out. Mr. Harrison is the man with a family in France. Lady Bloom is the woman with the dogs."

"What about the woman with the baby in the country?" I asked.

He regarded me closely. I smiled subtly, for I had him stumped.

"I shall not disclose that," he said seriously. "I am no gossip."

"Surely you cannot know, man," Lord McGregor said, his eyebrow lifted in disbelief.

Lord Cameron spared him a glance before standing suddenly. "Would anyone like tea? Rosalynn, Miss Cox?"

So it was 'Miss Cox' again? Well, good.

"Yes," Rosalynn said with a wave of her hand. Her eyebrows pulled together in frustration. Regardless of how dignified she was, she was undoubtedly as curious as her brother and it pained her that he knew something and wouldn't share it.

He turned to me and I said, "Yes. Cream and sugar, please."

Lord McGregor followed Lord Cameron toward the tea table and Rosalynn turned to me abruptly. "He knows."

"Or he is pretending," I offered.

"No." She shook her head and sat back, chewing her lip thoughtfully. "I know that face. He is happy he knows something we do not. Perhaps…" She gave me a sidelong glance and it took two beats of the clock for me to make the connection she had formed in her mind.

"No."

"But—"

"Rosie, no. If you tell your brother about my bargain, it is sure to become common knowledge. I would become sport for the young men once they find out that I cannot say no."

She sighed, slumping back in her chair momentarily. "You are right. I simply must find another way."

"Perhaps it is best if we do not know who the woman is. The other secrets are silly; this one is serious."

But Rosalynn seemed not to hear me, so wrapped up she was in her own thoughts. The men delivered our tea, and I glanced around the room in search of Freya. When I finally found her I nearly dropped my cup in surprise to see her speaking to Major Heybourne.

"What is it?" Lord Cameron asked. He'd appeared to have been watching me, and I pushed away the pleasure swirling in my stomach from that realization.

A smile touched my lips. "Oh, nothing. A friend of mine is here that I did not previously notice." I turned to Rosalynn, shaking her out of her trance.

Her eyes were wide and doe-eyed.

"Come, I have someone I want to introduce to you."

She was intrigued. "Oh?"

"Yes, and you will recall I spoke of him once. About Bath... and bright red punch at the Assembly Halls."

Enlightenment lit her face. "Oh yes! He is here? But I must meet this man."

"He is speaking to Freya now."

We left our teacups with Lord Cameron and Lord McGregor and crossed the room.

Major Heybourne stood tall, hands clasped behind his back and eyes crinkled in delight. We made eye contact moments before we approached their group, and his smile widened.

"Major Heybourne," I said. "How did I miss you at dinner?"

"I arrived late, I am afraid," he said sheepishly. "I snuck in during the musicale."

Mrs. Hurst grinned at the Major. "Better late than not to have come at all."

That was a strange sentiment. Most of London's hostesses would believe the opposite to be true. Unless, of course, they had thought the man in question to be a suitor for their daughter. Mrs. Hurst was positively beaming, her gaze dancing between Major Heybourne and Freya.

Freya, on the other hand, looked exceedingly uncomfortable. "Major Heybourne, allow me to introduce my dear friend, Lady Rosalynn Nichols."

He bowed and she curtseyed, her eye meeting mine on the way up.

Rosalynn smiled innocently. "How very fortunate we are to meet you, Major. We've heard so much about you."

I could have kicked her. If we had been sitting around a table I certainly would have. At the present, I had to make do with an icy stare.

Major Heybourne, however, found nothing to be embarrassed by. He reared his head back and loud, rolling laughter poured out.

I could not help but smile in return. Largely due to relief that he hadn't been offended by Rosalynn's implication that I told her of his bumbling dance.

"I'm sure you have," he said, wiping his eye.

Mrs. Hurst looked decidedly uncomfortable. She glanced between the Major and Rosalynn, and then to Freya, who was on the outside of understanding as well. I was not about to explain the situation to everyone, but the proper hint might help Freya make the connection herself.

"I had the fortune of making Major Heybourne's acquaintance in Bath," I said, eyeing Freya.

She looked between me and the gentleman, enlightenment clearing her gaze.

"Major Heybourne was just telling us how he is moving to London," Mrs. Hurst cut in. She looked to Freya, whose cheeks pinked.

Oh, dear. Had approaching with Rosalynn ruined an opportunity for Freya? Given her discomfort, I could only think I had aided her. Her mother's panicked face told another story.

"I was about to ask Miss Hurst here if she would like to accompany me on an outing to Gunter's tomorrow," Major Heybourne said, eyeing Freya. He turned to me suddenly with a warm smile. "Shall we find ourselves a few more gentlemen and make an outing of it?"

"That would be delightful!" Freya answered before anyone else could try and demure. "Perhaps Rosalynn's brothers would be willing to be our escorts. Or we could invite Mr. Fenway."

Why in heaven's name would Freya make that suggestion?

Rosalynn must have caught my stunned face. "I'm sure my brothers would be glad for an ice."

"Splendid!" Major Heybourne said, rolling back on the heels

of his shoes. Mrs. Hurst gave a tight smile, but Freya seemed very pleased.

CHAPTER 17

The carriage pulled up in front of our house, and I stepped away from the window to retrieve my bonnet. Rosalynn's note had said that she secured escorts and would instruct everyone to meet at my house, where we could all walk down to Gunter's Tea Shop together.

Billington was coming up to fetch me when I closed my door and skipped down the stairs and directly into the presence of Lord Cameron. I lost my balance in the act of trying to refrain from bowling into him, and his arms came up to steady me. His hands were strong, his grip firm, and my breath caught.

"Oh!" Surprise backed me up a few steps and out of his hold. I couldn't shake the lingering warmth from his touch, and I swallowed hard.

His dark hair was pushed away from his forehead and a satisfied smile lit his mouth as he glanced around our foyer. Something about his curiosity made me want to shove him out the door, but I settled for a quick curtsy and moved past him to walk down the steps myself where Rosalynn and Lord McGregor were waiting.

"Shall we go?" Rosalynn asked.

"What of Freya and the Major?"

"Major Heybourne sent a note. He planned to pick up Freya in his phaeton and meet us at the tea shop."

Lord McGregor stuck out an elbow and Rosalynn placed her hand on it softly, turning toward Berkeley Square. I clasped my gloved hands quickly behind my back and followed them, Lord Cameron falling into step beside me.

"Have you read the paper this morning?" he asked.

Could I ignore his question and maintain proper etiquette? The answer, unfortunately, was no.

"If you are referring to the dramatized article about my performance last evening and apparent new love interest then I must say, you are every bit as bad as that writer."

Lord Cameron chuckled. "You are a captivating subject. I cannot help but find it entertaining."

"Of course not. It is not your privacy being invaded."

He halted. "How is your privacy being invaded? The article has not mentioned anything that did not happen in public. The writer is not announcing what you ate for breakfast or whether you spent hours in your family's library reading *The Green Door*. They are reporting on various activities which were witnessed in public."

"But why me?" I asked, my arms shooting out in exasperation. "Rosalynn gave the amazing performance, not I, and she was not even mentioned. And it was Rosalynn who cursed in public, momentarily silencing the entire room! But yet they found it necessary to report on my mediocre pianoforte playing and new suitor?" I gripped his sleeve in frustration. "Major Heybourne isn't even my suitor!"

He looked down at my fingers fastened onto his wrist and I immediately let go, jumping back as though his arm had turned to hot coals. Heat suffused my cheeks and I began walking toward Gunter's, quickening my pace and hoping to leave my outburst behind us.

His long legs caught him up swiftly. "I can see why that would be confusing, and I wish I had an answer for you."

"Do not let it bother you, Lord Cameron."

"I'm not," he said.

I tried to pick up the pace again, glad I wore my sturdier half boots for the excursion.

"You are truly angry about this?" His voice was incredulous.

I wished he would give my feelings a little more credit. First, he could not believe that Rosalynn and I had a secret worth hiding, and now he was shocked I would be upset that my name was being bandied about London newspapers.

I stopped and turned to him. The sun hit my nose, and I squinted to see into Lord Cameron's dark eyes. "Why shouldn't it matter to me? Am I meant to shove down every feeling I have which is inconvenient? I am human, too, Lord Cameron. I cannot shut off my senses so easily."

His brows drew together. Even while he considered my claim to basic humanity, he was exceedingly handsome. I kicked myself for the thought. Of course he was attractive. Rosalynn's entire family was beautiful. But he was also being rather thoughtless.

I shook my head. There would be no getting through to him, so I needn't try. "Let us agree to disagree and not bicker further. I do not want my first ice ruined by these petty disagreements."

"Deal," he said, holding out his hand. I stared at it a moment. Shaking hands implied equality; to acknowledge that both parties had equal say in the agreement. Was he mocking me?

Hesitantly I complied and he closed his large fingers around my own, sending a warm shiver up my arm. We shook once and I slipped my hand back, rushing to catch up to Rosalynn and Lord McGregor.

"I have one more question for you," he said when he reached my side.

I glanced at him briefly, his own hands clasped behind his back as he strolled alongside me.

"Are you going to choose an ice or sorbet?"

"This is absolute heaven," I said after swallowing a bite of strawberry sorbet.

"I do not think I could live this close and not visit every single day," Freya said, giving me a meaningful look. "You have much self control, Elsie."

I grinned. "That was before I'd tried it."

"I would love to accompany you here any time you'd like," Major Heybourne valiantly offered.

"You are too kind, sir," I said.

I took my last bite of sorbet and lifted my head to make eye contact with Lord Cameron. His eyebrow was raised as though he was saying, "not a suitor, eh?"

I held his gaze a moment longer and then turned to Rosalynn. "Shall we walk through the park?"

"Yes, let's."

We returned our glasses and left behind Gunter's and its fantastic array of treats. We crossed into Berkeley Square. Freya drew my arm around her own and held tightly.

"How was the drive?" I asked quietly.

"It could have been worse. He is a kind man."

I lifted my eyebrows. "And therein lies the problem?"

She gave me a telling glance.

Lord McGregor came alongside us. "Will I have the pleasure of seeing you both at Almack's tomorrow evening?"

"Yes," I said.

Freya nodded.

"Fantastic. I must request a dance from each of you, then."

A volley of barking cut off our responses as a small dog ran between our gowns, spraying a smattering of mud on us when it passed.

"Good gads!" Lord McGregor exclaimed, pulling us to the side. The small dog circled the tree before us, barking excitedly. He halted behind the tree and peeked out, before he growled once, rearing back his lips to show sharp yellow teeth.

"Stay back!" Major Heybourne shouted, pushing himself in front of us. My gaze caught a large dog closer to the street reciprocating the growl, straining against his master's lead.

I struggled against the Major's grip when the lead snapped, the large, hairy dog suddenly springing directly at us.

"Quick! Save the dog!" I yelled, breaking free of the Major's arms and lunging for the tree. Strong hands gripped my arms, holding me back and I turned to see Lord Cameron, his face set in disapproving lines, refusing to let me go.

"He is in danger!" I yelled, to no avail.

The monstrous dog leaped past us, shooting at the tree and chasing the smaller one away. We watched them dart around the park, the small dog quick on his feet but no match for the larger one's strides. It only took moments for him to pin down the small, dirty rascal. I took advantage of Lord Cameron's slack to rip free and dart across the lawn, lifting my hem to avoid tripping. I looked about me for a weapon, but there was nothing. Not a total surprise, since we were in the center of the metropolis.

"Get off!" I yelled at the large dog. An evil glint in his eye mocked me, and he turned his head at the sound of my voice. I went for the collar around his neck when another man approached, his breath coming fast and a broken leash in his hand.

"Your dog?" I asked.

"M'masters," he responded, out of breath. He got a hold of the collar, and I dropped to the ground to pull the small, defenseless dog free.

A searing pain sliced down my arm as the large dog fought his master. I ignored the red blurring the edge of my vision and pulled the small, shaky pup into my lap. We scooted away from the claws of the monster while his man muttered apologies, managing to pull him away.

"You're hurt!" shrieked Freya, her hands coming up to cover her mouth.

Blood trickled down my forearm and began pooling on my gown. I shifted the frightened dog in my lap and looked away, repressing the queasiness in my gut. The dog found comfort in my arms and nestled in further, yelping suddenly when I shifted.

Rosalynn gasped. "Elsie! Push it aside!"

"I cannot. He is hurt." I tried to sound calm so I could, in turn, soothe my friends. It did not work.

"But the blood," Freya said. "It's everywhere."

I glanced down to where the red sticky substance had covered my wrist and bled all over the skirt of my gown. The pup's fur was matted and tinged red, though I could not tell if the blood was mine or his own. I looked up, my vision beginning to sway, when Lord Cameron knelt in front of me. I had never been one to keep my wits about me when faced with blood.

I used his dark eyes as a base to keep me grounded, and he said softly, "Miss Cox, are you well?"

"Yes," I lied. "Though, this poor dog…"

The next thing I knew, black was closing in around me, clouding over my thoughts and into my vision until the darkness took over and I fell, suddenly, asleep.

CHAPTER 18

Voices swirled around me, some of them familiar, though they melted into a blur. My eyes blinked open, and I instantly recognized the pale green ceiling of my drawing room with gold trimming and ivory accents.

"Mother?" I asked. She peered directly over my face, lying horizontally as I was, on the sofa.

"Awake! Doctor, come, she's awake," Mother squeaked.

An older man with thick, white sideburns bent over me, peering into my eyes. He lifted a finger and directed me to follow it, then stepped away and murmured to my mother. My arm was stiff, and I ran my fingers along it, surprised to find my forearm wrapped in linen.

Rosalynn knelt beside me, clasping my hand in hers. "How are you feeling?"

"Sleepy," I replied, letting go of her hand to push myself into a seated position. She helped me upright, and I closed my eyes until the room quit spinning. Opening them again hesitantly, I blinked a few times to clear my head and took in five peering faces, not counting my mother and the doctor speaking near the door.

"What happened?" I asked, feeling out of sorts.

"An enormous dog attacked you!" Mother said, anxiously coming to perch on the edge of the sofa.

The outing came back to me, and I shook my head, then regretted it instantly. The pulsing headache made my stomach churn. "No, he did not attack me, he attacked— but wait, where is the little dog?" I could hear the panic rise in my voice as I noticed the sheepish faces around me.

"We left it at the park," Lord McGregor explained from the far side of the room. Lord Cameron, standing between him and the window, was the only face which did not look abashed.

I stood quickly. That was a mistake. The blood rushed from my head and I swayed, a little woozy, coming to sit hard on the sofa again.

"I must go get him," I said wearily, dizzy from my foolish effort to stand with such haste.

"You will not do anything of the sort," Mother said.

"But he was hurt."

Freya and Rosalynn exchanged glances.

"We can go and look for it," Rosalynn offered hesitantly. "But I'm not sure we'll have much luck."

Of course they wouldn't have much luck, for they surely wouldn't look sufficiently. If they were comfortable leaving the frightened thing at the park in the first place, they could not possibly care as much as they needed to in order to find him. An idea formed on shaky legs in my mind and I glanced from my friends and back to my mother.

I tried to make my voice sound as drained as I felt—which wasn't much of a chore. "Actually, it's fine. He is probably long gone now." I swallowed, fully aware I had every ear in the room —including Lord Cameron's skeptical one. "In fact, I am quite fatigued. I think a nap will do me just right if I am to rest up before Almack's."

"Tomorrow is Wednesday," Rosalynn informed me.

"And I am exceedingly tired," I countered.

Major Heybourne stood at once. "I must fetch my phaeton, but I will be back shortly for you, Miss Hurst."

"We can take her home," Rosalynn offered. "Our carriage is already here."

He gave Freya a searching look before glancing back at me—I tried to look sufficiently exhausted from my ordeal—and then nodded once. Mother called Billington for Rosalynn's carriage, and we waited a few minutes for it to be brought around.

"Please send me a note in the morning," Rosalynn said, squeezing my hands.

I nodded. Each of my friends stopped at the sofa to wish me farewell, except Lord Cameron. He was the final one to leave, yet still, he stood by the window, searching my face as though trying to find the answer to a question only he knew. Lord McGregor gave him a questioning look from the door and cleared his throat loudly.

Lord Cameron tore his gaze from me. "Yes, let us be off." He nodded to my mother, and then to me, and strolled right out.

"I shall call you a bath," Mother said, standing. "Then you must rest the remainder of the evening." She shuffled toward the door, muttering, "I'll write to the Durhams. We cannot be expected to attend dinner this evening."

"No!" I shouted. Mother spun back, confused. I backtracked. "I only meant that you and Father should not have to cancel plans with your friends over this. I am well, only tired."

She searched my face.

"Truly," I said, standing—albeit, much more slowly this time. "I will take that bath and then I vow I shall sleep the rest of the afternoon."

"Very well," she said slowly. "I will speak to your father about it."

Once she left the room, I slouched onto the couch again. I needed a bath, a bracing cup of tea, and then I would be restored sufficiently to go out and find that dog.

"Shall I braid your hair, miss?" Molly asked, brushing my long, wet mane. I was refreshed and clean, except for my bandaged arm that I had kept from the tub, and wrapped tightly in a dressing gown. I spent the duration of my bath determining whether or not I could trust Molly.

She painstakingly spread out my night clothes on the bed behind us. If I did not trust her with this secret, who would help me dress? There was only one option open to me. I had to take my chances.

"If you would, yes please. And then wind it into a knot?"

"For bed, miss?"

"No," I took a deep breath and caught her questioning eye in the mirror. "I must go out."

"But your Mama—"

"Yes, I know. She thinks I am going to bed." I had relayed the entire episode at the park while Molly had washed my hair. "But you see, I have to at least try to find the dog. He was hurt, and so scared…"

She sectioned off my hair and began a plait, avoiding my face in the mirror. I could see the uncertainty playing across her features.

"Mother and Father leave for the Durhams in an hour, and it will still be light out. I promise I will be back before dark, and no one shall ever know I left in the first place. Or that you helped me dress for it."

Her gaze shot to mine. "Very well, but you can't go out alone. I'm going with you."

A smile spread over my lips. I had made the right choice. I settled into her ministrations.

"We'll find the mongrel much faster with two sets of eyes," she continued. "Now, why don't you describe him to me so I know what to look for."

CHAPTER 19

Wearing the darkest of our gowns, Molly and I tripped down the servants' staircase, sneaking into the foyer on the main level during the servants' dinner. Mother and Father were off to the Durham's and Billington was down with the servants eating so we were free and clear. Molly had told our butler I needed rest and she was going to keep an eye on me with her mending, asking not to be disturbed. We could only hope they would have no reason to question her request.

Shadows of empty tree branches stretched across the road like claws. While it was not yet dark, the sun was well on its way to making its descent.

"We haven't much time," I said, walking briskly toward the park.

"What are we doing with the dog once we've got it?"

I stopped in my tracks. Looking at Molly, at a loss, I admitted, "I hadn't thought that far ahead."

"Perhaps we worry when we get to that point, then," she offered.

"Yes. Good plan. We may not even find him." Though I certainly hoped we would.

We reached the park of Berkeley Square minutes later, my gaze sweeping the lawn for any shivering, small ball of dirty fluff. We crossed the street and made our way toward the tree where I had first seen the dog, but it was vacant. Turning slowly to sweep the park again, a figure caught my eye on the far end that had a familiar gait. I squinted my eyes but could not make out who it was.

We continued to search for a good while until Molly made the suggestion, "Perhaps we should cross to those buildings and check the alleys."

The concept had merit. Though it was far more dangerous than searching in an open park. I nodded reluctantly and we set off for the row of shops across the street. A carriage rambled up the road, and I sunk backward when I recognized the family crest on the side of the door.

Grabbing Molly's hand with my better one, I pulled her back toward the park. Evidently, I was not quick enough, for a moment later I heard Lord Cameron's voice call behind me.

"Were you looking for this?"

I spun immediately, Lord Cameron leaned out of the open door of his carriage, my small, dirty dog wrapped in a blanket in his arms.

I exclaimed, dropping Molly's arm and running to him heedless of my reckless appearance.

"How did you find him?" I asked, gently taking the dog from Lord Cameron's arms.

"With a great many hours of searching."

I looked up sharply, but he had a teasing glint in his eye. He was jesting, surely.

"I can take him from here. Thank you, Lord Cameron. I am much obliged."

"And where will you take him?" he asked.

I halted. How feasible was it to hide a dog in my room?

"Home," I said. "We can care for him, can't we Molly?"

"Yes, miss." Her head bent in deference. That wasn't quite the reinforcement I had been looking for.

The little dog shook in my arms. I stroked his head, my good arm supporting his body.

"He is unwell," Lord Cameron said. "It's best he be seen by an animal doctor."

"Do you know of one?"

He chuckled and my breath caught, the deep sound making my stomach flip. "I've got a good one at home, though that is on the other side of the country."

"Drat."

He looked thoughtful, the fading light shadowing his face. "I could find one, though I think it more suitable for you to bring the mongrel to my house."

That would not work. Mother could not return to find me missing, and I was not about to leave this poor dog again. "I need to return home right away."

"And I feel more qualified to take on the care and responsibility of the animal."

I scoffed. "You? Who left him defenseless, hurt and frightened?"

"At the time it was not the dog who was my priority." His meaning was thick between us and I had not realized how close he stood until now.

"I believe myself more qualified to care for him, Lord Cameron. It was I who chased him down and saved him."

The muscle jumped in his jaw and he turned away for a moment, his mind seemingly working around the problem. But I was not a problem to be sorted, and I had a mind of my own.

"We keep horses too, and I am confident my butler will be able to find a doctor for the dog, if needs be," I said. "I shall walk home with my maid now. Please consider my gratitude for your help today a sufficient thank you, for I do not think I'll find time to write a proper note with how incredibly full my arms are at present."

Concern flicked in his eyes. "Is your arm well?"

"Well enough," I said through gritted teeth, my arm beginning to battle my head in which ailed me more. I gave a half-hearted chuckle. "I am not weak, sir."

A smile played on his lips. "Of that, Miss Cox, I am infinitely aware. Very well, you may have things your way. But if you need me, you know I am only a note away." With a dip of his hat, he hopped back into his carriage, tapped the roof with his knuckles, and was off, leaving me in the street with my maid and a dirty dog.

"Well, that was certainly unexpected."

Molly scoffed. "I'd say, miss. What are we going to do?"

I began walking and she hurried beside me. "We are going to give this dog a bath and assess his injuries."

"How do you know it's a he?"

"I don't." I shrugged. "But I think we'll find out soon."

"Very good, miss." Molly hastened to keep up with my quick steps. "Only, are we really bringing a dog into the house? What will the missus say?"

"She won't say a word." I smiled. "No one will even know he is there."

"If no one knows he is here, then they are all deaf," Molly said, wiping suds from her forehead with the back of her wrist.

Exasperated, I threw a towel over the pup and wrestled him to the ground, hoping he did not have any severe injuries that I was making worse in the process. Getting him clean had been an ordeal. Dirty water now covered my wooden floor and wardrobe. The wall and vanity were splattered with muddy droplets and our gowns were similarly messy.

"I am glad you thought to roll away the carpet first," I said.

Molly's head turned to take in the mess and she grimaced. "A bath in the stables might've been wiser. I best start cleaning up."

"Thank you, Molly."

She turned sharply toward me, and then laughed, shaking her head. "'Twas an adventure, I'll give you that."

I rubbed down the dog, her sad eyes pulling at my heart. Molly discovered during the bath that I had been wrong all along. Chagrined, I considered her face for the right name.

"You are certainly not a Sally or a Becky," I said, tilting my face to the side. The dog tilted her head, mirroring my action. I tilted my head the other direction and she followed suit. "You clever girl," I said, delighted.

Molly came back in the room with a pail and rags. "I've got the perfect name," I said. "Watch this."

I showed Molly the head tilting trick and she had the grace to look impressed.

"What is her name then?"

"Copycat."

"But she's a dog."

"I know," I said, defensive. "It is ironic. And anyway, I shall call her Coco."

"Oh! Coco is sweet. And fitting. Her coat is the color of morning chocolate now that she's clean."

I looked at Coco again and had to admit this was true. It was a shiny dark hue, matching her equally dark eyes. In a way, she resembled Rosalynn.

"Shall you like to be called Coco?" I asked the dog. She gave me a beseeching look and barked once. "I will take that as a 'yes,' then. Oh dear, she must be starving."

"Allow me," Molly said, dropping her rag and wiping dirty

hands on her apron. She moved to my discarded dinner tray and sorted through the leftovers, surely looking for something appropriate for the pup to eat.

I took Coco to the fire and sat before it, using my hairbrush to comb her coat. So far there were no abrasions, so I could only hope the blood we washed off had come from me. I gently poked and prodded all of her limbs, and then her abdomen, but she did not protest once.

"I believe she is in fit physical condition. If my amateur evaluation means anything."

"I agree," Molly said. "She would've whined more in the bath if anything was broken."

She set a plate before us on the floor with meat chunks pulled from dinner and a bowl of water, and Coco jumped from my lap and dove in. When she finished licking the plate clean, she climbed back onto my lap and cozied in, falling asleep in a matter of minutes.

Gathering her in my arms I stood slowly, gently laying her at the foot of my bed. Once Molly helped me to dress in my night clothes, I peeled back my blanket and slipped inside. Coco moved suddenly and I froze while she positioned herself over my feet. A smile lifted the corners of my lips, and I drifted off to sleep.

CHAPTER 20

"Is it wrong of me to call that fortune?" I asked Molly, simultaneously moving my breakfast tray away while trying to hold Coco down.

"Come," Molly said sharply. Coco sat on her hind legs, waiting patiently while Molly set a plate on the floor in front of the fire full of sausages and eggs and a bowl of clean water. Coco glanced once more at my plate before hopping down from the bed and devouring her food.

"Because I am not happy, exactly, that my mother is ill," I continued, fingering the bandage on my arm. "But really, a summer cold is not all that horrid. And certainly she will want me to avoid her for fear I could catch it."

Molly said nothing. She continued to pull out my day dress and lay it on the edge of my bed.

"Am I a terrible daughter?"

She looked up, shocked. "Of course not."

"Then will you put that dress away and pull out something better for walking? I am going to take Coco out."

"Yes, miss."

I finished my breakfast and let Molly help me prepare for the day. When I was ready, I left Coco, Molly shushing her whining, and snuck out to check on Mother.

I knocked on her bedroom door before opening it slightly, poking my head inside. "You are ill?" I asked.

"Oh, dreadfully," she said with feeling. "If this is the end, do not let them bury me in London!"

"I wouldn't dream of it," I said severely. "Are you in need of anything?"

"No, and do not set foot in this room, Elspeth. I cannot have you catching cold and dying before we find you a proper husband."

I sighed. "If I am not to keep you company, then may I call on Freya?" I still needed her permission before I was able to leave the house.

"Very well," she replied with long-suffering fortitude.

"Thank you, Mother."

I raced back to my room, scooping up Coco before she could run into the corridor.

"I think she needs to go outside, miss," Molly said, concern on her brow.

"I will take her in a moment. I need to find my reticule."

"No, miss. *Now.*"

I glanced down at Coco's writhing body and understood her meaning. Immediately racing for the corridor, I took the servants stairs all the way down and out the back where the horses were kept. Coco leapt down the minute I reached outside and took care of her business.

Drat, I hadn't even considered that component of caring for a dog. By the time Molly followed me outside with my bonnet and reticule, Coco was finished and sniffing along the flowers at the side of the house.

We set off for Freya's, and Coco was just as talented at staying close as I had hoped. She veered a few times, but nothing kept her away from my ankles for very long. We reached the Hurst's home in double the time it usually took, but that was no matter. It was nice to have Coco along. Standing on the empty street, outside Freya's tall and imposing home, I found myself at a sudden loss.

"Oh dear. What do I do with you, Coco?"

"You can't take her inside?" Molly asked.

"No, I do not think it is proper. If only I had a leash, I could control her better."

"I can stay out here with her while you visit," Molly offered.

"I do not know how long I shall be, and I do not want you to lose her if she runs off. Perhaps it is better for you to take her home."

Nodding once, Molly bent and scooped up Coco.

"After I show Freya how gorgeous she is now," I said. "A small visit cannot be so bad?"

The butler showed us into the drawing room. Mrs. Hurst was seated on the couch with embroidery in her lap. Her face paled when we stepped through the door, and I realized my mistake at once.

"Oh Elsie, you've found him!" Freya dropped her own needlework and crossed to Molly.

"He's actually a she," I corrected. "Meet Coco."

"Where is she to live?" Freya asked, scratching Coco on the ears.

"With me, of course. Molly is going to take her home now, I only wanted you to meet her."

Freya turned to me, confusion on her brow. "But I met her yesterday."

"Yes, well, she has since had a bath. She is a new woman now."

Molly curtseyed once and turned away, but Coco was not as happy to leave. She jumped from Molly's arms and leaped onto the couch beside Mrs. Hurst, eliciting a scream from the woman.

"Oh dear," Freya said, bustling to the sofa to move Coco away from her mother. "I forgot! Mama is allergic."

Freya thrust Coco into Molly's arms, who all but ran out the door. I turned toward Mrs. Hurst, my cheeks burning. "I am exceedingly sorry Mrs. Hurst, I had no idea."

"No, well, you wouldn't dear," she said, regaining her composure. "I stay quite clear of the things if I can help it."

Mortification lay over me like a hot blanket and I stood, uncertain.

"Oh come in, dear," she said finally, her good nature restored.

Gratefully, I crossed to the light blue armchair and lowered myself slowly. Freya returned to her needlework but shot me an amused glance which I was not quite ready to return.

"You are here without your mother?" Mrs. Hurst asked, bringing a handkerchief up to her sniffling nose.

"She has caught a cold, I'm afraid."

"Poor woman."

Freya looked up. "Will you be missing Almack's this evening?"

"I suppose so," I answered. I had been looking forward to the break, anyway.

Mrs. Hurst tsked. "Nonsense, you shall come with us. It is settled."

Freya grinned into her lap. I had no one on my side there. "Very well," I agreed. "Now, tell me how you achieved that fantastic floral archway, Mrs. Hurst. It was positively gorgeous." Which, it was. All the additional flowers on the night of the musicale caused the overwhelming smell that, in fact, still lingered.

"No, dear. A hostess never tells her secrets. I can't have my ideas copied now, can I?"

"Isn't it flattering when others use your ideas?"

"No," Mrs. Hurst said simply. "That is called stealing."

CHAPTER 21

I did not stay long at the Hurst home. With Mrs. Hurst remaining in the drawing room and not giving Freya and me a chance to speak alone we quickly ran out of topics. Especially after Freya brought up *The Green Door* and her mother shot it down, labeling it uncouth.

I took tea at home alone. My father was holed up in his study doing who knew what, and when I checked on Coco, she was fast asleep, likely still exhausted from the ordeal of her attack and subsequent rescue. Either that, or all of the food she was consuming was making her comatose.

A spark of an idea formed in my mind, and I sat back, mulling it over for merit. By the time I decided to go forward with it, Coco was awake and yapping on the other side of my door. I slipped inside, finding Molly on the floor tossing a small object to the other side of the room, only for Coco to fetch it back to her and yap for Molly to throw it again.

"What a clever dog you are," I said, closing the door behind me. "What do you say to a ride in the carriage, Coco?" I glanced up. "Molly?"

"Yes, miss. Let me get your bonnet and I'll send for the carriage."

"I already did." I knelt down and scratched Coco behind the ears. "Would you like to see where my Aunt Georgina lives, Coco? Splendid. Let us go, then."

The carriage pulled up in front of Aunt Georgina's building. I turned to Molly while we waited for the footman to discover if she was at home for visitors. "You may take Coco to the park, if you'd like." I gestured toward the park we had passed.

"Yes, miss."

I was unaccountably nervous when the footman returned to tell me that Aunt Georgina would love to see me. I was led into a fabulous drawing room, immaculately designed to mimic the Egyptian style, with Aunt Georgina in the center of it all seated on her throne.

Well, it was a plush armchair. But it was golden.

"Good day, Aunt Georgina," I said, moving to kiss her cheek.

"Darling, what took you so long?" she asked, peering behind me. "Your mother does not come?"

"My mother has a cold."

Amusement danced in the older woman's eyes. "Ah, I see. She is indisposed and you took your chance to come and visit your old aunt."

"Never say 'old,'" I laughed, sitting on the settee across from her chair.

"Oh child, I am not afraid of aging." She talked with her hands waving about, reiterating her finer points. "Of course, I'm dignified. I'm also old."

I was distinctly uncomfortable but trying very very hard not to be.

"Now," she continued, pointing at a pile of newspapers on a table in the corner of the room. "Tell me how much of that is truth, and to what degree they've been exaggerated."

My cheeks grew warm, and I cleared my throat.

Her delicate white eyebrow arched up. I had the distinct feeling Aunt Georgina was a no-nonsense type of woman. She could see through any falsities anyway, so there was no sense in trying to hide the truth.

"They are pretty accurate, embarrassing as it is to admit. However, the number and strength of my suitors are highly exaggerated."

"I have a hard time believing that, Elspeth."

I shrugged. "I am not in the market for a husband."

Aunt Georgina cast her eyes toward the ceiling. She moved to the rope and pulled, requesting tea from the servant who responded.

"Young lady," she began, settling herself into her chair again. "Many young women come to London saying silly things like you just did with the hope that the right man will prove them wrong and sweep them from their feet. But life is not a gothic novel, and highwaymen do not turn out to be handsome earls in need of a wife. You can build a satisfying life with a number of the boring young men you dance with every night."

Squaring my shoulders, I reiterated, "You misunderstand. I made a decision at a young age to never sign over my life to another man. Aside from humoring my mother and yielding to a fondness for dancing, the only thing I wish to acquire in London this Season is a decent set of freckles."

She sat back in her chair, spinning her quizzing glass around her finger. "You are in earnest."

I let my gaze speak for itself, trying to infuse it with strength and dignity. The tea arrived and Aunt Georgina poured. I took a moment to recover from my outburst, restored after a gulp of tea.

"Do you wish to remain alone forever?"

"No," I answered. "I will probably settle down with a few close friends in a quiet country cottage where we can become the eccentric old ladies that everyone loves to gossip about."

"Like me," she said.

I flushed. "That is not what I meant."

"That does not make it less true. Now," she stood, placing her teacup on the tray. "Come. I've something to show you."

Aunt Georgina walked to the door before shooting a look over her shoulder.

I stood quickly, swallowing the remainder of my tea before following her out into the corridor and up the stairs. The wall was lined with gilded frames, men and women painted in a time well before our own. I trailed behind Aunt Georgina. She paused in front of a portrait of a young girl dressed in white, preparing for her debut.

"This is your grandmother," she said, her gaze locked on the young face. "You resemble her greatly, I believe."

I came to stand beside my aunt. It was a portrait I had never before seen, and the resemblance was striking. We shared the same honey hued hair, sloping nose and pointed chin. My eyes were not her bright blue ones, but my pale face and high cheekbones could have been a direct match otherwise.

"My father's mother," I said.

She nodded. "My sister."

We stood shoulder to shoulder for some time, our breathing falling into rhythm while we gazed at the woman I'd never met. She had died during Father's birth, causing him to be an only child and me to not have any cousins on his side. From all accounts, she was a lovely person, but Father did not know her, and I had never had much of a relationship with anyone else who did.

To be perfectly honest, I had never before considered her very much at all. Guilt fell onto me swiftly and I let it reign, for it was quite deserved. Without her, I would not be here. And I had never stopped to think of her.

"Come," Aunt Georgina barked, moving down the corridor to a door at the end. For all of her age, Aunt Georgina was a spry woman. She led me into her dressing room and pointed to a settee before the fire. I took her gesture to be a command and sat, watching her fiddle around in the bureau on the far wall.

"This belonged to her," she said quietly, coming to sit beside me. She held out a beautiful coral cameo on a gold filigree setting, the chain swinging beneath her hand.

I took the necklace, marveling at its superior craftsmanship. "It is beautiful."

"So was she," she said tenderly.

I reached for her hand and took it in my own. "You miss her."

"Immensely. She was my dearest friend." She laughed, sniffling in what I imagined to be a rare moment of vulnerability. "Dare I say, my only friend?"

"That cannot be true," I scoffed. "Your ballroom was filled when I graced it last."

"When you saw it for the first and only time, you would more honestly say."

Indeed, I had been correct. Aunt Georgina tolerated no nonsense.

Her smile was warm when she turned it on me again. "I do not blame you, dear. The blame rests fully and completely on your mother."

Well, I had not been expecting that. "Oh?"

"As you well know. Now, we best go and finish our tea. I will probably have callers soon."

I moved to return the necklace and Aunt Georgina's hand came around my own, closing it instead. "You keep it. She would want for you to have it."

My eyes pricked with emotion and I nodded simply, afraid opening my mouth would let out a squeak. Moving to the mirror over the bureau I unclasped the hook and slid the necklace into place. Touching it with the tips of my fingers where it sat over my breastbone, a warm, instant connection to the woman in the portrait wound through my heart.

"Will you tell me about her?" I asked when we moved down the stairs.

Aunt Georgina eyed me. Evidently, I passed the test, because she gave me a warm smile before leading me back into the Egyptian drawing room and to the settee. She weaved tales of two young girls growing up on an orchard in the countryside, getting into scrapes when they could sneak free of their governess and staying up late designing tales fit for a spook house.

"I do that, too," I said, excited to find common ground with my grandmother. "It is an odd sort of pastime for me, but I enjoy creating stories."

"Do you write them down?" Aunt Georgina asked, taking a biscuit from the tray.

"No, I haven't the patience for it. But my stories are entertainment for me so they serve their purpose."

"I always believed Charlotte would write a novel one day, her stories were so rich. They would have me laughing one moment, terrified the next, and crying by the end."

The door opened and the butler stepped inside. "Are you home for visitors, ma'am?"

Letting out a sigh, Aunt Georgina looked to me.

"I really should be getting home. I need to prepare for Almack's tonight."

"Very well. Let them in, Jackson." To me, she said, "Do come to my soiree on Friday. I should love to show you off again."

"You are holding another ball?"

"A little card party, dear. And don't seem so shocked. I needn't answer to anyone but myself, and I enjoy entertaining."

"I wish I could introduce you to my friends," I said wistfully. Aunt Georgina was precisely the sort of strong, independent woman we all hoped to become someday. "They would like you immensely."

"Bring them."

My face flooded with color. The cheek! Had I really begged an invitation for Rosalynn and Freya? "I couldn't."

"Are these the friends you shall settle with in the countryside to become eccentric old ladies together?"

"Yes," I said quietly, embarrassed I'd been so bold.

"Bring them. I should love to meet them as well."

CHAPTER 22

"Your eyes are like stars, dusting the night sky. Your nose, like a hill in the sweet summer breeze."

A hill? Was that meant to be alluring? I looked along the back wall but saw no one from whom I could beg rescue. Before me, Mr. Howe continued to make up for his faux pas at the last assembly by sprinkling words of affection all over me. When he begged a dance and I feared for my toes, requesting we sit out the set instead, I had not realized I would be submitting my ears to an assault in their stead.

"And your hair, like soft grass blowing in the wind…"

"Mr. Howe," I said suddenly. "I find myself in need of refreshment."

"But the supper just—"

"Yes, we recently had supper, but I was not quite so hungry then. Now I feel like I shall expire without a bite to eat."

He stood, bowing. "Allow me."

I relaxed, wondering how we let the dancing go on for so long. It was unfair. No, that was untrue. It was my fault for trying to come on too strong at the beginning of our conversation. I had hoped it would scare Mr. Howe away like it did Lord

McGregor. But alas, it appeared to have only encouraged him instead.

He returned shortly with a plate of cake. I took a bite, and it was nearly inedible. Ignoring Mr. Howe and his soft puppy eyes, I set it down on the bench beside me.

"Now," I said, pasting a smile on my face. "Tell me about your estate. You are from Derbyshire, yes?"

His eyes lit up and he delved into a monologue about the latest features of his home and the superior shooting to be had. When he began making comments about the size of the nursery and school room, I saw the mistake of my words. I had only encouraged the poor man even more.

Swallowing, I searched my mind for a suitable set down. I simply had to say something that would throw him off of my scent. But he was so nice, I didn't want to hurt him.

"And I cannot have the dogs inside the house, for I am terribly allergic. But we have a good breed trained and ready to go in the stables at any time."

I latched on. "Allergic, you say?"

"Oh yes, horribly so. My throat begins to close and breathing becomes difficult."

I shook my head slowly, conjuring a sad look to accompany it. "I am so very sad for you. How do you keep your feet warm at night? I vow if my dog is not curled over my toes I'd surely never fall asleep."

Mr. Howe blinked a few times, his face still. "But surely you do not require a dog in your room."

"No."

He visibly relaxed. I continued. "Not just any dog. My dog, Coco." He tensed again, and I pressed forward. "She is the sweetest little terrier, with fur the color of chocolate."

"Chocolate, you say?" he ran a finger around his collar, his Adam's apple bobbing.

"Yes, and she is just as divine."

The set came to a close, finally, and Mr. Howe stood. "Shall I escort you to your mother?"

"She is unwell this evening. You may escort me to Mrs. Hurst," I supplied. I would have felt bad for the man if I was not enjoying an overwhelming sense of relief.

Mr. Howe deposited me by Mrs. Hurst's side and beelined for the opposite side of the room. I was hoping he wouldn't lick his wounds too long. It seemed I could not let an assembly at Almack's pass without utterly offending or embarrassing him somehow.

Freya returned to us flushed and happy, on the arm of Mr. Fenway. He bowed his departure and she grinned, sidling up to me, unbothered by a few loose curls falling from their pins. "You shall never guess what I just heard."

"Then you may as well tell me."

She pouted. "Boo, you are no fun. Very well." She leaned in to impart her secret. "The Author of *The Green Door* is not only a woman, but she is a high society matron herself!"

"Do you think she is the high society matron? The one belonging to the actual green door?" I asked.

"That would be my guess. Now how shall we discover who she is?"

We both considered the matrons lining the edge of the ballroom as if one of them would jump out and proclaim herself the authoress.

"You are either looking for someone or avoiding someone," a deep voice said behind us, "and I cannot tell which."

I turned to face Lord Cameron, a smirk on his lips while he dipped his head politely. He wore a navy jacket and buff breeches, his hands clasped casually behind his back. Had his shoulders always looked so broad?

I lifted an eyebrow. "How do you know we are not admiring the varying gowns?"

"Are you?"

"No," Freya said. "We are trying to discover the matron who wrote the book."

He nodded, seeming to know what she meant despite her cryptic explanation. "Are you having any luck?"

I sighed. "No, of course not. If she wanted everyone to know who she is, she would not have signed it anonymously."

He seemed to consider this. "Unless she was waiting for the book to become popular before taking the credit."

I eyed him, but he glanced indifferently at the dancers.

"I doubt she will ever make herself known," I said, watching his face for a reaction. "She has made plenty of enemies, has she not?"

He turned, unable to hide the annoyance on his brow. "Because she has invaded their privacy?"

I could not fathom why this was a constant argument between us, or why he cared at all. "Because she has laid bare their most guarded secrets for the world to mock. Do you not think these people are affected by the book, whether their identity is obvious or not?"

"I think they should not have these secrets if they do not want them made known."

"How very rational of you."

"How, Miss Cox," he said, stepping closer, "do you make that sound like an insult?"

My head tilted back to look him in his dark eyes. "Perhaps because I meant it to be."

I turned to Freya, but she was gone. Somehow she had stepped away and was lining up for the next dance, and I had been unaware.

"Dance with me?" he asked, his breath sending a shiver down my neck.

I jumped at the closeness of the words, stepping back with a light chuckle to offset my embarrassment.

"I didn't mean to frighten you," Lord Cameron said, holding

out his hand expectantly. I wanted nothing more than to refuse him on principle alone, but I could not devise an excuse that would not be breaking the bargain. And I could not deny the part of me that wanted to swirl in his arms.

Instead, I placed my hand on his elbow and followed him to the dance floor. When the musicians began to play a waltz, I was shocked. Lord Cameron delivered a rakish grin and slid his hand into mine, gripping it.

He glanced to my arm, the bandage underneath causing my long glove to look stuffed and puckered. "How is your injury?"

"It is healing. The ointment left by the doctor has done wonders to soothe it."

"And the dog?" he asked.

"Coco."

"Bless you."

"No, her name is Coco."

His dark eyebrow hitched.

"She plays a trick," I explained. "Oh, nevermind. It is not such a silly name for a dog."

He spun me toward the center of the set, momentarily away from the gossipy women hiding behind their fans. I looked over his shoulder and saw Cecily dancing with Lord Fischer down the line, the dandy gazing at her with unabashed interest.

"You are to keep her then?"

It took a moment for me to realize he was referring to the dog. "Yes. I am fattening her up and giving her a place to sleep."

"And what do you receive from the bargain?"

"She keeps my feet warm while I sleep."

His eyes darted to mine, and a blush crept up my neck. Something which seemed so innocuous when speaking to Mr. Howe suddenly felt awfully forward and direct. I turned my head, watching Cecily deliver her charms to her partner like a parrot on a perch. Whyever was she so interested in him? Cecily was beautiful. She did not need to settle for a self-obsessed man with only a title and no fortune. If the gossiping matrons were to be believed.

"You are concerned about something?"

I whipped my head around, Lord Cameron's gaze searching mine. "No. Only watching the other dancers."

"Perhaps one in particular? Have you a beau among the patrons tonight?"

I glanced at him sharply. "Not that it is any of your concern."

He was all innocence. "I would not say that. There is nothing wrong with looking out for Rosie's friends. Particularly those with no older brothers to fill that role."

I tossed him a wry smile. "No, indeed. There is nothing wrong with that."

The moment separated us in a flurry of twirls, and I breathed deeply through the respite, gathering my wits about me as I returned to him. His eyes scanned my face while we moved. He did not need to watch where we were going, but knew innately. My hand was all too warm enveloped in his and I swallowed, grateful my glove would hide my perspiration.

The instruments came to a stop and Lord Cameron's hands dropped from mine. We turned and clapped for the musicians before he took me back to Mrs. Hurst.

"Should you be free tomorrow, I would like to take you to the park."

I tried to cover my surprise. "To Hyde Park, sir?"

"No, Berkeley Square. I have a mind to see Coco for myself."

My hesitation was futile, as I only had one answer I was allowed to give. "Yes, I would like that very much."

My voice did not sound wooden and stiff like it usually did in such situations. I chose not to wonder why.

"Very good." With a dip of his head, he was off.

"Elsie, you will never guess what I just heard!" Freya said, pulling me away from her Mama and toward the relative privacy of the wall behind her.

"I believe I have heard those words recently," I said drily.

I glanced up to see Rosalynn walk a straight line from the other side of the room toward us. I had not seen her since before supper. She had been dancing the entire evening without pause. She had a glint in her eye and a determination to her step.

"You shall never guess—"

"No, Rosie, I was already about to say it."

Rosalynn pouted. "Very well."

Freya turned to me, gripping my hand in both of hers. "You know the man in the book? The one left at the altar of his elopement when his bride took off with his valet and was never seen or heard from again? He was Lord Fischer!"

"No," I said, my jaw unable to pick itself back up. "That cannot be. He is the most self-concerned, self-aware man I know."

"And he was left at the church," Rosalynn said, Freya nodding along.

"How sad for him." I searched the ballroom once more for his bright clothing and conceited smile. I finally caught sight of him speaking with a couple of men, Cecily still by his side.

"It looks as though he has gotten past his heartache," Rosalynn said. "I do not know if I could bear to be seen in public after such an embarrassing anecdote about me was passed around."

"What else could he do, go into hiding? That would simply confirm he was part of the book. At least this way he does not know that anyone has figured it out." I hastily added, "If, indeed, it is true."

We watched while whispers passed behind fans around the room like a soft breeze. Eyes, widened in shock, darted to Lord Fischer as the gossip wound its way through the Fashionable World.

"It looks like it has gotten around," Freya said.

We stood in a line, watching the secret complete its round and land on Lord Fischer's party. A man approached their group, saying something hilarious to the laughing circle before Lord Fischer's face, momentarily, slipped. He regained composure, laughing along with the rest of them, his eye darting to Cecily periodically.

"Oh, poor Lord Fischer," I sighed.

"Poor him?" Rosalynn scoffed. "What about Cecily?" Who was, at that moment, curtseying to the party and moving away from them, her head held high and disappointment written on her features.

I lifted a shoulder. "If she cannot overlook the scandal then perhaps they were not meant to be anyway."

Freya eyed me. "Because of her experience in scandals?"

"No," I explained. "Because her name will never be spotless. She brings a fair share of disgrace to any relationship with those rumors from school. Her husband needs to be strong enough to support her and give her back some credit."

"Regardless, I am glad I am not mentioned in the book." Rosalynn laughed, but it was mirthless. "I could not imagine the shame of being discussed so brazenly among society."

I speared her with a look. She had the grace to look abashed. "It's different with you," she tried to explain. "The papers have never said anything directly hateful about you."

I tried to understand how saying that I guffawed like a caged bird was kind, but nevertheless, she did not understand. Regardless of the subject, it was uncomfortable to be so openly discussed. It was as though the articles gave Society the license to analyze my life and my choices; regardless of how wrong they were about my choice in men.

"Well, I feel for them. And I vow that if one more article unfavorably mentions my name, the paper will regret it."

CHAPTER 23

Laid up in bed with her cold, Mother was unable to read the papers before I properly disposed of them—save for one article. Which was a very good thing, indeed.

Alone in the breakfast room, I pushed an egg around my plate while I contemplated the options available to me. The article this morning had been blunt in its description of Almack's the night before, including the men I had danced with, the men I had sat out of the dances with, and who was going to be taking me to the park today.

Just how did this writer have access to that information? I strained to remember who had been nearby when Lord Cameron requested the outing for today, but I had been slightly dizzy from the waltz, and it could have been any number of people.

But more importantly, why did anyone even care? The gossip articles had become less about exciting things going on with socialites and had narrowed down its focus to my every move. Granted, I was keeping busy, but not busy enough to warrant such pointed focus.

Now, I had to make due on my promise. Whoever was writing these articles was going to pay.

Pushing away from the table, I folded up the article I saved from the fire and tucked it into my gown. I filled a napkin with sausages for Coco and returned to my bedroom, only to find her happily chomping away on eggs and kippers brought up by Molly.

"She has no taste, does she?" I said thoughtfully, eyeing Coco as she ravished the eggs. She licked her plate clean and trotted over to sniff the napkin of sausages I held in my lap.

"She's going to be a fat one, she is. Mark my words."

"Better fat than starving," I rebutted, opening up the napkin and letting her eat her fill. Which, incidentally, was all five of them.

"Do you need to change your gown, miss?" Molly asked, standing beside the clothes press.

I fingered the edge of the long sleeve I had chosen to cover my bandage. I would likely only need the gauzy dressing for a few more days, for which I was immensely grateful. A bulging forearm was not attractive. "No, I am going to take Coco for a walk shortly, so this dress will do just fine."

I sat on the edge of my bed and watched Coco sniff around the floor momentarily before moving in front of the unlit fireplace and curling into a ball on the cushions Molly had laid out for her there.

"She's right at home, she is."

"Exceedingly so," I agreed. "Right from the very beginning. Molly, can I ask you a personal question?"

She looked up, her dark hair falling out of its bun and framing her face. She was a lovely person.

"You may choose not to answer," I said in preparation, "but do the servants talk about me? I mean, to other servants. Some very personal things about me are making their way into the newspaper."

Molly looked me square in the eye, something I was not quite accustomed to with her, and said, "I've heard nothing coming or going with other households, miss. And if you excuse my saying, those articles sound like they talk about things us servants wouldn't even be there to see happen. I'm not sure how it could be coming from downstairs."

She made an especially valid point.

My shoulders drooped. "I suppose I only wanted to find an explanation."

"An easy explanation," she corrected.

Shamed, I stood, clasping my hands before me. "I will await Lord Cameron in the drawing room. Will you discreetly bring Coco to me when he arrives?"

"Yes, miss."

Leaving her to finish straightening my room, I escaped the embarrassment of our conversation. Pulling the article out once again I scanned it repeatedly, hoping for some clue that would lead me to discover the writer. I did not want to become the next person victimized by merciless gossip the way Cecily had been or Lord Fischer last night. The way things were moving with this columnist, it was increasingly possible that were I to slip up in any manner, my mishap would be bandied about London.

Not that I was planning to make a mistake, but knowing I had a spotlight on me made it all the more uneasy a prospect.

Lost in thought, I jolted at the sound of a boot hitting the metal fire poker. Lord Cameron stood across from me, leaning beside the mantle and grinning.

"How long have you been there?" I asked.

"Quite long enough to wonder what in heaven's name you are so deeply concentrating on."

I stood, wiping my hands down the front of my skirt to smooth the wrinkles and consequently, my thoughts. I pulled on the tug rope and requested the footman to send for Molly and inform her that Lord Cameron had arrived. If he was confused by the request, then he did not show it.

"We must speak in code," I explained once the footman had departed. "No one knows that I have Coco in the house."

He tried to temper his amusement, but I could see it clearly in his eyes. "I have a hard time believing you to be successful."

"Well, even if the servants have figured it out"—which even I had to admit was a distinct probability—"keeping my mother in the dark is the main objective."

As luck would have it, my father came in the room, utter confusion written on his tired face. "Lord Cameron," he boomed, stepping forward to shake his hand. "To what do we owe this pleasure?"

"I have come to take Miss Cox on a walk to Berkeley Square, sir."

"Indeed?" Father turned to me, his eyebrow raised. "Capital, I say."

Molly came down the corridor, Coco in her arms. I shot her a pleading look. She halted, unsure, and I turned toward my father, where he stood beside Lord Cameron and out of view of my maid.

"Father," I emphasized, "I believe we must be on our way if we are to avoid the afternoon heat." Molly immediately spun toward the front door. She would likely be waiting for us outside.

"Yes, yes." He nodded, so obliging. "Best be on your way." I had never seen him so accommodating before and a sliver of me resented Lord Cameron for being the reason for it. A large slice of me resented my father more.

Lord Cameron's amusement, however, was quickly tipping the scales back toward him.

Father escorted us outside, never once questioning who might be chaperoning our outing to the park. Propriety required my maid to attend and she would join us once father retired inside. That he didn't seem to notice her absence in the meantime only served as evidence of just how pleased he was with my outing. I wanted so badly to nip his enthusiasm in the bud, but I would have to wait until Lord Cameron was not around if I didn't want to embarrass—or enrage—my father.

Lord Cameron walked beside me down the street, his hands casually clasped behind his back. Molly let Coco loose when the dog saw me and began eagerly barking, and Lord Cameron paused momentarily before tipping his hat to her. "You are much improved after your bath, Coco. But where is your leash?"

"She hasn't one."

He turned startled eyes on me. "Whyever not? How are you to protect her against a vicious hound this time?"

In truth, I hadn't thought of that. "Well, I suppose that is why you are here." I laughed at his wry expression. "She minds well enough," I added. "We've taken a number of walks since she has come to live with me."

"A feat, indeed."

We both watched her lope ahead, sniff a patch of grass, and then slowly meander back to us. I called for her when it was time to cross the road and she jumped into my arms daintily. I was proud of her for her supreme obedience and was absolutely going to reward her in the morning in the form of extra bacon.

"I must admit," Lord Cameron said, drawing me toward a bench and gesturing for me to sit before lowering himself beside me. "I find myself amazed."

I nodded. "Coco has turned out to be something of a delightful surprise."

"Yes. Her, too."

I glanced up sharply, but his face was a work of stone. I blushed at the insinuation but could not find anything within myself to base it on. I swiftly shoved away his artful flirtation.

We watched Molly toss a stick for Coco to chase, the small dog fetching it with enthusiasm, over and over again.

"Do you miss Kent?" Lord Cameron asked.

"Yes," I said, nodding. "It's lovely. Quite a contrast to your Scottish wildland."

"I beg your pardon," he said, affronted. "I am an Englishman through and through. The ability I have to throw a stone from my rooftop and hit Scotland with it has nothing to say for my roots."

I eyed him sideways. "True. I suppose I ought to keep my opinions to myself when I've scarce gone further north than Cambridge. I am gathering my opinions from Rosalynn's descriptions."

He scoffed lightly. "Slightly biased, I assume."

I lifted a shoulder. "She loves her home, though you may not hear her say so."

He straightened on the bench, turning his head away to watch Coco ignore Molly's stick and sniff at a tree, her small tail wagging furiously. "Because of the people who live in it."

"No, she loves her family," I defended. "She merely suffered being the only female with a pack of—"

"Tyrants?"

I narrowed my eyes. "I was going to say brothers, but 'tyrants' is also accurate."

Silence engulfed us in an awkward, thick cloud. I searched for something to say, but I did not know how to convince him Rosalynn cared. It was strange to me that he was unaware of it, and I considered the possibility that he did not know her as well as he might have had they remained together; a definite byproduct of children being sent away to school for the majority of their growing up years. Can a close relationship be built on summers and Christmas holidays?

"I suppose we ought to go," he said.

I was mortified. Clearly I had overstepped, but it was an

innate reaction to defend Rosalynn. Though I found myself enjoying the easy, artless conversation more than I cared to admit. I plucked up my courage. "We needn't yet. I apologize if I overstepped by presuming to know Rosalynn's mind."

"No, that's not it." Lord Cameron pointed to the far side of the park. "It appears that Coco wants to eat that squirrel."

CHAPTER 24

We raced for the tree on the opposite side of the park where my dog barked ferociously, her tiny paws scraping at the trunk in an attempt to climb. Molly was running toward them but was not yet halfway there, while the squirrel, safely up in the branches of the tree, raced back and forth in a taunting rhythm.

By the time we reached them, Molly was trying to pull Coco away, but every time she got her arms around the dog, Coco would jump back down and resume her post at the base of the trunk.

"Coco, come," Lord Cameron demanded with all of the authority being the son of a duke instilled in him.

I was utterly shocked when Coco disobeyed. I did not believe it possible to contradict such a command.

"Well, she is your dog," he said wryly.

I tried not to read too much into that or what it said about my obstinate personality.

"Perhaps I ought to go find a rope," Molly suggested, breathless.

Lord Cameron stepped forward, sneaking up behind Coco while she barked relentlessly at the poor squirrel and scooped her up in one smooth motion. He pivoted away, and I struggled to keep up with his long strides, taking Coco from his arms after we safely crossed the road.

"You naughty girl," I said softly. "You have been bullied before. You really must know better. I am ashamed of you and you've lost your extra bacon treat."

I felt the burn of Lord Cameron's gaze and caught laughter dancing in his eyes.

"Must you judge me?" I said, instantly regretting my words for how taken aback he looked.

"Judge you for caring for your dog? Miss Cox, the only thing about you I judge is the silly pact you and Rosie made when you were school girls." His lips formed a sarcastic smile. "You know, the impossible one that was ill created and ill-sustained."

I was never so vexed in all my life. So many angry thoughts floated through my mind that I immediately determined the best course of action would be to say none of them at all. If Lord Cameron had shown me anything from the very beginning of our acquaintance, it was that he was not open-minded and would not welcome my radical ideals. There was no sense in trying to convince a brick wall that the garden before it was lovely; the brick wall would never hear or see anything to begin with.

Disappointment warred with irritation within me, quickening my pulse. I had begun to think of Lord Cameron as a friend.

Setting my gaze forward and holding Coco closer to my chest, I hastened toward my house at the far end of the street. Lord Cameron picked up his pace to match mine.

"Are you truly offended? That was meant to be a joke."

I stopped in my tracks to face him head on and he had to

backtrack a few steps to meet me. "Do you mean that honestly?"

He shifted from one foot to the other, his gaze landing somewhere over my head. He was not the tallest member of his family, and though he was of a good height, he only reached a head's length over my eye line.

He could not answer me, which I knew would be the case. I turned and continued to my house.

"Miss Cox, do not be silly."

"Heavens, no. Silly? I should never. I should always be amiable."

He ran a hand over his face and I took a twisted pleasure in seeing him so irritated.

"I am sorry if what I said bothered you."

I scoffed. "But are you sorry you said it? No. You think me naive. You simply cannot imagine that a young woman would choose not to wed, or that I would believe there could be more out there for me than to do someone else's bidding for the rest of my life."

"No, I cannot," he said, agitated.

"Then we are done here," I said, reaching my front steps. "Thank you for the walk, and good day."

He remained behind when I mounted the stairs to my front door, Molly racing up before me to open it and let me inside. Every part of me wanted to look back at him before the door closed, but I proudly refrained. I caught his outline in my peripheral vision and was glad I had not given into the temptation.

I slouched against the back of the door, Coco still clutched in my arms, when a shriek pulled me from my brooding.

Mother stood at the base of the stairs across from me, one hand clutched to her heart and the other firmly supporting the banister.

"Elspeth, what are you doing in this house with that creature?"

"Mother, this is my dog. Her name is Coco and she is very well behaved." I held her out for inspection, my mother's mouth drooping in shock. After a minute I said, "I shall be in my room if you need me," and took myself upstairs.

CHAPTER 25

"She's a lovely thing," Freya said, scratching Coco behind the ears. She knelt before the makeshift bed near the fireplace while Rosalynn paced from my bedroom door to my window and back. I sat on the trunk in front of my bed and watched her pace, growing dizzier the longer she walked.

It was the morning after my park escapade with Lord Cameron, but I found I could not relay the whole of it when Rosalynn initially asked how it went. She was confused about why he had asked me in the first place, but since I was just as ignorant on the matter, I was hardly the person to ask. His motives in my mind were as simple as wanting to see Coco, which was accomplished. If his secondary goal was to rile me up, then that was also perfectly achieved.

"Are they going to let you stay?" Freya asked Coco, though I knew she was really asking me.

"It matters little what my parents say. I could not possibly give her up." I watched Rosalynn grow more and more restless. "Besides," I said absently, "it is not as if my household claims a legitimate reason for not having a dog. No one has an allergy to speak of."

Rosalynn stopped suddenly at the window, looking out over the park. I turned to Freya, who was scowling deeply at Coco.

"Gracious," I said. "Whatever is the matter?"

Her expression immediately snapped back to normal, shooting me a wide smile. "Nothing, I was only wishing Mother was not allergic."

"You shall not have to live in the same house with her for the rest of your life."

"It would be my luck to marry a man who is allergic, too," she said wryly.

Rosalynn spun, a fierce look in her eyes. "What did you say?"

I froze at the indignation in her tone. Freya looked dumbfounded but was not given a chance to answer when Rosalynn continued, her brows pulled together in bewildered outrage, the fire in her eyes blazing. "You spoke of marriage as if it were an inevitability. And you"—she turned on me—"are not shocked by it. Has the bargain with your parents truly desensitized you to the issues we face as women in this imbalanced world? Have you both sincerely let go of the pact we made as the Sisterhood of Deserving Females?"

My mouth hung slack. Rosalynn's gaze darted between Freya and me before turning back toward the window. Her chest heaved with indignation, and I sought the words to soothe her, while also speaking the truth.

"Your silence is answer enough," she spat.

"Rosalynn, wait," Freya said, her hand reaching for Rosalynn's as she passed us. "It isn't like that!"

Turning at the door, Rosalynn sucked in a quiet breath, stemming the flow of tears which were trying to burst forth. "Am I the only one capable of staying strong? I thought I knew you better than this."

Silence hung heavy at her exit, and regret that I had not spoken right away swallowed me whole. I still did not know why I had said nothing.

Freya sat unmoving on the floor, her hand absently petting Coco while her gaze leveled off in the distance. I allowed her the silence and privacy she evidently needed, waiting for her to come to her own conclusions. Part of me hoped the explanation she had would suffice for me as well.

It felt like hours but was likely only minutes before Freya came to. She stood clumsily, wiping her hands together and then down the front of her gown.

"I must be getting home," she said quietly.

Concern filtered through my gut. "Freya," I said softly. "Do not let her words offend you so. You have your own life to live, and you must feel the ability to do so freely without the judgments of others. We were children when we made the pact. You could not have known then how you would feel now, and it is not for Rosalynn to determine your future." I stepped forward and picked up her hand, squeezing her fingers lightly. She had yet to make eye contact with me and my heart constricted, worried for her. "Is that not the basis of our whole pact: that we may determine for ourselves what we want from life?"

Nodding absently, Freya slipped her hand from mine. "I shall see you at your aunt's soiree. Good day, Elsie."

I watched her walk from my room, feeling as forlorn as Coco looked. There had been a shift in my world in the past ten minutes. I did not know exactly how it was going to present itself in the form of my relationships with my friends, but I knew it would never be quite the same again. Words had been said which could not be called back, and things were left silent that could have filled the chasm that grew between us. Grief exhausted my body and I slumped onto the floor, faintly aware of Coco's nose pressing into my side.

The one thing—the Sisterhood of Deserving Females—which drew us together and created a solid bond of friendship and support, was also the thing that was tearing us apart. I could only hope the damage was repairable.

I stepped to my window and watched Freya depart, her maid following close behind her. She shuffled down the street with her head bowed and her shoulders slumped like an errant child returning from a scolding.

Pivoting away from the window, I leaned against the wall, sliding down until my gown gathered around my knees and my head rested against the armchair beside me. Coco trotted over to me, nudging my elbow with her wet nose until I lifted my arm and took her onto my lap.

"You do not judge me, do you Coco?" I said, recalling Rosalynn's sharp eyes. "You love me unconditionally. I shall never be so fortunate to find another like you, shall I?"

Her beady eyes looked up, the confusion on her face reminding me that I was speaking to a dog.

"Perhaps I could get another dog and be surrounded by unconditional love."

She stood as though affronted by the concept that her love was not enough for me and crossed to the door, scratching at it with her paw.

"Have I offended you? Oh, never mind. Come, you little rascal, and let me take you outside."

CHAPTER 26

"We shall have to get new gowns made, tomorrow at the very latest." Mother was seated on the green brocade armchair, a stool lifting her feet and a fan in her hand cooling her face. Her nerves had not yet caught up to her body in terms of recovery, though she was going to rally enough to accompany me to Aunt Georgina's card party that evening.

She glanced longingly at the tea tray, prompting me to offer, "Would you like some tea, Mother?"

"Oh, I suppose so," she said weakly. Evidently, she was planning to milk this illness as long as she was able.

Father entered the room while I poured cups of tea. "Would you like some tea?" I asked him.

"No."

I glanced up sharply, the severity of his tone making my back set up. Instinctively, I pulled inward, guarding myself against his impending anger.

His glare pierced me, clocking my every move. "I've been informed that you have been keeping a dog under my roof for days without my knowledge or consent. What do you have to say for yourself?"

I tried to make myself small. It was the best way I knew to cater to his anger. He would be magistrate, and though he asked if I'd like to defend myself, we both knew he did not want or appreciate justifications.

"I am sorry, Father. I should have asked you first."

His face turned red in irritation. He sputtered, spit flying from his lips. He coldly said, "You will dispose of it immediately. I will not have a dirty stray in my house."

"Yes, Father." I lowered my face, tears born of frustration streaming down my cheeks. I waited for the receding footsteps to sound before I finished preparing my mother's tea, leaving my cup unattended. I had lost my appetite.

"We will leave before noon tomorrow so as not to wait in any monstrous lines," Mother said, accepting my cup.

I looked her in the eye, pleading with my gaze for her to say something. Anything would do. I only wanted to know that it bothered her, how he had to control everything. He hadn't even known Coco was there, so how was her presence in my room negatively affecting the household?

"We can take the dog out with us when we go," she said, shocking me. Yet still refusing to meet my eyes. "I think there ought to be a place we can leave it when we run our errands."

Was this her way of speaking up? She was giving me an extra day. Father had said "immediately" when he ordered Coco's eviction. Mother was now saying that tomorrow would be fine. I could have kissed her in gratitude. I decided not to push my luck and nodded instead, worried my voice would reveal my emotion.

Pulling out my handkerchief, I dabbed at my eyes, settling back onto the sofa and drawing the needlework bird I had been working on into my lap. I sat quietly and stitched, for once unconcerned with the boring repetition.

After enough time had passed in silent companionship, it was time to prepare for Aunt Georgina's card party. Mother had not been surprised by my mentioning it as she had already received an invitation. It appeared that once our presence was made known, Aunt Georgina invited us to all of her social gatherings. Why we had never before gone to them, and, subsequently, why Aunt Georgina had been so shocked to see us arrive at the ball—was solely on Mother's shoulders. Though I could not imagine why she would not want to attend. Aunt Georgina was wonderful.

Billington stopped me, a brown paper-wrapped parcel in his hands. "This arrived for you earlier, Miss Elsie."

Surprised, I accepted the small package from his hands and took it up to my bedchamber to open while Molly readied my clothes for the evening. Untying the twine, I slid it from the parcel. Unfolding the thick, brown paper, my eye caught on a thin, well-cut strap of leather. A white card fluttered to the floor and I bent down to retrieve it, reading the simple note within.

Perhaps this will save a few squirrels.
-C

Lord Cameron had gifted me a leash for Coco. I was unsure whether this was kind or obnoxious, but my chest warmed regardless, my gaze skittering over the loopy C on the card. I stowed the leash with Coco's other things, tucking the note into my vanity drawer, decidedly not considering the implications of the gift. Lord Cameron saw a need, and he had simply done what any practical man would do: filled the need.

I put on my white gown with lace capped sleeves and coral ribbon lining under the bust, the long silk skirt flowing down with coral rosettes dotting the hemline and a sheer overlay shot through with golden thread. It was perhaps my most flattering silhouette, which was explanation enough of why I had postponed wearing it. With the wretched newspaper and Mother's bargain, I tried not to draw attention to myself whenever possible.

Molly worked my hair into ringlets with the hot curling tongs, gathering them on my head and weaving through a white ribbon that set off my honey-colored hair. Opening the drawer of my dressing table, I pulled out the necklace Aunt Georgina had given me, handing it to Molly to clasp around my neck.

My reflection looked more dignified than I felt, and I hoped the illusion would last all evening. There were many questions in my life and fewer solid truths at the present. Confidence in my appearance was one way I was able to face society with a semblance of bravery.

"Father has commanded that Coco must be sent away," I said at last, fiddling with my gloves rather than meet Molly's eye. "I have until tomorrow, but she must be gone before noon. This will be our last night with her."

I hazarded a glance and winced at Molly's pain. I had been correct. She had also formed a connection with the pup.

"Yes, miss."

"I am going to do my best to place her in a good home. I refuse to put her back on the street where we found her."

"I wouldn't imagine anything else," Molly said, surprising me. I swallowed the lump in my throat and turned toward Coco, her sad eyes nearly undoing me.

"Be good, you," I said, sniffling discreetly. Then I turned and fled.

CHAPTER 27

Regarding my bargain, I found myself in even deeper trouble at a night of card games than I ever had before at any ball. The requests to partner in a game of whist were endless, and I was the fortunate lady who said yes to every single one.

Aunt Georgina was in her element, floating from table to table or holding court on the sofa near the refreshment table. When I first arrived and greeted her, she noticed my necklace right away and a suspicious sheen glazed her eye. We shared a brief hug and I promised to introduce my friends to her the moment they arrived.

Which, presently, was impossible.

I had played four rounds of whist with four different partners, was currently in a game partnering Mr. Fenway, with his obnoxiously flirtatious glances, and had Lord McGregor lined up next. Lord McGregor was the final man on my list for the time being.

Rosalynn had yet to arrive, but Freya was busy making rounds with her mother. Aunt Georgina did not seem to be forlornly awaiting my introductions, however, so I tried to remain calm.

"Do you have a love for cards, Miss Cox?"

I glanced to my right, where Cecily sat daintily, her partner, Lord McGregor, focusing on playing his turn.

"I find it entertaining."

She innocently tilted her head. "Though not, perhaps, with much time to devote to the craft?"

I connected the dots slower than I was proud of. She was trying to tactfully say I was horrible at cards. Well, when distracted like I unfortunately had been that evening, it was only natural I would lose so terribly.

We continued to play, Mr. Fenway very kind about my horrid choices and obvious lack of attention. When Lord McGregor and Cecily won by a landslide, the men switched chairs, thus switching partners.

I shot Lord McGregor a commiserating look. "I apologize, sir. It is certainly not my lucky night."

"Ah, but I can honestly say it is mine," he graciously replied. "What other man can boast two such lovely partners back to back?"

Cecily and I both looked at Mr. Fenway.

"Besides Mr. Fenway, naturally," Lord McGregor said with a grin. He shuffled and dealt our cards, and we got ourselves off to a decent beginning.

"You have not seen Rosalynn yet this evening, have you?" I asked.

Lord McGregor glanced up from his cards, his copper brows pulling together slightly. "I was unaware she intended to come."

I had not thought of that potential. Perhaps she had changed her mind following our disagreement. I focused on my hand of cards, trying to show Cecily I was not generally as hopeless at whist as I had so far proved.

I caught Freya's eye as she sat on the sofa near Aunt

Georgina, and she gave me a tentative smile. I returned it with much more enthusiasm, glad to know that she, at least, was not angry with me.

We nearly won the round, but Mr. Fenway and Cecily pulled ahead by a few points. Before either of the gentlemen could be polite and offer another round—to which I would've been forced to accept—I stood from my chair. Both gentlemen hastily followed my lead. "Thank you for your company. I must greet my aunt."

I crossed the room, aware of the extra eyes that followed me. I had anticipated some praise for this particularly exquisite gown, but nothing to what I was receiving. It was disconcerting to say the least.

"Your gown," Freya gushed when I approached. "I vow, it is the loveliest I have seen this Season."

"It is not a ball gown," I said. "There have been far superior gowns. It is only difficult to recall them at present."

She looked ready to argue but I cut her off as we approached her mother. "Mrs. Hurst, how lovely to see you. Have you met my aunt?"

"Yes, yes. I know Miss Stuart," she said.

I'd never heard her called by anything other than "Aunt Georgina" before, and the "Miss Stuart" did not fit her regal white hair or bright, intelligent gaze in my eyes.

"I haven't yet," Freya said excitedly.

I reached for her hand. "Then allow me to do the honors."

We stepped over to the corner where a few older women were gathered near Aunt Georgina. They scattered slightly when we approached, much like hens.

"Aunt, allow me to introduce my dear friend, Miss Freya Hurst."

Freya curtseyed most becomingly under Aunt Georgina's watchful eye. She stood tall and welcomed the appraisal, a grin stretching her lips and revealing her straight, clean teeth.

A single nod indicated the end of the evaluation. "Pretty thing," Aunt Georgina said decisively. "And you are doing well this Season?"

A blush pinked Freya's cheeks, and she darted a glance at me briefly before looking away. "I do well enough," she said finally.

"Shall I fetch you a refreshment?" I asked Aunt Georgina.

"Yes. Lemonade, please."

Perhaps leaving the two of them alone was not my finest moment. But it was a quick trip—the footman immediately handed me a glass of lemonade when I approached—and I was back in minutes, startled to find Aunt Georgina and Freya in deep conversation.

"I may never have a dog, for Mama is deathly allergic, but if I did, I vow I would want one just like Coco."

Had she relayed the story of Coco's discovery in the park? I tamped down the pain that shot through me. "Actually," I said, clearing my throat. "I must find another home for her. Father has forbidden me from having a dog."

Aunt Georgina looked dumbfounded; Freya was shocked. "Whatever for?"

I shrugged. "It is not for me to know. Nor is it for me to ask questions. I shall have to simply hope I will find a good solution in the morning. I have until noon."

"Oh, child," Aunt Georgina said. "What a horrid thing. You must bring her here."

"You cannot want a little terrier, Aunt. She is sweet but has her fair share of energy."

Aunt Georgina preened. "Then perhaps a little will rub off on me. It is decided, she will come here for the time being."

I dared not hope what that could imply. She could mean it was an acceptable arrangement for a few days. Or she could mean it was appropriate until the end of the Season when I would earn my independence.

I would not ask her to clarify now. Better to let her fall in love with Coco before I begged to impose long term. "Very well. Thank you."

She waved a hand nonchalantly. "It is nothing. I employ far too many servants, anyway. Best give them something to do."

Freya shot me an amused glance and I returned it, freezing when I caught a pair of deep brown eyes on the far side of the room: Rosalynn. My heart quickened when I noticed the man escorting her, his perfectly messy hair and discerning gaze sweeping the room. My pulse thrummed, and I turned abruptly, pushing away the feelings I did not want to own up to.

It was unfair, really, how the heart seemed to have a mind of its own.

"Freya," I said, hoping to guard the nerves in my voice. "Rosie is here."

She spun on her heel, her hopeful eyes seeking out our friend. It had to be a good sign that Rosalynn showed up at all. I was going to hold onto that thought as long as I was able.

She turned worried eyes on me. "Should we approach her?"

"Yes," Aunt Georgina said, startling both of us. "I do not pretend to follow what is happening here. But if she is the other woman you promised to introduce me to, Elspeth, then you best bring her here."

"Yes, Aunt."

I crossed the room slowly, in control, Freya by my side. Rosalynn stood near the door, speaking with her brother and Lord McGregor, who had reached them before we did.

"You must partner me," he was saying. "I should like to show off, and with you, there is no other course."

Rosalynn's lips formed a pretty grin. "Because I am superior at all card games?"

"Because you are particularly talented at whist."

She glanced to me briefly and then opened her mouth to respond when I stepped forward. "My aunt should like to meet you first, if you have a moment." I hoped such a request could not go ignored. Particularly as she was the hostess.

Rosalynn speared me with a look so full of varying emotions that I could not decipher what she was feeling. I simply was grateful when she nodded.

"Forgive me," she said, turning to Lord McGregor. "Perhaps you could save me a game."

He bowed. "Of course."

She stepped between her brother and Lord McGregor, much the regal queen, and followed me toward my aunt. I was surprised to see Lord Cameron close beside her when I turned to make the introductions, but I hoped it was not apparent in my face.

Aunt Georgina nodded at Rosalynn's curtsy and winked at Lord Cameron's bow. My jaw dropped at her forward behavior, but upon noticing her twinkle and his amusement I tried not to be so thoroughly shocked. That was perhaps one of the benefits of being an eccentric older woman: one could be as brazen as she pleased.

"And you have known each other quite some time, I am told," Aunt Georgina said, indicating all of us.

"We were at school together," Freya supplied. "I am fortunate to have gained an instant connection with the both of them."

"Fortunate, indeed." Taking a sip of her lemonade, Aunt Georgina smacked her lips and placed the glass on the small table beside her armchair. "Well, you simply must come here often. I love to have visitors, and the dog will grow sorrowful, I am sure, without a thorough petting every so often."

Rosalynn exchanged glances with Lord Cameron. He gave her a brief shrug.

I said, "She is referring to Coco."

"Whatever for?" Rosalynn asked.

"She has been evicted," Freya replied.

"Elsie?" Lord Cameron expostulated, his eyes wide as saucers.

"No." I tried not to be offended. "I am not homeless, only Coco. Father has told me I must find a new home for her, and Aunt Georgina has graciously offered to provide one. I am eternally grateful."

"It is nothing," Aunt Georgina said. "Now I find myself interested in playing a hand of whist." Her eye was fixed on Lord Cameron, and he obliged her. "I hate to leave you here, but there seems to be a place opening just over there. It was lovely to meet you, and welcome to my home."

She walked away on his arm and I turned toward Rosalynn, hoping to find grace within her countenance.

Instead, I found delight.

"Your aunt is lovely," she said, Freya nodding agreement.

"I knew you'd both love her. She is extraordinary, to be sure. Quite the epitome of doing what she wishes and saying what she will. I believe she does not care a whit for what others may think or say of her."

If only I could be so brave.

Silence reigned for a moment, none of us knowing quite the right thing to say. The conversation earlier in my bedchamber could not be undone, and the things that were said were now laid out before us. I did not feel the need to defend my actions, for I did not feel I had done anything wrong. Freya, on the other hand, looked exceedingly sorrowful.

She stepped forward and placed her hand under Rosalynn's elbow. "Forgive me? I have let myself get wrapped up in the glamour of the Season and I fear I let my priorities get away from me."

"I am not your mother," Rosalynn said slowly, not unkindly. "It is not for me to say how you should live your life. I was bothered by other things and reacted more severely than I should have. I vented my anger on you both, and neither of you deserved my censure. Let us put it behind us and move forward with respect and support as we have done in the past."

Freya and I stood in stunned silence. That was not the reprimanding I had come to expect from Rosie, nor was it the guilt she could have heaped upon us. It was humble, and it was the truth.

I pulled her into a brief embrace, aware of our setting and the many watchful eyes. I spotted an open sofa a few paces away and pulled them both toward it, seating ourselves against the wall where we might talk at our leisure.

"I believe," Freya began quiet but steadily, "if I have the both of you by my side, I may very well accomplish anything."

CHAPTER 28

The evening was winding down and Mother had shot me multiple loaded glances throughout the past hour which clearly said, "I should like to go home now."

I did my best to pretend not to see them, thoroughly enjoying the card games and company of my dearest friends. We lost Rosalynn to Lord McGregor not long after she arrived, but Freya and I were able to partner a few times and had since been reunited with our third.

"I haven't mentioned yet how stunning your gown is," Rosalynn said, leaning back in her chair slightly to survey me. We had finished a round of cards and lost our fourth player, Cecily, to Mr. Fenton. "Odd choice to pick something so breathtaking for a night of cards. And I don't believe I've seen that necklace before."

My fingers immediately went to the cameo necklace, and the reason I had chosen my gown—it matched the necklace so perfectly. "It was my grandmother's," I said, trying to ignore Lord Cameron's approach to our table. He pulled out a chair and sat across from me.

"Whist?" he said, beginning to shuffle the cards Cecily had left behind.

Freya leaned forward and picked up my necklace, squinting her eyes and tilting her head slightly. "It is gorgeous," she said.

"So lovely," Rosalynn agreed.

"Aunt Georgina gave it to me." I picked up my cards and began to sort them into proper order. "I'm not sure if my father even knew of it before." In fact, he probably still didn't, since he chose not to accompany us that evening in lieu of a night at his club. Again. But I kept that to myself.

"Did he not know her well?"

I glanced up from my cards to see what Lord Cameron had played. "She died on the day of his birth."

"Tragic," Freya said sadly. "I cannot imagine not knowing one's mother."

"I very well could," Lord Cameron said wryly.

Rosalynn shot him a glare. "You speak as though Mother is a nuisance."

"No, darling Rosie." He leveled her with a look. "She would have to be around much to earn that title."

"Of course she is not around much," she snapped. "Do you blame her?"

Freya shot me a discreet look, and I played my turn, hoping for the conversation to shift with it. I was not in luck.

Lord Cameron's mouth hung slack, his eyebrows inching higher. "You think her blameless?"

Rosalynn straightened her already perfect posture, her gaze trained on her cards. "I find I can sympathize with her, yes."

He laid his cards on the table, not heeding the need for secrecy. Standing up, he did not take his eyes from his sister's face. "We shall never agree on this subject and I am tired of arguing with you. I will ask you to complete your business and be ready to leave when our carriage is brought around."

He strode out the door in long, fluid motions, Rosalynn staring after him as though he'd gone mad.

Perhaps he had.

"What was the meaning of that?" Freya asked, braver than I.

Her gaze remained fixed on the door while she answered the question softly. "My mother has left for home, putting my brothers in charge of squiring me about for the remainder of the Season. Evidently, Cameron is bothered by the responsibility."

Lord Cameron had escorted Rosalynn to more functions so far than her mother had, so that was not entirely believable. I had only seen the duchess a handful of times, myself, the majority of those in her own home. The root of their disagreement clearly had something to do with their taking sides. Though I'd no idea what it could be about.

Freya wrinkled her softly freckled nose. "I was under the impression that Lord Cameron enjoyed social activities."

"They are a necessary evil," she countered. Standing, she dropped her cards on the table and exhaled in frustration. "I suppose I must go."

She left to take leave of Aunt Georgina and I stood. "Would you like more lemonade?" I asked Freya.

She glanced up from collecting the cards. "Yes, I would."

A footman, standing at the ready, poured the beverages and I took them, narrowly avoiding dropping them when I turned around and nearly ran into a man's black jacket. "Forgive me," I said, hurriedly setting the glasses on the table and pulling out my handkerchief to wipe the drops of lemonade that sprinkled his jacket.

"It is nothing," Lord Cameron said, immediately stepping out of my reach.

My cheeks went hot and I slipped the handkerchief back into my reticule. Why had I attempted to wipe the man clean? I could not believe I had touched him like that.

"I apologize," he said, his voice oddly formal, "for the outbreak a moment ago. It was uncivilized."

"I do not find emotion uncivil, Lord Cameron. We all feel it, even when we'd rather not."

His gaze focused on me, and I felt the odd sensation that he knew my mind. I stepped back slightly and he opened his mouth to speak, only to clear his throat and glance away instead. "Nevertheless, it was impolite."

I had no response for that. I could not contradict his truth, but was it equally crass to admit it had not bothered me?

Picking up the lemonade glasses again I prepared to turn away when a sharp elbow in between my shoulder blades shoved me forward and the contents of both glasses arched in the air, landing squarely in Lord Cameron's face.

Sputtering, he wiped at his eyes with his fingers while I pulled my handkerchief out again and pushed it into his hand. He seemed to jump at my forceful connection, but I did not care. For all I knew the lemon was severely burning him, and I would not be responsible for blinding a lord.

He wiped at his eyes, producing his own handkerchief when mine grew sodden. By the time he finished his ministrations, I became aware of the distinct quiet in the room and all eyes on me. A slow blush crept up my neck and into my cheeks when Lord Cameron met my gaze.

He seemed disturbed, though not upset. He appeared frustrated, but not angry with me. I could not quite understand how I had reached that conclusion and even when he turned to listen to the footman who came to probably tell him his carriage was waiting outside, I could not tear my eyes away from him. He gave me a slight nod, smiled genially to the room at large and then swept out the door, Rosalynn soon behind him.

"We are leaving now," Mother said into my ear between clenched teeth. I startled softly and then meekly followed her from the room, keeping my gaze lowered, careful not to draw further attention to myself.

In the carriage on the way home, mother spoke softly into the darkness. "I cannot wait to see what is said about you in the papers tomorrow." She sighed, long and drawn out. "Or perhaps it is better left unknown."

"It was hardly my fault someone bumped into me," I defended.

Mother was unconvinced. Shaking her head, she muttered, "I just don't know what we are ever going to do with you."

CHAPTER 29

The bell jingled above the door when we stepped into the fashionable modiste. Two women were being assisted near the bolts of pale fabric in the corner and a shop girl was sweeping up bits of thread and fuzz on the wooden floor.

Mother immediately moved toward a bolt of deep burgundy satin, fingering the shiny fabric between her gloved fingers. It was the perfect shade to set off her brown hair, darkened with age. Until the portrait of my grandmother was revealed to me, I had always thought I looked more like my mother than my father. I wondered now if Mother had ever seen her mother-in-law's portrait, and if she was aware of just how much I had inherited from Father's side of the family.

"You should order a new gown, too," I said, prompting her. The burgundy satin was exquisite, and because the focus had been on my come out since arriving in London, I was quite sure Mother was due a new gown. She deserved to treat herself after everything she put up with.

"Perhaps I will."

I turned away, perusing the various spools of lace lining the wall. Mother had not kept true to her threat last evening and had scoured the papers this morning for mention of my lemonade debacle. We had both been shocked to find that it was overlooked. In fact, the card party, in general, had been absent from gossip.

It was confusing, but I was not going to try and figure out why it had been left out. I was simply grateful for it.

"But did you hear what happened last evening?" A small voice carried from the opposite side of the room. "She threw her drink into Lord Cameron's face."

My body stiffened and though I was not near my mother any longer, I could feel her holding her breath from where I stood.

The woman continued. "I heard he propositioned her and she was showing him how she felt about his invitation."

I pulled in a sharp breath. Glancing to Mother, she gave me a sharp shake of her head and I tilted my own in question. How could she let these women discuss me without any defense? The falsehoods about me aside, Lord Cameron did not deserve to be spoken of in such a light, particularly when it was untrue.

The other voice chimed in, laughing, "She should be so lucky. I was there, actually. But I missed the ordeal."

The second voice was familiar. I knew it well. I strained to hear the rest of their conversation, but they had begun whispering and I was unable to decipher their words.

Mother approached me and spoke quietly. "We will not supply any more fodder for their gossip. Do not engage."

I obeyed, but I couldn't help glancing toward the ladies when they wrapped up their business and left the building. I did not recognize the profile of the first woman; irritation filled me anew when I saw the second. Luckily she did not look to me, for if she had I no doubt would have opened my mouth and given my opinions on those who do not stick up for others. Particularly when she was well aware I had spent my final months at school defending her.

Cecily Hapworth was far less loyal than I.

The remainder of our time choosing fabrics and flipping through fashion plates was something of a blur. I flitted between anger and hurt, doing my utmost to feel less of the latter.

When we arrived home, Mother dropped her bonnet and gloves at the door before saying, "I shall nap until the ball tonight. Do not wake me."

"May I take the carriage out?" I asked, swallowing. "I need to take Coco to her new home."

She turned on the stairs, confused. "Who?"

"My dog."

"Oh, yes. Just be back in time for dinner."

I nodded. She had forgotten about Coco. Perhaps there was a chance Father had forgotten, too. Though I was not prepared to test that theory. I went upstairs and gathered Coco into my arms, her favorite toys and blanket collected in a basket and waiting near the door. The leash poked out slightly and I found my gaze drawn to it. The temptation to sneak it out of the basket temporarily took me, but I shook off the absurd notion at once.

"Come now, Coco. Let us go and meet your new mother."

I pulled on the rope to call for Molly. Coco bounded off my lap when the maid arrived and I tried not to feel hurt by her disloyalty. It was impossible not to recognize that Coco had been around Molly more than she'd been with me. I shot my maid a glance in the carriage while we jostled our way over to Aunt Georgina's house and noticed the decided sheen in her eye.

I rubbed behind Coco's ears. "We shall simply have to visit Aunt Georgina regularly." I turned my attention to the dog. "And you will have to behave so she does not turn you out on your ear."

"It has been quite a few years since I have lived under the same roof as a dog." Aunt Georgina sat on the golden armchair in her drawing room, eyeing Coco who sat on the floor in front of her with guarded calculation, tilting her head slowly to the side. Coco mirrored her head in a tilt and Aunt Georgina's eyes flashed in amusement. I let out a silent sigh. It was going to work out.

"You're quite the spunky little thing."

I scooped Coco up and settled her onto my lap. "And you are quite the popular hostess," I said, eyeing Aunt Georgina from the side. Her soft smile was knowing and she bent down to busy herself with the tea.

"I appreciated your diversion at the end of the evening," she said, her face even. "Of course, you couldn't have known that I had gotten myself into a horrifically boring conversation with the mother of a shockingly ugly debutante. She asked me if I would sponsor a ball for the girl. Can you believe the gall of it?" Handing me a cup of hot tea prepared just the way I like it, she continued to pour a cup for herself. "Your little outburst was the distraction I needed to change the course of the conversation."

I lifted my cup in a salute. "You're very welcome."

"Now," she said, settling into her chair. "Explain what really happened, because I am certain you did not intend to throw your drink into Lord Cameron's face."

Sipping my tea, I took my time in responding, my free hand rubbing Coco's back. "No, it was not intentional on my part. Though rumor would say otherwise."

"What rumors, exactly?" a deep voice said from the doorway, forcing the hair on my bandage-free arm to stand on end.

"Speak of the devil," Aunt Georgina said quietly. She set her teacup down and fixed her smile on Lord Cameron. "Were your ears ringing, sir?"

"Yes." He smiled, his dark eyes fixed on me, and waited to be invited in.

Aunt Georgina dragged the moment out and I found it uncomfortable, though Lord Cameron, in utter contradiction, seemed entirely at ease. He must have moved past whatever had been bothering him the night before.

"Do come and sit down," she said finally. "Will you join us for tea?"

"No, thank you. I have already eaten." Depositing himself on the settee directly across from me, he crossed an ankle over his knee and settled into his seat.

"Have you removed all of the lemonade from your person?" Aunt Georgina asked, a smile playing at her lips.

I flushed, positive I was beet red. Lord Cameron, graciously, chuckled.

Aunt Georgina clucked, changing the subject once more. "Now, did you see Mrs. Hapworth and her horrid feather? I wanted to rip the thing from her hair and toss it in the fire."

I tuned out their conversation, finding myself confused by Lord Cameron's presence. It was not exactly the thing to inquire about why someone chose to visit another. But really, what would he have to speak to Aunt Georgina about? He had only met her yesterday.

"And you must meet my new housemate."

I glanced up to catch surprise flit over Lord Cameron's face.

Aunt Georgina laughed with abandon. It startled me in its intensity, but a quick glance at Lord Cameron assured me he thought nothing of it. Mother was correct, though I hated to admit it. Aunt Georgina was an eccentric.

"I did not mean Elspeth, silly boy," she continued. "I meant the dog."

"The dog has a name, Aunt," I said, pulling Coco closer.

Lord Cameron smiled at Coco endearingly. "She is well behaved, but I would keep her away from large dogs or squirrels."

Aunt Georgina stilled imperceptibly. "You speak as though you know her."

"Indeed, I do. I assisted in her rescue, as a matter of fact." His gaze flicked to mine before settling on the dog again. "I spent a good deal of time searching for the creature when Miss Cox desired to locate her. It appeared to have been worth the effort."

Silence took the room. Aunt Georgina eyed Lord Cameron suspiciously, and then me. After a long, slow sip of tea, she asked me, "Why was that not in the papers? I had thought I was able to keep tabs on your activities thus far."

As a matter of fact, that was a valid question. It had not been in the papers at all. "I can only assume whoever has been informing on me was unaware of the episodes in the park."

Her thin eyebrows shot up. "There was more than one?"

"As Lord Cameron suggested," I said, tearing my gaze away from Aunt Georgina and looking to the man himself, "I would avoid large dogs *and* squirrels."

CHAPTER 30

"Preparing my hair has never taken so long before, Molly, is everything all right?"

She shot me a look through the mirror. She knew something I did not.

"What is it?" I demanded.

She shrugged. "Your mother requested extra plaits."

That would explain all of the loops.

"Do you know why she felt a sudden need for additional plaits? Your normal creations are quite extraordinary."

She glowed slightly under my praise. "I gather that the Season is more than half done and it is time to reveal your potential."

I peered at her, my eyes squinting. "Those are not your words."

"No, miss. They aren't."

At the completion of my toilette, I turned to bid Coco farewell before departing, only to feel the sting of disappointment at the empty hearth. Perhaps Aunt Georgina was planning on going out that evening and would say farewell to Coco, snuggling her in the process.

Or perhaps Aunt Georgina planned a night at home and could keep Coco's company for the duration. Coco's new home just may suit her better than her old one. What a dismal thought.

When we reached the ball, Father helped me out of the carriage and turned back for Mother's hand. We mounted the steps with slow precision. Considering how we appeared from the outside, it was undeniable that we should seem the perfect family. Mother had been a beauty in her youth and though the years had added lines to her face and rounded her figure, she was still very handsome, particularly with Father and his dashing smile beside her. Of course, the picture was not complete without their dutiful daughter following close behind them.

It was impossible not to love them, I admitted, but equally difficult not to resent them.

I scanned the ballroom when we made our entrance but did not land on either Freya or Rosalynn. Disappointed, I smiled at Lord McGregor while he approached and accepted his dance. I was eager to be away from the throngs for a moment with a safe dance partner whom I was positive felt no feelings for me.

"You wound me, Miss Cox."

"Oh?" I raised an eyebrow in inquiry.

His face was devastated, but his eyes told a different story. "I caught you searching for someone when you first arrived, and your lack of excitement at my approach validated that I was not the lucky man."

"Who is to say it was a man I was looking for?"

Lord McGregor gave me a knowing look, amusement lurking in his smile. "Lady Rosalynn has not yet arrived."

"I came to the same conclusion." I took his hand and the instruments began to play.

Lord McGregor expertly led me around the floor, a companionable silence taking residence between us. I much enjoyed the waltz and found it was exceedingly more enjoyable with a partner who did not have leering eyes or wayward hands like some of the others in the past. I was grateful to realize Lord McGregor and I had settled into a cheerful camaraderie, the awkward incident in front of my house now long past, and, hopefully, forgotten.

We had nearly reached the end of the dance when he spoke. "Have you seen her since last evening?"

He must have meant Rosalynn, for we had not talked in the interim. "No, but I can see that you are worried. May I inquire why?"

His throat worked and he swallowed, his glance flitting behind me. "She was quite upset. I was hoping she...that someone had checked on her."

"And you could not?" I probed. The dance came to a close and we stopped right in the center of the room.

Lord McGregor looked harassed and I regretted my final words for a moment before I glanced over his shoulder and saw my mother's gaze trailing my father as he left the room. He had done his time by her side and was off, as he usually was, to find the gambling room for men only. Men. They could be so selfish. Everything in life revolved around them.

Except, at that moment, Lord McGregor worried over Rosalynn, and for the life of me, I could not find an ulterior motive. He simply cared for her, desired to be assured of her wellbeing.

He picked up my hand and escorted me toward my mother.

"Really," I said, genuine curiosity overriding my good manners. "What is it that has you so concerned?"

He turned pained eyes on me and suddenly it all clicked, and I felt so utterly stupid for never before connecting the pieces.

"You love her," I said simply, though perhaps not quietly. His arm stiffened under my hand, and I was grateful the people near us did not seem to have caught my words.

"I would thank you to keep your accusations to yourself."

I snapped my mouth shut. It was neither the time nor the place to delve into the finer points of Lord McGregor's feelings, nor how utterly unsuitable and unrequited they were. Did he know about Rosalynn's pact and the binding Promise Juice? Was he aware that his was a hopeless cause?

We reached my mother and no sooner had he bowed than he turned to disappear. I was sure I had made him angry. Though at me or himself I did not know.

"Elspeth," Mother said in her sickly sweet tone. "I have a man here who would like to meet you. His name is Mr. Wendel and he comes from America." She emphasized the final word as if it was an exotic location and not a colony of our cast-offs.

I turned to the gentleman, handsome in a black jacket and subtle ivory waistcoat. His hair was fair and long, and his eyebrows were bushy and full of expression.

I curtseyed. I had yet to meet an American before. And from the stories I had heard, he was not what I had imagined.

"A pleasure to meet you," he said, bowing. His voice held a weird tinge to it, and I found myself praying I would not be asked to dance.

"May I request the next set?" he said.

"Yes," I replied, swallowing a sigh and placing my hand on his outstretched arm, allowing him to lead me out to the quadrille.

My eye caught a daring red gown at the entrance of the ballroom and I turned sharply when I recognized the glossy, dark hair which accompanied it. Rosalynn.

The set of dances was pure and utter torture. I moved about the floor watching Rosalynn flit from person to person, sparkling and smiling while she flirted and laughed, unabashed at her utter disregard for Society's rules.

What was her mother going to say?

It occurred to me that it was perhaps irrelevant what her

mother thought, for her mother was no longer in London. According to the uncomfortable argument between her and Lord Cameron the evening prior, the Duchess of Clifton had returned home.

When Mr. Wendel returned me to my mother, I thanked him heartily and turned away before he could request anything further. My back was apparently enough of a dismissal and one that, thankfully, Mother had not noticed.

"May I go and search for Rosalynn?"

"You must dance, Elspeth," she reminded me, flipping open her fan and lazily airing her face. "The Season has not yet ended and you must dance every single dance."

"That was not the agreement," I reminded her. "I am to say 'yes' to every request. There is no requirement that I must fill the dances myself."

Her beady gaze lifted over my head, and a throat cleared behind me. I squeezed my eyes closed for a moment, hoping whomever had approached had not heard the last of our conversation. I turned.

"Rosalynn is dancing just now," Lord Cameron said, taking my hand and bowing over it. "Will you join me for this set, Miss Cox?"

Nodding, I followed him away from my triumphant mother. We lined up for a minuet and he gazed at me a moment, his face a work of stone. I was sure he was going to say something but his mouth remained firm. It was perhaps the first dance we shared in which we remained silent throughout, and I found my nerves winding more and more as the music dragged on. The minuet ended and a country dance began. The intensity of his gaze burned and I could not smile for the trepidation that overcame me.

He had explained why I could not go in search of Rosalynn when he approached me. There was zero doubt in my mind that he had heard the whole of my remarks, finally discovering the secret I'd been holding close to my heart. It was what he planned to do with the information which terrified me.

Our song came to a close and we bowed. I turned abruptly and hastened toward the door that led to the corridor. My plan, though hazy, was to locate a servant and request direction to the ladies retiring room.

I was successful and slipped inside the room safely, but not before I caught sight of Lord Cameron entering the corridor, his eyes searching, and landing on my own through the closing door.

CHAPTER 31

The room was empty. I paced the length of it, sidestepping the sofa and circling back. My mind had filled to its brimming point and I was trying to make sense of everything that had been revealed, whether to me or someone else.

Rosalynn, the object of Lord McGregor's romantic feelings, had shown up in a bright red dress. And her brother, unwittingly, had eavesdropped on the very secret I depended on remaining secret to protect myself throughout the rest of the Season.

I simply needed to compartmentalize and undertake one thing at a time.

Starting with Rosalynn.

I peeked my head through the door and the corridor was clear. I tilted my head and listened for a moment, smiling at the thought of Coco copying me if she had been standing beside me. Silence.

Stepping through the door, I jumped when Lord Cameron materialized from the other side of it. Drat. I had not seen him.

"What has you smiling?" he asked.

I gave him an exasperated look. He had no right to question me on anything personal at the moment.

He leveled me with a gaze that I read instantly; he was not going to play games with me. In retrospect, he never really had.

"Please do not repeat what you heard," I asked, ashamed slightly at the pleading in my tone.

He reared back slightly. "Of course I won't repeat it."

"Then why did you follow me out here if not to try and glean more information? Is that not what you've done from the moment you learned I possessed a secret? Heaven forbid I deigned to hide it in the first place."

His eyes brightened and his hand came around my forearm, pulling me further away from the ballroom and around a corner.

"That is the secret I tried to pull from you at that dinner?"

Was there a point in trying to hide it now? He had, in a sense, promised me no nonsense. I owed him the same. "Yes. It is part of a silly bargain and I am more than halfway through it."

"And what do you receive at the end of it?" He looked so eager, so hungry for the knowledge that I nearly swallowed my words.

Instead, I blurted it out, unheeding the small warning bell within. "My independence. My financial independence, I should say. And the opportunity to govern myself."

He was unconvinced. "Your father will never allow that."

"He has already agreed to it."

Lord Cameron looked impressed. "That is, perhaps, worth losing the ability to turn down dance partners."

"No, sir. It is not only dance partners. It is any request by an eligible male."

"Any request?"

I lifted one shoulder. "If I want my freedom before I am thirty years old, then yes."

His eyes took on a dark gleam as he raked my face, stepping slightly closer. The corridor suddenly seemed small and overly chilly, made worse by the goosebumps traveling up my arms. I realized just how far I was from Society, and how utterly alone I was with a man. My heart raced. It would be dreadful if we were discovered alone.

"Do your parents not see the danger in such a bargain?"

"There is no danger," I argued. Except to my peace of mind and love for dancing. I had begun to dread it more than enjoy it of late.

"None at all? So if I were to ask you to walk in the park with me, you would be required to oblige?"

"Indeed, I was."

His brown eyes glittered with interest. "And if I were to ask you to dance the waltz with me, you would absolutely say yes?"

I nodded. He seemed to be moving closer, though I did not see how. His hand came to rest lightly on my elbow and my breath became shallow and rapid. I held myself still, afraid if I moved it would break the spell.

His voice lowered. "And if I begged a stolen kiss, you would not turn me away?"

My breath stopped altogether, snatched away by his intense chocolate eyes and his fingers grazing the bare skin of my arm between where my glove ended and sleeve began. A shiver raced down my arm and I swallowed a lump, searching his gaze while he searched mine.

This did not count. I could say no if I wished to. But did I?

I leaned forward. His head bent, coming so close he nearly kissed me. His lips were a hair's width away, and my body swayed forward of its own accord, yearning for him.

Our lips met, his kiss soft and warm, sending fire through my body. My eyes drifted closed. I forgot to worry about my revealed secret as Cameron kissed me, one hand gliding behind my neck as the other slid behind my back, pulling me toward him as my pulse rapidly thrummed in my ears.

My arms remained limp at my sides and warmth raced

through my body, filling me with comfort and light. Cameron pulled away, and I immediately missed him. My eyes remained closed and I commanded my heart to calm, the smell of his shaving soap lingering and enticing my senses. I opened them slowly, startled to find a shocked expression overtaking his usually congenial face. I tried to step back but he tightened his grip around me.

"Do your parents know how foolish this is?" he said, his voice deep and dangerous.

Stunned, I tried to step back again. But still, he would not release me.

He lowered his voice. "There is a vast difference between accepting a man's hand in a dance and allowing him the privilege of ravishing you."

Ravishing me? Shame and humiliation flooded me. My feelings had been real. Had he merely meant to teach me a lesson?

"Unhand me," I said, furious. I put my hands to his chest to push him away but he held on firmly.

"Do you think if the wrong kind of man got you into an embrace, he would simply unhand you because you requested it?" He was spitting fire. "You do not simply say 'yes' to every single request. Not only is it foolish and unsafe, but it is utterly senseless."

With my hands rising and falling quickly against his chest, I managed to spit out, "I can see that now."

Instantly he released me. My euphoria had not only been beaten down but further stomped on and coated in mud. Fire blazed within me, but not the enjoyable kind from being tenderly held in his arms. I locked in on his gaze as surely as he had mine, our chests heaving in time.

"I have the intelligence to determine which offers even my mother would not expect me to agree to," I said through bared teeth. "Do not ever touch me again."

I stepped around him and down the corridor, glad he

remained behind and I had a moment to correct my face before returning to my Mother. I had been so utterly stupid, so caught up in senseless feelings. He was not worth risking my reputation for. I entered the ballroom to the loud sounds of a boisterous country dance and located my mother straight away.

"Where have you been?" she said from behind her fan.

"The retiring room. I feel unwell. May we go home?"

My face must have been enough evidence, for she raked me over with a look before nodding. "I'll send a man for our carriage, and for your father."

She turned away to summon the footman standing at attention near the wall and I caught Lord Cameron's gaze as he stepped through the door. Though his lips were fixed in a firm line, his eyes were soft and laced with what appeared to be regret. I found I could not tear my gaze away while he stepped along the wall toward his sister, the feeling of his lips on mine so fresh, my mouth still tingled. Mother returned, a word from her dragging my attention back and I followed her from the room.

It was clear I could never trust Lord Cameron again. I could live with that. Though if I were to consider the entirety of the episode, I found myself pondering my chosen life path, and wondering if I could live without kissing as well.

CHAPTER 32

Freya was missing. Not in the sense that nobody knew where she was, but she had disappeared from Society functions and her butler delivered a practiced spiel when I tried to visit, relaying that she was not home for visitors.

But I was not simply a visitor. I was her dearest friend.

When the Hurst butler turned me away for the sixth day in a row, I requested my coachman to drive me to Rosalynn's home instead. The morning was drizzly and cold, and I tucked the newspaper clippings into my reticule to keep them safe and dry from the wet London weather.

I mounted the stairs with no little apprehension. I had yet to see Lord Cameron since the ball the week prior, and I was afraid for what I would discover when I did see him. The butler opened the door and ushered me into the corridor, saying, "She is in the music room, Miss Cox."

I nodded and followed him, chasing the music that bled down the corridor. Rosalynn was in a daze when the butler opened the door to announce me. Her eyes closed, she played the pianoforte by memory. I held a hand up to halt him and he backed away. I let myself inside and settled on the sofa, relaxing into the rhythm of the intricate piece I had not heard before.

When it came to a close, I sat up and watched her face, the exhaustion rimming her eyes evident in dark circles. I crossed to the instrument and laid a hand on her shoulder, whispering, "Rosie?"

She opened her eyes but did not startle. "How long have you been here?"

"Only a few minutes." She scooted over on the bench and I sat beside her. "That was lovely."

A smile tipped half of her lips and she slouched forward slightly. It was so unlike her that I feared something was horridly, dreadfully wrong. "What is it?"

She sighed, leaning back as though she was watching a memory I could not see. "Where do I begin?"

"Perhaps the beginning?"

She looked at me sharply then, and I could see the calculation in her eyes. Was she gauging how much to tell me, or whether she could trust me? Both of the thoughts hurt, and I shoved them aside. "When have we ever kept secrets from one another?"

Rosalynn stood, and I thought I had pushed too far, but she only moved to the sofa. I followed her over, pulling my feet under me and tucking my skirts around them.

"Where is Freya?" she asked instead.

"She is not home for visitors."

Rosalynn nodded as though it made sense.

I had never before felt so left out. "What is going on? I feel like I have missed something, but I do not know what."

"No," she said. What did that mean? No, I did not miss something? Or no, she could not tell me?

I pulled the unflattering newspaper articles out of my reticule and smoothed them out, laying them on the bare seat cushion between us. "Have you seen these? My mother is considering leaving Town."

Rosalynn glanced at me sharply. "That seems a drastic measure."

"So you've read them."

She did not answer, only picked up the clipped papers and shuffled through them. In the days since the ball—and that horrid, delightful kiss—the articles in the paper had changed their tune. The jokes became barbs, the 'facts' significantly exaggerated, and I was painted to be a high society hussy who could not refuse the attentions of any man.

Thankfully, the writer of the articles seemed unaware that I literally could not refuse; I was simply illustrated as a flirt. Not that that was any better.

"Mother is livid," I said. "She cannot determine if the better course of action is to flee Town or face them head-on."

"You are not a coward," Rosalynn said, setting down the articles. She hadn't done more than glance through them. I was correct, she had read them before.

"No, I am not," I agreed. "I have been fighting to stay in London."

"And your father?"

I lifted one shoulder. "It is the one time I would like him to step in and tell Mother we will not run away and all he has done is make himself scarce." I had a theory that Father was disturbed by the accusations against my virtue and chose to avoid me altogether instead of punishing me.

That was punishment enough, however, for it only fed my desire to defend myself.

"What am I going to do?"

"Push through," Rosalynn said stiffly. "We've already come this far, there is no sense in wasting our efforts."

I wanted to ask what efforts she had been making, but there

were many other questions which took precedence. I was simply formulating the best way to approach them.

"Shall we drop the facade, Rosie?"

She looked up sharply. She was so on edge. "What do you mean?"

I sighed, then began to count off using my fingers. "Your argument with Lord Cameron at my aunt's card party. You've worn nothing but red gowns since the ball last week, which defies all convention and basic etiquette—you essentially painted a target on your back and still, you were not discussed in the papers. Explain that to me. And then Freya's absence the last few days and the fact that I was turned away from her door. Which you seem to understand." I threw my arms in the air in exasperation. "What am I missing?"

"Come now, Elsie. It is not nearly so bad as you are painting. Is it really so shocking that I should shed the white debutante gowns the moment my mother leaves town?"

She had a point. "Yet still, it does not explain the argument with your brother."

"Ugh! Elsie, let it go. Why are you so focused on Cameron anyway?"

I went still. Was it obvious? "I'm not."

She avoided my gaze. "Then let it go. He's only my brother, a Tyrant. Beyond a few shared dances you do not know him at all, so quit wondering why we argued and let it go."

I felt like I had been slapped in the face. She was right, though her delivery could have been kinder. I had gone to her in search of an ally and support, but I only found an irritable, testy friend who was undoubtedly keeping secrets from me.

I stood, clutching the articles in my hand. "Very well. Shall I see you at Almack's this evening? Oh, I suppose not, since they will bar your entrance if you defy convention and wear anything less than reputable."

She said nothing, and I let myself out. I only hoped I had not walked out of her life so easily.

"You must have an opinion on the suitability of the high perch phaeton, though, surely," Major Heybourne said, the amusement in his eyes belying the hollow topic of conversation.

I tried to smile, but everywhere I looked eyes were avoiding me and mouths were whispering behind fans. Major Heybourne's hand tightened on mine and he spun me away.

"Do not let them get to you," he said deliberately.

"I was allowed through the doors this evening," I said. "So I suppose I ought to count that a success."

"You would never be so far removed that you would be denied entrance to Almack's," he said loyally. "The papers could not disparage you so."

"They already have," I countered. "And this new reputation is not a good thing. I have never before been so popular a dance partner. I vow I just may agree with my mother after this evening ends and flee to Kent."

His eyes were troubled, and he looked away. We continued to dance, though I effectively cut the conversation off at the hilt. Sorrow swirled in my gut. I did not try to be so morose, but I did not need to hide my feelings with Major Heybourne and he received the brunt of my despondency.

"How is Miss Hurst?" he asked. "I have not seen her for some time."

He did not need to say he had been turned away from her door. I knew it firsthand. And if she denied me, then surely she was denying the whole of London.

"I do not know," I answered honestly. "She will not admit me, and I have not seen her in at least a week. It would be untrue if I said I was not worried."

His eyebrows drew together. I tried to rally. "She is equal to anything, though. If she has gone into hiding it must be for a good reason, and she will be recovered quite soon, I am certain."

"You sound confident."

The tune came to a close, and I delivered my most genuine smile. "I suppose I am."

He took my arm and escorted me back to my mother. "Perhaps we should join forces. She cannot turn us away if we camp out at her door."

"No, but my reputation could not withstand any more gossip, I fear. Particularly of that caliber."

His rueful gaze was enough of a confirmation, and I flinched at the rawness of it. At least I knew I could always count on him for honesty.

We passed by Cecily as she was led to the dance floor on a man's arm who I did not know. She caught my eye and looked away without acknowledgment. I tried not to be hurt. It was silly to let her actions bother me simply because I had defended her once.

On deeper reflection, I suppose I had only spoken the truth at the time. Regardless of her treatment of me, I would do the same again.

"What is going on over there?" Mother asked as we approached. We turned in unison to see a commotion at the entrance. Voices were raised and a man began forcibly pushing his way inside. I caught a glimpse of his face and sucked in a breath, my eyes involuntarily shooting toward Cecily.

Her face was pale as she stood in the center of the dance floor facing the door, where Lord Fischer was trying to get inside, calling her name. He said something to her but over the commotion of the room, it was impossible to understand what it was. I saw a flash of dark hair when Rosalynn snuck around the outer edge of the room away from the men, and I left Mother's side to join her.

"You are here," I said simply, not knowing quite where we stood.

"Only just arrived," she said, her breath coming rapidly. "They tried to turn Lord Fischer away and he threw a veritable fit."

"That I can see." I watched her face a moment. She seemed distracted, but not upset. Were we meant to pretend our earlier argument had not occurred?

"No," she said, leaning closer. "At the door. He was determined to get inside. He said he needed to explain to Cecily before it was too late."

We watched as a few men grabbed him by the arms and removed him from the room. Many fans were hard at work cooling off ladies from the excess of excitement. "Why here, though?"

Rosalynn shrugged, distracted. "Her parents probably forbid an alignment with him. His name is being bandied across every gossiper's tongue in London."

"So is mine," I said, "but I have not been refused entrance to Almack's."

She speared me with a look. "You have done nothing wrong. That gossip is speculation on who you will marry, not an attempt to elope."

That was true.

I opened my mouth to agree with her when her brother approached behind her and my breath caught in my chest.

Lord Cameron was here.

CHAPTER 33

"Lord Cameron!" I wanted the floor to swallow me whole. Did I have to squeak?

He bowed.

Rosalynn turned to him impatiently. "I do not see her. I suppose we must try her at home tomorrow."

"Freya?" I asked. Both siblings looked at me; neither responded. "She is not here," I continued. "In fact, I have not heard from her in days."

"Drat," Rosalynn said under her breath, fingering her pale pink gown. "I wore this for nothing. I suppose we can go home."

"I am not ready to leave yet," Lord Cameron said, his gaze coming to rest on me. "Are you spoken for the next dance, Miss Cox?"

My mouth went dry. Rosalynn was not paying attention, but if she was would she notice my rapidly beating heart? I was angry with Lord Cameron. At least, I was supposed to be absolutely livid. But I found that the only feeling I had when his brown eyes sought mine was lightheadedness. That could not be good.

"Miss Cox?"

"Oh, I am afraid I cannot. I promised this dance to Mr. Wendel."

"The American?" Lord Cameron all but yelled, his eyes growing enormous. "He is *here*?"

I shared a look with Rosalynn. Whatever could his outburst be about?

I nodded, which only made Lord Cameron's fury grow. He stepped closer to me, pushing Rosalynn aside, and said in a low, dangerous voice, "Do not tell him a word. Not a single word. Do you understand me?"

Taken aback, I leaned away from his vehemence.

"Miss Cox, promise me," he continued.

"Whatever for?" Rosalynn asked, her hand on her hip and eyebrows pulled together in anger.

Lord Cameron did not grant his sister a response. Instead, his eyes bored so heavily into mine that I found myself nodding against my will. I left them to return to my mother and was chastised to find Mr. Wendel waiting for me and the first song of the set already begun. I apologized for my tardiness, blaming the commotion of Lord Fischer's removal. Mr. Wendel accepted the explanation graciously. When he asked my thoughts about the patronesses of Almack's refusing Lord Fischer's entry, I merely deflected, obeying Lord Cameron's demand to keep my opinions to myself.

Why I felt compelled to do his bidding, I knew not. That I wanted to obey him was reason alone to resent the man. So whyever did I not?

The dance was boring and after a few indifferent responses to his inquiries, Mr. Wendel quit asking me questions, instead engaging in conversation about the assembly hall and its dry cake. I laughed at his jokes, though they were not funny, and smiled while I curtseyed, though I was not enjoying myself. I had not given Lord Cameron the opportunity to beg the next set, and I was irritated with myself for hoping he would still ask. He'd yet to apologize for his actions, and I would do well to remember that.

If I was not careful, I would have to admit I actually wanted to be around the man. I stopped dead in my tracks, the person behind me ramming me in the shoulder while the man that was meant to spin me stepped on my foot instead, shoving me to the side.

I let out a yelp of pain and immediately Mr. Wendel was by my side, helping me to a chair along the back wall.

"Are you well, Miss Cox?" he asked. "Shall I retrieve your mother?"

"No," I said hurriedly. "She mustn't be bothered. I shall be fine in a moment. I only need to catch my breath."

He looked dubious but relented. I followed Lord Cameron with my eyes while he crossed the room, spoke to Major Heybourne, and then walked away.

It was with utter disappointment that I watched Major Heybourne approach, his face a mixture of compassion and joy. "Miss Cox, perhaps I can have the next set?"

"I do believe I will be sitting out, sir. My foot needs a moment to recover."

"Then allow me to accompany you."

I nodded and he gave Mr. Wendel an exceedingly pointed look until the small man bowed crisply and walked away, the final strains of the country dance coming to completion.

"You hurt yourself?" Major Heybourne asked, seating himself beside me.

I glanced away, the throbbing in my toes beginning already to ebb. "I will be fine. Thank you for rescuing me once more."

He dipped his head in acknowledgment before turning to sweep his gaze over the room.

It would have been prying and rude to ask if he was looking for someone in particular, so I swallowed the question. Besides,

I had a strong inkling that he held a fondness for Freya. If only she returned his feelings.

We chatted throughout the duration of the set of dances, amiably discussing our favorite events of the Season thus far.

I caught sight of Lord Cameron dancing with a young lady, smiling down at her with his cordially tilted lips, and my body clenched. I did not want to think too deeply about my innate physical reaction, but I could not deny that since the kiss I had not really been able to think of him again without feeling some level of keenness for a repeat performance.

And I hated myself for it.

What would Rosalynn think if she knew how I felt? How would Freya react to this break in our pact? These developing feelings were far richer and heavier than any basic reaction I had previously had for an attractive male.

Before, I had believed myself able to live a single life. But now I wanted to be around Lord Cameron. I looked for him when I arrived anywhere, and my heart was light when he was nearby. This must be it. This must be how women were trapped into relationships and marriages and then shoved aside, belittled and ignored later.

I would not be like the rest of them.

Panic seized my heart and tears started behind my eyes. Of course he was not interested in me, but at this point, that was irrelevant. I was so thoroughly ashamed for the way I had been feeling. I stood abruptly and searched for my mother, spotting her nearby. I started toward her and jumped when Major Heybourne came upon me. I had forgotten all about him. Mumbling an apology, I reached Mother and clutched her arm, beseeching her to read in my eyes the sincerity in my words. "I should like to go home," I said softly.

She glanced at the women she was chatting with and then back to me. "Very well."

I was pleasantly surprised by her quickly agreeing. She must be tired of battling Society as well.

I kept my gaze from the dance floor. We skirted the spinning gowns and made our way to the exit. I caught Rosalynn's eye, dancing near the end of the row, but merely received a brief smile before she was gone again.

Shaking, I wrapped my shawl around my shoulders and followed Mother out to our carriage. I was unsure what I was going to do next, but I knew it had to involve accepting and squashing whatever developing feelings I was entertaining for Lord Cameron. I would not give my power to him or any man.

"What is it?" Mother asked the moment we took off, her shoulders swaying in time with the moving carriage.

Borrowing time, I glanced out the small side window, biting my lip. I was not going to lie, though the idea to feign a headache was very desirable. "I was overwhelmed," I explained. I tried to further deflect the conversation. "Did you hear any gossip? I am determined not to let it bother me, but I should like to be prepared to face what I must."

The grim smile I could see on her lips in the dim light was telling. "It is being said that you were propositioned."

"By Lord Cameron?"

She nodded.

"But that is untrue."

"Yes, we know. But it did not help that you were seen speaking to him tonight."

This could be the very thing I need. "So I must avoid him?"

"At all costs. At least while his name is thus connected with yours."

I turned away. I couldn't like this. It was unjust. "That is not fair to him, Mother. He has done nothing wrong. I was elbowed in the back, or pushed, or something. It was an accident. To say I had purposefully thrown lemonade in the man's face for such vile, imagined reasons is preposterous. Are we not condoning the lies by refraining to dispute them?"

She did not answer me. By the time we made it home and went into the house, I was convinced she was not going to say another word. She surprised me by turning back once we reached the corridor to our bedchambers. "The damage is done and you cannot convince anyone otherwise. At this point, our wisest course of action is to say nothing and stay out of the spotlight. Your respectable actions and good name will speak for themselves in time."

And in the meantime, I would be part of the besmirching of another's name. I felt sick inside, but I said nothing when Mother turned away.

She shot over her shoulder, "Besides, men bounce back from these things. If the situation were reversed, you would never."

She had a point. Society was prejudiced, and Lord Cameron would come around well enough. He had not lacked for partners that evening, and he certainly did not seem put out by the rumors—if he knew of them. He was going to be fine.

I took a deep breath. *I* was going to be fine.

CHAPTER 34

My carriage rolled to a stop and I sidled up to the window. We were not directly in front of Aunt Georgina's house. My coachman hopped down and helped me step from the carriage. I walked the length of the street, halting before the empty carriage that sat unmoving before Aunt Georgina's door.

Perhaps this was not the best time to call if she had a visitor already. Indecision halted me on the steps when her front door opened and Freya stepped out. Her gaze trained on the ground, she did not notice me until I stepped in her path.

"Oh!" she said, jumping back in surprise.

"What are you doing here?" I hated my accusatory tone, yet I couldn't help but feel hurt that she would visit my aunt, whom she hardly knew, but refused my visits to her home.

Guilt pulled her eyebrows together. She glanced away. "I came to see Coco."

I waited for more but her lips remained in a tight line.

I stepped closer. "Freya, what is happening?"

"Nothing," she said, too quickly, tucking a loose curl behind her ear. She was lying.

Her fingers fidgeted as she toyed with her reticule, her gaze refusing to meet mine.

I moved out of her path, and hurt sliced through me when she dipped a curtsy and sidestepped me, climbing into her carriage with unladylike speed. Since when had our relationship stooped to such a level?

Her carriage rolled away as I mounted the steps. I was led into a drawing room bustling with chatter and felt minimal joy at the delight on Aunt Georgina's face when I was announced. I tried on a smile and approached her, glad to see Coco comfortably dozing near her feet.

"What a treat," she said while I leaned forward to kiss her cheek. A few women I recognized faintly were chatting on the sofa, their caps bouncing along with nodding heads as they gossiped. I was an outsider.

Taking a seat opposite them I allowed Aunt Georgina to introduce us and then spent the better part of a quarter hour listening to them discuss their daughters and nieces and rank them in terms of success in the marriage market. I held my tongue, wondering briefly if Aunt Georgina would have jumped in and spoken about me had I not been present.

When the women took their leave, I moved closer to Aunt Georgina's chair and settled in at the end of the sofa. Coco awoke in the bustle of goodbyes, and her ears instantly perked up when she saw me, trotting over to climb onto my lap.

"Are you being a good girl?" I asked, scratching behind her ears. She tilted her head softly and my heart ached. I had really been missing her superb ability to warm my feet at night.

Aunt Georgina settled back in her chair, arranging her skirts around her toes. "She's splendid. I hadn't thought I'd enjoy a dog."

"She makes for a nice companion."

"Indeed." Aunt Georgina had a decided twinkle in her eye. "But companionship is not something I lack."

"Clearly," I said through a grin. Nonetheless, I was grateful she had a bond with Coco.

We discussed the article from this morning's paper which described my popularity at Almack's and the brawl fought at the door when Lord Fischer tried to force his way in.

"It is not too terrible," Aunt Georgina said thoughtfully. "Though it almost feels as though they are trying to make you sound like a tart, and not simply a highly desired dance partner."

"I believe that is absolutely what they are intending," I said with feeling. This was the very reason I had chosen to come to Aunt Georgina's today. I needed sound advice. "Mother believes I must ignore the gossip and prove my good character through my actions."

"Your mother wouldn't know the right side of a social situation if it hit her in the face."

My eyebrows shot up. I had no idea Aunt Georgina felt so strongly. Apparently, the disdain between the women was mutual.

"When gossip turns hostile there is not much that can be done to undo the damage. Regardless of the truth, people believe what they want to believe. And they cannot unhear the nasty things people say"—she pointed to the basket of newspapers in the corner—"or write."

I slumped, my face falling into my hands. "How do these people live with themselves?"

"Easily."

I peeked between my fingers. Aunt Georgina looked smug.

She would, I suppose. She was a gossiping old biddy herself.

"What should I do then?"

She speared me with a glare. "Your name is not so muddied, yet. You will recover. Do not give credence to the naysayers, and stay clear from trouble. I have a feeling the papers will change their tunes soon enough."

"Oh?" I asked, my eyebrow raised in question.

Her smile was cat-like. "I cannot give away my secrets, dear. Now run along. I do not want your mother coming after you."

The footman announced my carriage and maid awaiting me outside and I kissed Aunt Georgina farewell, watching Coco crawl back to her place at my aunt's feet. I walked away from her with a healthy measure of contentment. Coco was going to be fine. She was finding her place here.

A man at the foot of the stairs moved aside as I began to descend, and I halted in the face of Lord Cameron and his calculating gaze.

"Miss Cox," he said with a stiff bow.

I returned the curtsy in kind. "Lord Cameron."

We faced off like two opponents, my heart beating rapidly within my chest. I wanted to ask what was bothering him, what had drawn his eyebrows together and formed lines between them, but it was not within my place. An even better question would have been what he was doing at my aunt's house, but I found I could not ask it. I did not want to seem as though I cared.

Neither, though, did he show any sign of moving.

"Are you well?" I asked, searching for a way into conversation. I had the lucky convenience of being at eye level with the man for the first time ever and it was both bizarre and powerful.

He nodded. Well, that did not work.

His gaze bore into mine, and he stepped closer, my hand tightening on the banister beside me. "Your little spill has caused quite a stir."

The blood slowly slipped from my face. He was actually referencing the incident with the lemonade and what people were saying about it? How utterly mortifying.

I swallowed. "I was hit in the back. It was unintentional."

"I know," he said simply. "I saw it happen."

"But you said nothing."

He shrugged. "I did not realize it would develop into such a scandal."

I fell into his chocolate eyes and hated how soft my voice sounded, how small I felt. Where was my strength? My standards? Wasn't melting into his gaze in some form handing my power over to this man? Besides, he had still yet to apologize for treating me so callously. "My mother has told me to stay away from you until the rumors have ceased."

Amusement glittered his eyes. "And will you?"

My mouth was dry; there was nothing for it, I cared for him. The way he stepped forward slightly, his face inches from mine while his hands stayed so concretely out of reach clasped behind his back, the smell of his shaving soap wafting to my senses and sending me back to our embrace. He was blocking my way but did not seem the least inclined to move. I glanced over his shoulder at the corridor that would lead me to the front door.

He seemed to follow my train of thought and chuckled softly. "I find that I do not like your mother's advice. Will you go for a drive with me tomorrow?"

I needed to be strong. Feelings aside, he hurt me and had yet to apologize. Regardless of the time apart between the kiss and now, he did not appear the least bit remorseful. "I'm not sure I will be able to get away."

His hand came up, halting me. "Was that a denial, Miss Cox? Surely you would not say 'no.'"

I had forgotten that he knew about my bargain with Mother. In truth, I had not even recalled the bargain at that moment. But he was correct to remind me. I was not allowed to deny a gentleman's request. Yet, I was also instructed to steer clear of Lord Cameron. Either choice I made would be going against my mother's wishes.

But when faced with the prospect of losing the bargain, I would not take any chances.

"I will accompany you," I said before stepping forward and inching around him. I needed to get out of the cramped stairway so I could breathe easily. "But I will not enjoy it."

He bowed low while I backed away. "Until tomorrow."

Hopefully, I thought, grateful for regular, even breathing once again. As long as I could get away with it where Mother was concerned. It was one thing to determine I hadn't broken the bargain. It was another to convince *her* of that fact.

CHAPTER 35

"You have *who* coming to pick you up?" Mother said, eyes bulging, teacup suspended above her knee.

"Lord Cameron," I repeated. After a few beats of stunned silence, I continued. "What was I to do, say no?" I speared her with a look, my eyebrow raised.

Her eyes flitted to my father, seated on the end of the sofa with his chin resting on his chest, moving up and down in slow, even motions. Whispering now, she set the teacup on the table softly. "You are to stay away from the man. Was I not clear on the matter?"

"And void our agreement? I weighed my options, Mother. I will not do anything that could lose me the bargain."

She rolled her eyes.

"You may not take it seriously, but I do," I said in defense. "When the Season ends and I have completed my side of the bargain, it will be worth it."

"Your entire side of the bargain," she said, a small gleam coming to her eyes.

I swallowed. What was she up to now? "Yes, Mother. My entire side of the bargain."

"You remember all of it?"

"I remember the requirement that I do not feel even a thread of interest for any man." I swallowed. My disloyal thoughts flicked to Lord Cameron. I shoved him from my mind. Yes, I had interest in him. But it could easily be squashed.

Billington opened the door to announce Lord Cameron and Mother sat up tall, her mouth forming a tight smile. When he entered the room, my heart began to gallop. I caught his gaze briefly before he bowed to Mother, and then a recently awoken Father who tried to pretend he had not been asleep this entire time. A few minutes of polite conversation while I tied on my bonnet, and we were on our way.

Lord Cameron helped me onto the seat of the curricle, my gloved hand tingling long after he walked around the horses and jumped up in a fluid motion to sit beside me. I trained my gaze forward as we took off, and I found it difficult to think of a topic of conversation. What had gotten into me? The moment I admitted to myself that I harbored an attraction for Lord Cameron, everything was lost: my ability to speak, to look at him for longer than a moment, to breathe normally in his vicinity.

The silence drew out. With each passing second I worried Lord Cameron would read my hesitancy and know my feelings at once. I hurried to think of something to say.

"It is a lovely day," I said, squeaking my words out. My face flushed and I bent my head, counting loose stones on the road as we weaved through the midday traffic.

"Not as lovely as my companion," he replied with no little amusement. "Come now, Miss Cox. When have we been so formal?"

I looked up at him, his familiar smile soothing my nerves. We had known each other distantly for quite some time. He was the next sibling older than Rosalynn and had often accompanied her to and from my home in their carriage, though he never remained longer than a quick meal. Our deeper friendship was only recent. But he was correct. Formality between us had long since been abandoned. He could see my nerves, and I hoped above all things that he could not guess the cause of them.

"You are wearing the cameo again," he said, his gaze darting to my neck and back to the road. "You favor it."

I nodded. I had taken to wearing it most days. I could not explain why, but I felt a connection to the necklace as though I could siphon strength and support from the woman pictured there. It was a reminder of the sacrifices and strength of my grandmother, but also of women in general.

"Would you care to share what has gotten into you today? You are quieter than a mouse."

"It is fortunate that you can put uncomfortable experiences behind you so thoroughly, but I find I cannot so easily forget." The words were out of my mouth before I could control them and I clamped my lips together.

He stiffened on the seat. "I suppose it would be better to discuss it, but I had hoped we might just put it behind us."

"Ignore it, you mean?" I corrected. "I am not worthy of an apology?"

His head whipped toward me so fast I heard a slight crack in his neck. His hand came behind to rub it and he winced. "I suppose I deserved that. Have I not apologized?"

I gave him a wry smile and our carriage pulled into Hyde Park. "No, sir. Surely you would remember such a thing."

He looked thoughtful as he continued to rub the back of his neck. "I apologize for taking advantage of the situation and taking liberties that question my standing as a gentleman. I intended only to show you the folly of your agreement. I hadn't planned to actually...I never meant to kiss you, Elsie." He glanced at me before turning his attention back to the road. "I'm still not sure how that happened. But I should not have become so carried away. To say that I've regretted using you so abominably would not be doing it justice. Indeed, I am deeply ashamed."

Silence sat between us. His implication caused my breath to hitch, and I did my utmost to appear unaffected. But he made a valid point. Had he kissed me, or had I, by leaning in, kissed him? We both held some of the blame.

Silence pressed on us and we waved at passing carriages, nodding at lone riders and walkers beside the path. But Lord Cameron did not so much as slow down to greet acquaintances. He merely drove the length of the park and turned to repeat the process.

I swallowed, carefully weighing my words. "You are not sorry for your harsh words, though?"

"I am not sorry," he said swiftly, "that I brought to light a danger you may not have considered."

"Well, I had certainly not considered *you* dangerous before, Lord Cameron."

"And you do now?"

"Certainly. I have discovered far more than perhaps I should have." Like how pleasant it was to share a kiss.

He looked thoughtful, stopping the curricle momentarily to swap greetings with a man he knew from his gentlemen's club. He begrudgingly introduced us, and I felt the unhappy sensation of leering eyes upon my back as we went our separate ways, pricking my skin like an abundance of tiny needles.

Lord Cameron must have sensed my discomfort. "Not all men are honorable."

"But you are?" I could not help but add.

"I would never hurt you," he said severely.

I swallowed. Had he not already? I changed tack. "You saw who pushed me into you at my Aunt Georgina's card party. Was it an accident?"

"No," he said. "But I shall not tell you who did it. It was

perhaps not their brightest moment, but I know they meant no harm."

"However could you know that?"

"Just trust me."

That was not something which came easily to me. I settled my gaze straight ahead. The ride was not going at all as I had imagined it would. I noticed, for the first time, the many fingers pointing our way, and mouths moving in conjunction. I swallowed a lump of sand. Perhaps this was not my brightest idea. But what choice did I have?

"It appears that we are the center of attention."

"Is that terrible?" he asked.

"If you should like to regain your good name. I fear we are only adding to the ridiculous gossip."

"Perhaps," he said, avoiding my gaze. He seemed suddenly unsure of himself, hesitant, and I feared for his next words. "Unless we put those rumors to rest."

I sighed. "That is what my mother would like. For me to have nothing to do with you until they have dissipated."

He glanced at me. "I am referring to the opposite."

My mind tried to wrap around his words, but I found it didn't matter which way I spun them, I could not make any sense of his meaning.

He continued, "If I were to call on you, and court you, then surely they will see what is between us is authentic."

Surprise pressed on my chest. "You would court me to prove rumors false?"

He grinned. "No, but it would be a satisfying benefit to be sure."

I connected his implications instantly, though I did not find an easy way to believe them. If my ears had not misconstrued his words, then Lord Cameron had professed his interest in me. And he did so in a way that I was at liberty to accept or deny him.

Indecision warred within me. If I accepted, would I be going against my very beliefs, or would denying him on the basis that I made a pact six years prior be even more foolish and dishonest? Was not my bargain with Mother a very reason to accept, so I may give love a chance, as she intended?

I failed to notice that our carriage had come to a stop until a sweet voice called attention to my absent thoughts.

"We know one another," Cecily was saying. Had Lord Cameron tried to introduce us? I waited for her to explain how, but her lips were shut. Her father beside her on the barouche seat was now describing a decent horse he had recently purchased. Cecily gave me a perfunctory smile and looked away. Whatever had I done to earn her distaste? True, we had not gotten on splendidly at school, but I had stuck up for her when no one else would. That should have gained me some favor, surely.

Our farewells were not delivered quickly enough for my taste. Once we had gone out of earshot I said, "We roomed together at school."

"Oh?" Lord Cameron looked surprised. I did not blame him.

"Yes. She was not my closest friend, obviously, but I feel something must have occurred between us which I have no knowledge of. She plainly dislikes me."

His confused expression only grew.

"I defended her," I explained. "There were rumors...well, suffice it to say, I stood up for her when no one else bothered." *Not even your sister*, I thought. I sighed. "She repays me by listening to horrid rumors about me and refraining from saying anything in my defense."

"But surely you cannot know—"

"Yes, I do."

He looked at me and seemed to understand. "I see."

A few moments of silence followed us from the park and back toward my home.

"Perhaps," he said cautiously, "it would be beneficial to remember when we hear rumors that we do not always know the whole of it. It is easy to judge another's actions, but we cannot know their motives."

So he hadn't understood then. I wanted to explain I had not heard a rumor that she had listened to gossip about me, but had watched it unfold first hand in the modiste's shop. I swallowed my explanation, however, since it was both embarrassing and petty, and I did need to let it go.

"Thank you for coming out with me," he said, handing me down the step in front of my house. "Is it presumptuous of me to request your presence at the theater Thursday next? Your parents are invited also, of course."

"I am unsure," I replied. "I must check with my mother." Surely that was not breaking the bargain?

"I'll await a note." He bowed over my hand, and I mounted the steps in a daze.

Something had altered between us, and I found it was not altogether unpleasant. Terrifying, sure. But perhaps it was not entirely inappropriate to admit it was also pleasant. I swallowed a lump, handed Billington my bonnet and went upstairs to locate my mother. Nothing made sense, but I was determined to make my own sense of things, one way or another.

CHAPTER 36

Cameron had secured a private box and invited along his family, as well as mine. Rosalynn had denied the treat and his father and brothers had, allegedly, laughed at the idea. Since my father held similar contempt at the prospect of an evening at the theater, there was only Cameron seated to my left and Mother to my right.

I felt, very acutely, the gazes around the room that were trained on our box.

I had convinced Mother to let us accept the invitation on the basis that if we were seen to be courting then the other rumors would be proved false. She accepted, though unconvinced, and I looked forward to my first experience watching a play of this magnitude.

A bustle behind us caught my attention and delight spread through me when Aunt Georgina stepped through the velvet curtain into the box and Cameron stood to assist her into a seat beside Mother, whose face tightened into a semblance of a smile.

"Good evening, darling," Aunt Georgina said, using a walking cane she did not need and settling herself comfortably, spreading her vivid purple skirts around her. "I have not been to the theater in an age. You are such a gem, Lord Cameron, to think of an old woman such as myself."

"It is my honor to escort the three loveliest women in all of London," he said gravely.

Aunt Georgina smiled, amusement in her eyes belying her frivolous air. Mother's mouth twitched into a smile which she tried to hide but could not. It was apparent that flattery was the way to win her over, and Cameron came to the same conclusion. "Mrs. Cox, do tell me you enjoy the theater. I find myself thrilled at the prospect of the comedy this evening. I've heard tell it is the most entertaining show to hit the stage this year."

"As long as it is not vulgar," Mother said with an air of authority.

"Yes, certainly."

"I find," Aunt Georgina said, not minding the volume of her voice, "a little vulgarity often adds enough flavor to keep things interesting. I should think *The Taming of the Shrew* would be quite boring if they hadn't Katerina to tame."

"Yes, well," Mother said, flustered. She flipped open her fan and began to rapidly air herself, casting her eyes about for a change of topic. She was immensely relieved, it appeared, when the play began.

And I was too, for Cameron had settled once more beside me and spent the humorous moments of the play chuckling softly and leaning slightly toward me in shared mirth. His shoulder brushed mine, sending warm flurries through my stomach.

Intermission was a dazzling affair, glasses of champagne in the lobby and hordes of socialites laughing and speaking to one another, about one other. I overheard my name numerous times in affiliation with Cameron's and I did not know whether to be pleased or horrified that we were continuing to fuel the gossip.

Cameron sidled up to me, watching Mother chat with a few

acquaintances across the room. "Have you enjoyed yourself thus far?"

I grinned at him, unable to stop myself. "Yes. It is even better than I anticipated. And I feel I must tell you, I had high expectations to begin with."

"I'm pleased."

The interesting part was that he truly seemed it. I changed the subject. "Rosalynn was not interested?"

"No." He glanced at me and then took a sip from his glass. "She is not quite happy with me at present."

"She has been acting strangely for some time." Instantly I regretted my words. It was exceedingly disloyal of me to speak about her this way, and to her brother of all people. It was a line I should not have crossed.

Whether he sensed my discomfort or felt a degree of his own, he did not continue down that line of conversation.

Loud laughter jarred us from our *tête-à-tête* and we both turned toward the American, Mr. Wendel, his head thrown back as he roared in mirth, his circle of friends smiling politely. For such a short man, he really could bellow. Cameron immediately pivoted away. Holding my elbow, he led me back to the box and we took our seats, my mother and aunt still socializing in the foyer.

He set his gaze on me, struggling to hide his annoyance. "How have you enjoyed London?"

"Well enough," I said cautiously. "Though perhaps I would have been happier if my name had remained my own."

His eyebrows pulled together. "In what way?"

Had we not gone over this before? "Those dratted newspaper articles. It is terribly violating to be so discussed."

His silence was not very comforting. "I should think the popularity was helpful."

"Then I should think you do not know me at all, sir." Which, in fact, was partially true.

The women returned shortly and the rest of the play was enjoyed. Cameron was subdued. He laughed, but it was not the authentic chuckle of before. I could feel the strain, but could not place the cause.

It was further discouraging when the evening ended and he delivered us home in a silent coach. Walking us to the door, he bowed handsomely, placing a chaste kiss on the back of my gloved knuckles, and then skipped down the steps and into his carriage without a backward glance.

I tried to swallow my worry. I couldn't help but wonder, though, what I had said to put him in such a mood.

Father was gone when we returned home—to his club for an evening of gambling, no doubt. He had not been so addicted to the sport as to cause us any trouble, but he enjoyed his cards as well as any man.

"That was not so terrible," I said to Mother when we mounted the stairs toward our bedchambers.

"Did you hear what was being said about your old school friend? Cecily Hapworth, I believe it was."

Calling her a school friend was a bit of a stretch, but I merely shook my head. Cameron and I had gotten out of there before hearing any gossip ourselves.

"It appears that she has eloped with Lord Fischer."

I gasped. "You cannot mean it."

Mother smiled like a cat, her head nodding furiously. "Apparently her father forbid their marriage, so they went off to Gretna Green and wed over the anvil. She is now Lady Fischer, and they stopped at her estate on their way home and picked up a child who she calls her ward."

I said nothing, but my mind was connecting the implications at a furious rate.

"It is widely believed she is the lady from *The Green Door* who had a secret child hidden away in the countryside."

"Perhaps they shall do well together, then," I said, shocked. "If they both were victimized by the book, they might understand one another better. At least I have never been the object of cruel and unjust hearsay."

"Mmm," she consented. "I suppose we'll know more when the papers come out tomorrow."

She had a point. I kissed her goodnight and trudged toward my own room.

I submitted to Molly's ministrations, wearily swaying while she brushed through my long hair, plaiting it for bed and tying a string at the end.

"The theater was magnificent," I said to her. It was clear that she was curious but unable to speak until I did so first. "It was exceedingly humorous. The costumes were striking and the sets so realistic."

She sighed. "That sounds grand, miss."

"It was," I agreed, climbing into bed. "And now I shall sleep for a week."

CHAPTER 37

Arriving at Aunt Georgina's home outside of polite visiting hours, I was utterly shocked to find, once again, Freya's carriage waiting in front of the door. I approached the drawing room behind Aunt Georgina's butler with some trepidation, but the fire of intrigue died the moment the door swung open to reveal Freya's distraught, sobbing form on the sofa.

Rushing to her side, I ignored Coco yapping by my toes and threw my arms around her, wondering why Aunt Georgina hadn't left her golden throne to console her distressed guest.

"Elsie!" Freya shrieked, backing out of my embrace and coming to a stand. "What are you doing here?"

I sat beneath her on the sofa, stunned. "You mean at *my* aunt's house?" I looked to Aunt Georgina for support but her face was as passive as the unlit lamp beside her. "I am visiting, of course."

Freya wiped furiously at her eyes. She turned to my Aunt and said, "I apologize but I find I must leave." When she reached the door, she turned and spoke softly. "Thank you." Then she was gone.

When the front door was heard to shut behind her in the distance, I turned to Aunt Georgina, my eyebrows raised in disbelief. "What in heaven's name was that about?"

"Oh, it was nothing," she said, waving her hand in disregard. "Now tell me, did you enjoy the theater the other evening as much as I?"

I stared at her. Could she really disregard my concern so easily? I had never before witnessed such a display from Freya, directed at me, no less.

Her pale eyebrows remained set. Plainly, she was not going to budge. I ran my hands along my skirt, smoothing it out as though it would clear up my confusion as well. Very well, I would play her game. I had little choice in the matter as it was.

"I would have enjoyed the theater more if the papers had not exaggerated the events. I did not succumb to Lord Cameron's flirtations during the show, as you very well know. And I certainly did not allow him to stroke my…" I blushed, lowering my voice, "my leg."

"Yes dear, I do know these things. I was right beside you."

I threw my hands up in exasperation. "But the rest of London does not! How am I going to show my face at the Nelsons' ball this evening when the whole of society believes I am a trollop?" A thought came to me. "Is that it? Is that why Freya ran out of here like a madwoman? My reputation is in shreds?"

"No." She laughed. "Of course not. That had nothing to do with you. You must know Major Heybourne's attentions are becoming exceedingly pointed."

I did not. I assumed he cared for her, naturally, but I had hardly seen Freya of late. How was I to know she was being courted to the point of distress?

Aunt Georgina rang the bell beside her chair and asked the answering maid to bring a fresh pot of tea. She then turned to me and said with all of the dignity and gravity she possessed,

"You must hold your head high and face the *ton*. If you run off, then you give credence to the rumors. They will merely talk behind your back if you leave."

"As opposed to gossiping right in front of me?"

She smirked. "I'd rather the enemy display their evils to me openly. That makes it easier to know whom to like."

Which, she did. Aunt Georgina did not give a whit for gossip, nor what society thought of her. It gave her a reputation of an eccentric, naturally, but it also gave her freedom and respect.

"Perhaps I am not as brave as I should be." I settled back into the sofa, petting Coco's ears when she jumped up and nestled in beside me. "I'm certainly not as brave as you."

Aunt Georgina's eyes narrowed, her lips pursed. She opened her mouth to speak but the door opened to admit the maid bearing tea and she shut her mouth again. After tea was prepared and administered, I waited patiently for whatever she was going to say, on the edge of my seat mentally and literally, but trying to remain undisturbed.

I had come to the conclusion that the conversation was over when she finally spoke, her words firm and undeterred. "You are only as brave as you choose to be. Courage comes from within. It cannot be bought or traded, but it can be feigned until it is real. Telling yourself you lack bravery, however, is nothing more than an excuse to not even try."

I stared at her, thoroughly put in my place. "That is easy for you to say, Aunt, you care not for anyone's thoughts."

"That is neither true nor helpful." She busied herself arranging her shawl, avoiding my gaze. "You do not always know what another is thinking. Anyone may put on a brave front, but that does not indicate that their courage comes easily. I have had years of putting up with gossip and hurtful barbs until I made the choice to surround myself with people I like. I do not lack friends now, dear, but that does not mean my life was always this pleasant. Nor my evenings so full and entertaining. I do, perhaps, entertain a tad more than most. But why not? It fills my heart and my days and gives me the companionship I desire. Do not waste your years caring too heavily about Society's feelings, when Society will turn around and dump on you the moment it suits them. Cultivate the relationships that matter, and pull them close to you in times of need. You will find that the rest of them quit caring so much about your affairs when you stop making them matter so heavily to you."

"How should I do that when my closest friends are pulling away from me? I have no one, currently."

"You do not have *no one*, darling," she said, leaning closer. "For you will always have me. And those worthless parents of yours if they choose to quit looking in a mirror for a moment and consider their daughter."

I chuckled slightly, then stood to go. "I've taken enough of your time, and you have given me quite a lot to think about. Thank you, Aunt Georgina."

She speared me with an intelligent look. "My door is always open, child, should you need it. For any reason at all."

Tears sprang to my eyes at the thoughtful gesture. I nodded for fear of releasing a storm of emotion and saw myself out, asking my coachman to drive me straight home.

I had a plan.

The letters dispatched, I asked Molly to pay special attention to my toilette, struggling to sit still while she piled curls over my head and expertly arranged them around pearl combs.

I was unsure if it would work, but Aunt Georgina's words about pulling my friends close around me had hit a chord within my soul, and I knew I could not give up on them yet. It was evident that both Freya and Rosalynn were struggling with personal predicaments, and it was equally clear that they did not feel capable of confiding in me. As much as it hurt, I needed to respect their privacy and remind them I was there if they needed me, whether they wanted to talk about it or not.

I had written to both Rosalynn and Freya, asking them to meet me at the Nelson's ball to discuss something very important. We were nearing the end of the Season, and I feared if we did not come to some sort of understanding now, then we would all drift away until our friendship had dissolved. And I could not let that happen without a fight.

"You are certainly dressed up tonight," Mother said when we loaded into the carriage. "I wonder if Lord Cameron is planning to attend."

"Is Father not accompanying us?" I asked, deflecting.

If she wanted to imply my reason for looking well was Cameron, then I would not be able to honestly deny it. But that was only part of it. More to the point, I felt the desire to show the whole of society that I was strong and defiant in the face of their judgment. Not that I expected her to understand.

"He is preparing himself to return home," she said, much to my surprise. "It appears the clubs have worn their enjoyment, as the balls did months ago. I should think we only have a week or so left before we will leave."

A moment of silence passed. When the carriage came to a stop, she said, "Oh do pick up your jaw, Elsie. It does not do to look like a trout."

I obeyed.

The Nelsons had outdone themselves, according to Mother's reports of previous balls. They liked to be one of the final events of the Season, to finish with a smash, but not so near the end that they did not receive a full room of guests.

And a crush, it absolutely was. I could hardly see the other side of the room, for the hordes of people grouped about the edges of the ballroom. How there was enough room left for dancing in the center was beyond me. I could not see the dance floor well enough to determine its size.

The downside to the overflowing ballroom was that it was nearly impossible to spot the person one was looking for; the advantage was that once I found them, we would be able to slip away unseen.

As soon as Mother was deeply involved in a conversation, I slipped away. Weaving through the groups, I kept my eye out for red ringlets and red gowns, hoping that finding either one of my friends would help me to spot both of them.

A hand came around my wrist, stopping me, and I turned, surprised to see Mr. Wendel and his awkward smile at the end of the arm. Pulling myself free, I dipped a quick curtsy and turned away when he blocked me once again.

"I am sorry, sir, but I cannot stop just now."

"Whom do you seek? Perhaps I can assist you," he said, his sly grin making me uneasy.

"Just a friend."

His eyebrow hitched up. "A secret assignation, perhaps?"

I could have slapped him for the inappropriate insinuation. I hoped the shock and disgust on my face proved how false he was. Choosing to retain my dignity over making a scene, I turned away from him without gracing his rudeness with a response and sidestepped the arm I saw reaching for me from my peripheral vision. Thoroughly disturbed, I hastened my steps around a group of ladies whispering to one another and sped for the other side of the room.

Heads turned wherever I walked, and I straightened my spine against the words I heard floating around the ballroom. My name, Cameron's name, and a multitude of insinuations were making their rounds.

There was a flash of red among the pale sea of gowns. Rosalynn stood near the back wall and my heart leaped at the tall dark-haired man beside her, his back to me.

Approaching Rosalynn, I could not control the grin that lit my face.

Disappointment filtered through me when the man turned and it was Lord Tarquin's face I beamed at like a lovesick fool. I had not seen him since that day, ages ago it felt, in their home. I hadn't previously noted how similar to Cameron he looked. But I supposed it shouldn't have been a shock, for all of the Nichols siblings were quite similar in appearance.

"You came," I said, pulling my gaze from Lord Tarquin.

She did not smile. "It seemed urgent."

"Have you seen Freya?"

"Not yet," she answered. Her gaze flicked to her brother and back. Someone passed behind me, pushing me toward Rosalynn.

"Perhaps we should try to find somewhere more private."

Lord Tarquin delivered a long-suffering sigh. "I'll be in the card room when you are ready to leave."

We followed him into the sea of pale gowns and dark jackets, through the doors and into the corridor. Lord Tarquin disappeared through a doorway further down and Rosalynn and I were waylaid by Major Heybourne, camped at the entrance to the ballroom.

"It is too full," he said simply. "I find I cannot make myself go inside."

Lost for words, I looked to Rosalynn for help, but she was distracted, waiting nearby.

"Have you seen Freya?" I asked.

"Yes," he answered, his gaze pulled back into the ballroom. "But then she turned around and left. I find I now have no good reason for entering such a crush. I suppose I shall take myself off. Good day, Miss Cox. Lady Rosalynn."

We curtseyed, and he walked away. Strange behavior, perhaps, but I did not blame him. The ballroom had been hot and stuffy, the smell of heated perfume clouding and making the large room feel small.

"I suppose she isn't here, then," I said, trying to rally. Even if Freya came and left, at least she had shown up. That had to be a good sign.

"Come. Let's find the ladies' retiring room," Rosalynn declared, leading me away. We found it shortly and slipped inside as a young woman and her mother were leaving.

Upon first glance the room was empty, I followed Rosalynn to a sofa and sat down.

"What is so urgent?" she asked immediately.

A squeal sounded behind us and we both leaped from the sofa, my hand rising to hold my racing heart as Freya stepped from behind the curtain on the back window.

"What are you doing?" Rosalynn demanded.

"Hiding from that horrible woman and her daughter," she responded.

Rosalynn was still angry, her chest rising and falling rapidly while her face took on an exasperated groan. "But why hide from *us*?"

Freya's eyes widened. "I didn't very well know it was you until you spoke, now did I?"

A laugh bubbled from my chest and rolled out, the image of Rosalynn and Freya so angry with each other over a simple fright simply too much to bear. It was the final straw in a series of high-strung events, and I laughed louder and louder, unable to stem my amusement. Sitting on the sofa, I clutched an arm around my midsection and laughed hysterically, only getting louder as I heard the others join in. It was ridiculous, really, and I was ever so grateful no one chose to enter the room at that precise moment, for we looked positively mad.

Wiping a stray tear from each eye, I leaned back on the sofa. Freya came out of her hiding place and sat beside me. Rosalynn crossed to the door and slid the lock into place.

"To avoid more horrible women and their daughters," she

said, by way of explanation. "Now will you tell us what the letters were about?"

"Us," I said, fixing each of them with a look in turn, Freya on the sofa beside me and Rosalynn across from us in a high back chair. "I do not pretend to know why either of you have pulled away from me, but I cannot like it." Rosalynn opened her mouth to argue but I lifted my hands, halting her. "You do not need to share with me the details of your troubles, but I would like to remind you I am here for you. I have been here for you since we were girls and nothing you could do or say would cause me to stop loving either of you."

I took a deep breath. Now came the difficult part of my speech. It was easy to remind them that I cared, but asking them to care for me was a much deeper level of vulnerability. "I don't know if you've been keeping up with the latest articles about me, but they have taken a turn for the worse. They are spouting lies that are ruining my reputation. My mother fears it is impossible to recover, and I learned this evening that we are unlikely to stay in London much longer. But I needed you both to know the things they are saying are false." I turned to Rosalynn. "And the things that have been said about Lord Cameron are untrue."

"Not all of them," she said quietly, her eyes cast down.

"What do you mean?" I asked, her expression planting a seed of doubt in my mind.

Rosalynn shifted awkwardly in her seat. The slow burn of dread began in my gut and grew outward. She could not hold eye contact with either of us and when her eyes closed tightly, I feared she was not going to explain.

Her voice was quiet. "Cameron is behind everything."

CHAPTER 38

The dead silence in the room was interrupted by a rattle on the doorknob, causing all three of us to jump. We watched the knob as it continued to rattle until whoever was trying to get in ceased, and footsteps could be heard receding.

"I feel like you ought to explain," Freya said calmly.

"I know." Rosalynn closed her eyes once more and blew out a long breath. She opened them again and set her gaze on me. "Cameron has been hassled by my father for the last two years to choose a career. He was uninterested in the church and the military, and he found the law dull. He turned to writing instead."

"I do not follow," I said, not ready to believe it. How many conversations had I shared with the man about my distinct discomfort with the spotlight those articles placed on me? "Are you saying Cameron has been writing the articles? But they make him look bad, too."

"No, not all of them. But he is responsible for your fame. He is responsible for many people's fame. He has been writing gossip articles for the newspapers for the last two years, and it was he that produced *The Green Door*."

I sat in stunned silence, waiting for the words to sink in. I registered what Rosalynn had said, but I could not convince myself to accept it. I did not want to understand. It would mean believing the worst about a man I was beginning to care about.

Freya shook her head. "But that book was written by a woman. You cannot expect us to believe that. Besides, you mean to tell us you've known who was hurting Elsie and you have said nothing?"

"He is my brother," Rosalynn said, affronted. "What was I supposed to do?"

"Warn us!" Freya stood, her disposition matching her fiery hair. "You could have told Elsie who she might avoid. I am disturbed that I considered you a friend." Shaking her head in disbelief, she scoffed. "If I had discovered that it was my own mother writing those things about Elsie I would have gone to her straight away and done everything in my power to stop it."

"Of course I did everything in my power to try and stop it!" Rosalynn jumped to her feet. They squared off, and I knew I should step in and do something, but I was numb.

Cameron? He had authored those articles?

"No, you did not do everything in your power," Freya said. "You did not warn us!"

"I did not find out any of this until after he had ceased writing them. The column was taken over by someone else."

Freya scoffed. "So that condones his past behavior? He still knows more than the rest of us, Rosie. He still would be able to give us the information we need to find a way to end it."

Rosalynn threw her arms out in frustration. "You cannot end the newspapers!"

They were shouting now and I was positive that if anyone was standing in the corridor they would be able to hear every word. My reputation was bruised enough, and now my pride alongside it.

I faced them and said with every last bit of strength I could muster, "I thank you for coming forward now, Rosalynn, and I would ask that you tell your brother I should never like to see him again."

I turned to go but she came around and cut me off. "No, Elsie, you do not get to say your piece and be done with it. I need to explain."

Freya laughed mirthlessly from the sofa, where she had slumped down again. "As if you have a right to anything now."

Glaring, Rosalynn ignored the barb. "I love my brother, but I do not condone what he did. I am furious with him and that he has taken advantage of you and the bargain with your mother. I came tonight to warn you, actually, to stay away from him. He's writing a sequel to *The Green Door* that heavily features a young debutante who cannot refuse any of her suitors. I could see you've been spending more time with him, and I needed you to know he is just like every other man, and his ulterior motives are probably infinitely worse. He will utterly ruin you when his book is published."

Blood drained from my face and Rosalynn began to sway in front of me. I felt cool all over and registered a look of concern on her features before her hands gripped me, leading me to a chair.

"Are you all right?" she asked.

"Of course she's not all right," Freya snapped.

I leaned my head against the back of the padded chair, closing my eyes to cut off the swirling and wishing I could close my ears to their bickering as well. Cameron's articles were bad enough, but this…how could he? How could the man who had incited such warmth in my soul turn around and use me so ill?

"Enough," I said weakly.

They did not hear. The arguing mounted until I could not

take it any longer and I sat up quickly, squashing the urge to smack both of them. "I said enough!"

They both paused, turning to me. I rubbed the weariness from my eyes and tried to sit up tall. The blood had returned to my head, for I did not quite feel so dizzy and faint. But to say I was well would be an overstatement.

"This arguing is not helping anyone. And there is a ball on the other side of the corridor, so I suggest we each take a few deep breaths and go find our mothers."

"I came alone," Freya said.

"I came with Tarquin."

I looked at Freya. "You came alone? No chaperone at all?"

She shrugged. "Father is away and Mama was unwell. I planned to slip in and speak to you and then leave directly."

"Probably for the best," Rosalynn agreed. "You do not want to be caught alone."

Freya speared her with a glare. "I care not for my reputation."

"Apparently."

Exasperated, I said, "Please, *enough*! This is not good. This is not us."

They both had the grace to look slightly ashamed. I cleared my throat. If anyone in the room had the right to be furious, it was me. And I certainly was, just not with either of them. "Tomorrow, Hatchards at noon?"

Freya raised her eyebrows. "After all of that, you want to go to a bookstore?"

"I need a reasonable excuse to leave the house and a store my Mother will not insist on accompanying me to."

They both nodded in understanding. After we all agreed, Rosalynn unlocked the door and we slipped back into the deserted corridor. Freya snuck away and when I made for the ballroom Rosalynn stopped me, pulling at my arm.

"You must know I did everything I could."

I had a hard time believing that since she did not even tell me when she learned the news. Her eyes were remorseful, but they did not erase the past. I wondered how much she knew about my courtship—if it could even be called that, now that I knew it was false—with her brother, and if she had believed me to be falling in love as much as I had believed it. A pang sliced my heart and I chose to file it away to consider at a later time. I was afraid if I thought much on it now then I would fall apart at the Nelsons' ball, which would not do me any favors.

"Where is he?" I asked instead. Lord Tarquin had not escorted her a single time the entire Season up until this ball.

"Something came up. He's not here."

"You know he has been courting me, though?"

"Yes." She stood taller. "And I tried to warn you that he is selfish just like every other man. Why do you think I shoved you into him at the card party? I was trying to show you his less charming side. He would not have made you happy, Elsie," she spat. "He is not different than the rest."

Evidently.

My heart broke again with every word she spoke. Hadn't she hurt me enough? Why did she feel the need to twist the knife her brother placed in my back? I walked away from her, into the crush of warm bodies with overly intricate hair and cloying perfume. I circled the room until I found my mother, the look of surprise on her face evidence that I looked unwell.

Leaning forward, she whispered, "Is it the rumors? How bad is it?"

I weighed my options and then spoke the truth, considering my heart, my ideals, and my reputation.

"I fear I shall never recover."

CHAPTER 39

Arriving at Hatchards before noon gave me plenty of time to pretend to browse the shelves and consider what I was going to say. I had been awake all night tossing between bitterness, anger, and despair, and I had yet to settle on a solitary emotion. While a small part of me hoped to see Cameron so I could tell him precisely how I felt, I was quite positive I should utterly break if I had to face him so soon, the betrayal still fresh and raw.

Freya appeared first and we escaped to a far corner above stairs where we could speak and not be overheard.

"Do you think Rosalynn will come?" she asked.

I lifted a shoulder. "I hope so."

Freya shook her head, her red curls bouncing. "I am not sure I can ever forgive her."

I wanted to ask why, but Rosalynn came up the stairs then, her face ashy and drawn as though she had seen a ghost.

"What is it?" I asked, afraid.

She shook her head, her voice soft and thin. "I don't even know how to say this. I am not sure I can speak the words aloud."

Concern filled me; something was gravely wrong. Selfishly, my first thought was that the second book Cameron wrote had been released before I had time to get out of London, but her eyes indicated something far more severe and I pushed the thought away.

"Do you need to sit down?" Freya asked.

Nodding, Rosalynn allowed us to lead her to a chair. "It is my brother," she said quietly, her eyes staring into the distance behind us. "There was a duel. This morning."

I looked to Freya, unsure if I had heard correctly. Hoping I had not heard her correctly.

"Your brother?" Freya asked, speaking the words my mouth could not form.

Rosalynn nodded. "The other man was unharmed and taken into custody. But my brother did not make it."

"Rosie," Freya said gently, her earlier anger forgotten. "Which brother?"

That seemed to startle her from her stupor. She looked between us. "Geoffrey."

Guilt pierced me at my profound relief. I glanced once at her sorrowful eyes and knew immediately she was devastated. He was the oldest brother, set to inherit the dukedom one day, and had been growing more and more angry and autocratic like his father. But regardless of his tyrannical behavior, he was still her brother.

I wrapped my arms around Rosalynn and pulled her into an embrace, pleased when Freya joined us. Soon Rosalynn was wracked with sobs, her body heaving while she dampened my shoulder, venting sorrow and grief.

We sat that way for quite some time, until the tears dried up and Rosalynn pulled away, using her handkerchief to wipe her nose and dry her eyes.

"I must go shopping," she said, surprising me. "I do not own a single thing in black."

"I can help," Freya said, shocking me further.

I glanced between them. It did not matter what mistakes we had made or secrets we had kept. When it truly mattered, we would always be there for one another. We sat in the book store and listened to Rosalynn share stories about her brother. Some we had heard before, like when he taught her to ride her first pony or showed her the hidden door underneath the stairway, and others she hadn't before shared, like when they hid on the roof and dropped spoonfuls of pudding onto unsuspecting servants.

My traitorous mind wondered where Cameron was and if he was receiving the support and comfort he needed as well. But I shoved the thoughts away, reminding myself that the Cameron I thought I knew was not the man he truly was. I turned my attention to rubbing Rosalynn's back and focusing on her stories.

When we finally stood to go, she looked weary but resolute.

She was going to be fine.

Rosalynn's carriage rolled away down the street and Freya watched it go, an unreadable expression on her face. She had gone from furious to supportive so quickly that I wondered where the negative energy went and whether she was merely shoving it aside to access at a later time.

"I suppose I should tell you," she said, pulling me from my thoughts. "It shall become common knowledge soon enough."

"Whatever are you speaking of?"

She turned to walk down the street, and I followed her, glancing over my shoulder to see Molly trailing behind us.

"Do you remember the man from *The Green Door*, I believe he was called Julius, who had a secret family in France?"

I nodded, unsure of where this was leading.

"Well," she said, sighing. "That is my father."

I halted mid-step. She could not have said what I thought I heard. "Pardon me?"

"It's true, Elsie. Mama discovered it a few weeks ago. She found some letters in a hidden drawer in Father's desk."

A few pedestrians passed by us, and I waited until we were alone again before speaking. "Was that when you began to pull away?"

Her nose crinkled up and she looked thoughtful. "I suppose. The secret was alarming, and I was so worried the truth would come out at any moment. I've been a nervous wreck."

"But it did not."

"It did actually, only yesterday. We received a caller that was hoping for a confirmation that Father was indeed the man from the book. It will make the rounds eventually. Mother is beside herself, so I could not convince her to leave home last night for the ball. And Father…well, ironically, he is off on business, which we have come to understand is what he terms visiting his other family."

That explained why Mr. Hurst was away so frequently. It also explained her withdrawn behavior of late. I had no idea what to say to Freya to comfort her.

"What will you do?" I asked.

"Mama wants to leave London, but we will not go home. She says she cannot bear to be there when my father returns. She has mentioned going to stay with her sister in Yorkshire, but I'm not sure I could handle all of my cousins." She shot me a wry smile. "My aunt has six boys."

"And Yorkshire is so far away. Come stay with me."

"That is kind of you, but nothing is set in stone quite yet. For all I know, my mother will grow a backbone and face my father head-on."

I gave her a disbelieving look. "And what would you have her do if she faced him?"

"Tell him to leave. He can go live with his other family in France and leave us the house and income to sustain us. He has been an absentee father my entire life, and now I know why. Part of me is relieved to have an explanation. But most of me is more determined than ever to never marry. You think you know someone, and then they turn around and do something like this."

I understood the sentiment entirely. Smiling, I tried for humor. "Poor Major Heybourne."

She widened her eyes. "Never say so. The man cannot take a hint! I have been straightforward with him from day one."

I linked my arm through hers and began walking back toward my carriage. "Can you blame him for falling so madly in love with you, though?"

She smiled reluctantly. "I suppose not. I am rather extraordinary, aren't I?"

We reached the end of the street in silence and I offered her a ride home, to which she refused. "But where is your maid?" I asked.

"I did not bring one."

I tried to temper my shock. It was one thing to arrive alone to a ball, but it was quite another thing to go out without a maid or a footman. "Does your mother know?"

Freya rolled her eyes. "She cannot tell whether it is day or night from all of her hysterics. She has no idea where I am and neither does she care. Her world fell apart, and she cannot even breathe without wondering whether I am legitimate. I've had to hide away these last weeks to avoid her obsessive hunting."

"Hunting?"

Freya smiled, though her eyes were flat, void of emotion. "For evidence. She will not sleep until she discovers whether her marriage was first or second."

Because if Mrs. Hurst was the second wife, then that would mean their marriage was invalid. Which, in turn, meant Freya would be illegitimate. I understood now, and my heart ached for the trauma Freya was facing.

I picked up both of her hands, willing her to see the sincerity in my eyes. "Do not leave London without telling me. Please write to me before you go."

She agreed, and I watched her walk away, a self-possessed gait full of confidence that I could never have feigned in the face of such conflict. But Freya was strong, and she was proving her fortitude and independence in droves.

"Wait!" I called before she could get far. "Didn't Lord Cameron tell us at that musicale that the man with a hidden family was Mr. Harrison?"

She turned, her eyebrows pulled together softly. "Yes, it was something like that."

"Then who is Mr. Harrison?" I asked, admitting I did not know to whom he referred at the musicale, and I still had yet to meet a Mr. Harrison since. It was not so strange at the time, for I had not been in town long and did not know many people.

Had he been casting us off the scent so we wouldn't discover Freya's secret?

Freya shrugged. "I haven't the faintest."

CHAPTER 40

I returned home to find my bedchamber in utter chaos. Clothes were strewn about, my trunks opened with items spilling onto the floor. The dressing table was littered with my basic necessities, jewelry lining the edge of the bureau.

If this was the work of a thief, then they were a very thorough thief to be sure.

Molly stepped from the wardrobe with my white and coral gown draped over her arm and I relaxed. At least my belongings weren't being stolen.

"Molly, what is going on?"

She paused, her eyes round and innocent. She clearly did not want to speak, but I looked at her, unwavering, and she relented. "I am packing your belongings, miss."

"We are leaving?"

She nodded, her eyebrows drawing together apologetically. "As soon as tomorrow, I believe."

I was stunned. That was entirely too fast. How would the servants at home even have time to prepare for us again?

"But that is too quick." I had just left my friends, but I had not said goodbye. And there was Aunt Georgina, and Coco. Not to mention Freya's distress and Rosalynn's grief. No. I simply could not leave yet.

I spun in the doorway and marched to Mother's dressing room. It was disheveled and teeming with maids packing away her belongings, too, though much less messy than my own.

"Where is my mother?" I asked.

The older of the maids turned to me in surprise. "She is in the drawing room, miss."

I raced down the stairs and into the drawing room, annoyed to find both of my parents placidly sipping tea on the sofa.

"We cannot go," I said, my chest heaving with indignation.

They looked to me, surprise plastered across both of their faces.

Mother regained herself swiftly. "It is settled. We will go home, ride out the scandal and come back next year and try again."

The idea of starting over with the scent of scandal about me was disturbing and left me queasy. "I cannot go," I said weakly. "Freya is—"

"Illegitimate," Mother finished, her eyebrow raised smugly.

I tried to cover my shock. Word had spread rapidly.

"No," I said emphatically. "At least, no one knows for certain. And can Mrs. Hurst really be blamed for her husband's deceit?"

"They pulled the wool over all of our eyes."

I could not believe what I was hearing. "Mother, how could you say that? We are living in our own sphere of false rumors and exaggerated scandal. How can you sit there and find humor in others' pain?"

She did not look the least bit chagrined, and I was disturbed to think I was related to such blatant disregard and superficiality. I stood tall, clasping my hands in front of me. It was time to make my declaration, and I was glad to have both of my parents' attention, regardless of my father's apparent lack of interest thus far. "I am going to remain in Town. If we are indeed leaving tomorrow then the Season for us has ended, and I can honestly say I have not rejected a single suitor, and I retain zero interest in any man."

I thought of Cameron and immediately hardened the wall around my heart. Mother hadn't said I could not have any feelings, she had said I must not have a single thread of *interest*. While my feelings for the man were raw and unclear at present—I did not know whether I would strangle him or simply walk away when and if I were to see him again—my interest in him had well and truly died a quick death upon learning of his deceit.

Father's face was a picture of confusion. "What the devil is she talking about?"

"The agreement," I said, looking to Mother to help me clarify.

Her eyes were focused on her embroidery and a hint of suspicion pooled in my gut.

"You know," I said with force, my hands gripping the back of the sofa I stood behind. "The bargain Mother made with me if I accept every invitation for this entire Season and do not find a husband, that I would be free to take my dowry and do with it whatever I wish."

The room was thick with silence. Mother's needle stilled halfway through the fabric. Father looked dumbstruck.

Suddenly he began to laugh, the sound loud and maniacal and causing me to startle. "What dowry?" he asked, laughing harder.

"What do you mean?" Mother asked sharply.

"It's gone," he said, his laughter dying. He swallowed. "All of it. The dowry, everything. Why do you think we are beating a hasty retreat?"

I could not help the tears that pooled in my eyes. He could not mean it, surely. He could not be implying that the gaming clubs he had spent every night in for the majority of our time in

London had swallowed up my independence, the money I was going to use to live off of for the rest of my life?

I turned to my mother, her face pale and drawn. She looked as sick as I felt. "That does not change the bargain. You promised, Mother. I get to have my independence, and I am not leaving."

"There was no bargain," Father thundered, getting to his feet. "I never heard a peep of this ridiculous hen-brained scheme and I surely am not going to endorse it now. You are going to marry, and you must marry well if we are to recoup our losses."

"I am not a pawn to do your bidding," I defended. "I am a person."

His ruddy cheeks jiggled as he spoke. "You are my child. You will do as I say."

We squared off, our faces mirroring anger and stubborn perseverance.

Billington came to the door, and Mother stood. "What is it?" she demanded.

"Miss Cox has a visitor. Shall I say she is not home for company?"

"Yes."

"No!" I said, turning to Mother. It could be Freya or Rosalynn, both of whom needed me. "Allow me to say my good-byes if you are going to tear me away so suddenly." I did not admit I was still trying to come up with a scheme to remain in Town. I was desperately grasping for whatever I could.

Mother looked to Father, thunder in his face belying his words. "Say your goodbyes, then. But do not think for one moment that you are going to get out of this. I say we are leaving, and that is final."

He knew me perhaps better than I had given him credit for. He stormed from the room, Mother glancing to me sharply before following him away, no doubt to control the damage however she could.

I nodded to Billington, who did not relay any surprise that he may have felt over the dispute he had witnessed. I stepped around the sofa, slumping on the cushion, my head falling into my hands. What was I going to do?

The door opened behind me, and I was surprised to find Lord McGregor, tall and handsome, taking up the bulk of the doorway. His hair was disheveled, his eyes weary.

"Oh, sir. I had not expected—" I swallowed. He was distressed, of that I was certain. "Please, come in."

He left the door ajar as a proper gentleman ought to do and came to sit on the chair opposite me. He seemed to read my face for a moment, and we sat in silence.

"I have come to ask for your assistance," he said.

I tried to remain impassive, but confusion was at the forefront of my blend of emotions.

He cleared his throat, leveling me with a beseeching look. "May I speak plainly?"

"Please," I said.

He ran a hand through his dark red hair, disheveling it further. It struck me at that moment that he was likely grieving the loss of his friend.

"Is it about Lord Stallsbury?" I asked, hoping to lead him into a conversation.

"No. Well, partly, I suppose. It's Rosalynn and her dratted stubbornness."

We sat in the quiet, and I let him form his thoughts. I was not about to pretend I understood his meaning. Of course, I knew her stubbornness well, but I did not think that was entirely what he meant.

"She is grieving for her brother now," he said quietly. "Of course, we all are. It is horrible and sad, and she will be forced to endure a few months of mourning before she can marry."

Did he not know, then? Surely Lord McGregor, close as he was to the family, must know about Rosalynn's pact. She did not try to hide her desire to never marry. In fact, she was the most vocal of the lot of us.

"I am sorry," I said, delivering a small smile. "I do not follow."

"Do you not?" He looked surprised. "I had thought she told you everything."

Well, that stung. "Apparently not."

"We were engaged," he said. "It was not made public as she needed to speak to her mother first, who is off at their estate at present. She wanted to discuss it with her mother before taking my case to her father."

"Did she think her father would deny you?" I asked, unwilling to fully believe what I had heard, but trying to play along. Lord McGregor must have misunderstood. There was no other explanation I was willing to readily believe.

"No." He rubbed his hand over his face. "I am like a son to him. Nothing would have made the duke happier."

"I thought we were speaking plainly," I admonished, "and I am more lost now than when you first arrived. Lord McGregor, Rosalynn is my closest friend and I have known she will never marry as long as I've known her. What you are trying to tell me is very difficult to believe."

"I see," he said. "Then she failed to tell you that I have been in love with her these past few years."

"Yes."

"And she did not tell you she has struggled with feelings for me, also?"

I shook my head, the sincerity in his eyes forcing me to believe his honesty. At least, that he honestly believed what he was saying to be true. "No, she did not tell me such a thing."

"Then perhaps you cannot help me after all." His shoulders sunk, defeated.

I shrugged. It was hard to know, without understanding the problem. "If you share your dilemma, then I may."

He glanced up and I winced slightly at the desolation in his eyes. "Rosalynn refuses now to move forward. She says with the mourning ahead of her it is vulgar to announce an engagement at present. I believe it could be the very thing her family needs to bring some light and hope into their lives."

"Their whole worlds have shifted," I said gently. "They lost the heir, their brother, their son. Lord Tarquin alone now has to come to terms with becoming a duke when he had previously not been required to face that responsibility, and the duke must shift his direction to another son. None of their worlds will ever be the same. Perhaps if you give them time to come to terms with the changes, then Rosalynn will be open to discussing the issue again."

"How selfish I've been," he said, shaking his head.

He stood and paced to the end of the room and back, and I watched him move in agitation, considering him in a new light. It was true he had marked attention for Rosalynn from the beginning, but I had only imagined that was because of their families' long-standing relationship. I had never looked for further feelings between either of them, but now it clicked into place.

"When you were beginning to court me," I said, blushing with realization. "You did not wish for a connection."

The side of his mouth lifted in a smile. "I was quite interested to know you better. I believed if I won you over then you would aid me in convincing Rosalynn to forgo that wretched pact."

So when I had come on to him, it scared him away unnecessarily. It was almost humorous now. Almost.

"I apologize. I was of no help."

He shrugged and resumed his pacing. "It is of little consequence now." He crossed to me and bowed. "Thank you for listening to the ramblings of a lovesick fool."

"I am honored," I said, standing beside him. "Now, please

tell me what she needs right now. Do I go to her, or leave her be?"

"I cannot know," he said, shrugging helplessly. "I tried to go to her and I fear I only made her more distressed."

I chuckled. "Yes, but I will not be trying to convince her to come out with an engagement she is not ready to yet acknowledge." If indeed, she was going to acknowledge it at all.

He smiled wryly and took his leave. I watched the open doorway for some time, weighing my options. When I finally came to a conclusion, I stood quickly and moved toward the drawing room door. I had to put my plan into action before I could talk myself out of it.

CHAPTER 41

The bargain had ended, and thus my obligations with it. I did not seek my mother out and request permission to call on Rosalynn. I had, however, informed Billington of my destination in case they needed to locate me. But whether Father wanted to agree to it or not, I was going to gain my independence one way or another. Mother had promised, and I was not about to let that go unchallenged.

The front door of the Nichols' home was shrouded in black, and I swallowed nervously before stepping inside. The butler led me to the music room, and I walked behind him, both hoping and fearing I would run into Lord Cameron. My mind traveled back to the time I had come to the music room to see Rosalynn and passed Lord Cameron in the corridor, calling orders to his servants.

I had disliked him then; I loathed him now.

Rosalynn was seated at the pianoforte, head down and arms wrapped around her midsection. The house was eerily quiet like we were the only two people there.

"Rosie?" I prompted softly when I had stood beside her for some time without any response.

She jerked her head up, her tear-stained cheeks glistening in the soft afternoon light. "Elsie."

She scooted over on the bench, and I sat beside her, my arm coming around her shoulders and pulling her closer. Her head came to rest on my shoulder. We sat in the silence for some time before she straightened up, pulling a handkerchief from her sleeve to wipe her eyes. I had not made a personal decision to be done with secrets only to keep another one. I waited for her to compose herself before I spoke.

"I had a visit from Lord McGregor."

She stilled beside me. "Oh."

"And I learned some interesting things." I promptly added, "From his perspective."

She was given a way out. If she wanted to deny anything, then I had created the opportunity for her to explain why Lord McGregor had thought such ludicrous things.

Deflating, Rosalynn would not look me in the eye. "It was not official," she said.

Well, that answered that question. Lord McGregor had told me the truth of their engagement. Not that I had really thought he'd made it all up. But Rosie had always been so firm in her convictions. I had wondered. A ruse on his part made more sense to me than the truth.

"I could not bring myself to tell you and Freya. I am such a hypocrite."

In a sense, she absolutely was. But I was not about to say so. "Did you think we would be angry?"

"I did not know what to think," she said. "It all happened so fast. I have struggled with my feelings for him for years now, and when he launched a campaign to prove to me that he was different from the others, I believed he would fail."

"But he didn't," I said gently.

"No," she laughed. "He most definitely did not. He won my heart instead."

Tears trickled down her cheeks once more. "I worried so deeply that not only had I set you and Freya up for a life of loneliness but that you would despise me for finding happiness myself with a man."

"I could never despise you," I said. "Both Freya and I made our own choices. I will not deny that you were quite the force to be reckoned with, even at twelve, but you did not compel me to drink that horrible Promise Juice."

Rosalynn burst into laughter, jolting me with surprise. I could not help but join in after a moment, imagining the three of us huddled in the chilly attic of our antiquated school, drinking globs of food and calling it juice.

"I sort of did force you, but it is kind of you to say otherwise. And it was horrible, wasn't it?" she said through a watery giggle.

"What was in it anyway? Besides stew, if I remember correctly."

She turned wide eyes on me. "I shall never divulge that information."

"Oh come now," I laughed. "You cannot seriously mean that."

She grinned, and I found that perhaps it was better if I did not know. I leaned my elbows on the edge of the pianoforte, resting my forehead on my knuckles.

Her voice sounded disembodied. "I spent so much time worrying that he was luring me in with his charms, only to steal my freedom and force me into the lonely existence my mother suffers from."

"But how do you know that won't be the case?"

A tender smile tilted her lips. "I suppose I don't. I can only trust him, and I love him enough to give it a chance."

"What happened to all men are pigs?"

Rosalynn laughed. "At one time I really thought that. But he talked me out of it."

It was shocking how many things were happening around me that I had not been aware of. I was saddened by her lack of trust in me, but I suppose there was nothing to say for it. Rosalynn did not trust easily. She built up a wall that protected her from her mother's standoffishness and her brothers' and father's brutality. If she made the decision to trust Lord McGregor, then I supposed there was nothing for it; I simply had to trust her.

Rosalynn sighed. "Freya, you, and I have all had negative experiences with men. None of us have fathers we truly admire. But unfair laws aside, not all men are equally good or bad in the same way that not all women are equal. Look at Cecily Hapworth and how she treated you in school after you stood up for her. It was unfair of us to recognize that some women are better people than others, but not to give men the same understanding."

"True." She made increasingly valid points. Cecily did not care that I defended her. When the situation was reversed, she did not do the same for me. But not all women were like that. I reached over and squeezed Rosalynn's hand. "I must wish you joy."

Her eyes were distressed, and I wanted to soothe away the sorrow. "We are going to wait to announce it."

I nodded, knowing. "Against Lord McGregor's wishes."

"Because I do not think it is the right time. I must still speak with Freya."

"And your mother?"

Confusion clouded her brow. "Oh," she said, smiling. "No, I only gave him that excuse because I wished to speak to you and Freya first, but I needed to gain courage. If I used my mother as an excuse, it was both reasonable and bought me enough time to decide for myself whether I was making the correct choice. It was plain to me that once my father was apprised of the situation it would happen regardless of my wishes. I could not give

Jack hope only to change my mind after. It would have devastated him."

Her eyes became soft when she spoke of him, and I knew. "You really, really love him."

"I do."

"Then I am behind you, whatever the outcome."

Rosalynn thanked me, and the tension eased that had built in my shoulders over the previous few days. I watched her cross to the rope pull and call for some tea before joining her on the sofa. The maid brought in a service and left the door ajar, and I found myself staring into the distance when a figure walked through the corridor, paused, and then stepped back to stand in the doorway.

My heart immediately plummeted to my stomach. I had thought my first reaction to seeing Cameron after learning the truth would be anger or hatred. I was utterly mortified when my eyes sought his chocolate brown ones and my body was filled with hurt and sorrow.

Rosalynn stopped adding sugar to my tea and crossed to the door. She said something softly to her brother and closed it, and I felt instantly bereft.

I wanted to run to the door and throw it open, to fall into his arms and comfort him over his loss. And I was irritated with myself for those feelings. I accepted the tea and drank it absently, listening to the silence while we sat companionably. It was enough for her that I was simply there, which was all I could give at present. I waited long enough that Lord Cameron could not still be waiting in the corridor before I stood to leave.

"My maid is packing at present," I said, regretfully. "I do not suppose I shall see you again. But please write to me, and I will try to make it back to London soon."

"We intend to leave as well, but I will keep you apprised of my situation."

She did not ask about the bargain or the cottage we had

planned to buy. Her mind was filled enough at present and I did not blame her, glad not to have to explain how horribly our plan had failed. She did not need to know of my father's reckless gambling or my mother's lies. She had enough on her plate.

She walked me out, and I embraced her near the door, glad to have mended our fractured relationship.

Cameron was waiting outside, leaning languidly against the railing at the bottom of the stairs. The sun was still shining, though beginning to make its descent. My breath caught when the magnitude of Cameron's rugged handsomeness hit me in a wave. His hair was messy, as if he'd run his hands through it repeatedly, and his eyes were downcast, tired.

I resolved to treat him with the dignity and respect that set us apart, for I was not the false floozy he had painted me to be in his wretched articles.

"Elsie," he said beseechingly.

Every decision I previously made went out the metaphorical window when he deigned to use my Christian name without proper leave, after all he had put me through.

I marched directly up to him and spoke with all of the fire in my being. "You forget yourself, sir. You have neither the right nor the privilege of addressing me so, and I beg you will consider our situations and take yourself off."

I stormed toward my carriage, the coachman opening the door and assisting me inside. My chest heaved in indignation but I did not feel better for the words I had said. I resolved to look away from him while I waited for the coachman to climb onto his perch, but faltered at the last moment and caught stricken, broken eyes that melted my anger and seized my heart.

The horses were prodded and we took off. I jumped to the other side of the coach, sidling to the window. I watched

Cameron's face until he disappeared from sight, aching over his grief-stricken, downturned face.

Had I been too hasty? I'd let my emotions govern me and hadn't even given him the chance to explain. Swallowing the bile rising in my throat, I felt the bitterness of regret.

He glanced up just before we turned down the street and caught my gaze. I feared that last fleeting look we shared would be burned into my mind for the remainder of my life.

CHAPTER 42

Father was gone. He had taken his horse and valet and rode out of Town earlier that morning. I had gone to Mother's dressing room shortly after, hoping Father's absence would make her more inclined to bend the rules, and I had been gratified by the agreement of one extra day.

I invited her along with me to bid Aunt Georgina farewell and she declined on the basis that she must oversee the remainder of the packing. I did not argue, for I knew Aunt Georgina would be equally grateful if she stayed away.

I stood in the foyer awaiting my carriage when a knock sounded at the front door. I waited a moment for Billington to see to it, but silence carried on, and when the knock came a second time, I pushed aside proper convention and opened it myself. I promptly shut it again when I came face to face with Cameron, a look of relief crossing his features before the door slammed against them. I had not expected to see him and I shook myself, opening the door again with a smile pasted on my face.

"Lord Cameron. May I help you?"

He seemed to see through my false cheer. I did not back down, but neither did I open the door further to let him inside.

"I had thought you would be gone by now. I hoped to speak with you."

I opened the door, and he stepped inside, closing it behind himself. I turned for the small morning parlor we had on the ground floor that we hardly used, and I knew would be void of people, if a little dusty.

I chose not to sit, walking to the center of the room and turning to face him, I clasped my hands in front of me and put on the bravest face I could conjure, mindful of Aunt Georgina's advice to feign courage if needs be. I was certainly feigning it now.

He stepped into the room, leaving the door ajar and removing his hat. He played with the brim in his fingers, spinning the hat slowly while his brown eyes tried to read my face. I hoped it was as impassive as I was trying to appear, for I was certain the boiling emotions within me would erupt shortly if we did not end this conversation soon. But after my rudeness the day before, I knew Cameron deserved a chance to explain himself.

His eyes were fixed on mine, his face solemn. "When I began to write those articles, I did not know I was going to fall in love with you."

Stunned silent, I took in his nervous form on the other side of the room and tried to make sense of his words. He stepped forward and placed his hat on the small table at the end of the sofa.

Clearing his throat, he said, "Ignorant that I was, I thought mentioning you in the papers would give you a boost in society. I believed I was doing you a favor, and you must understand that my actions were well-intentioned."

It made sense now, why Rosalynn was not mentioned during

the musicale despite her amazing performance and later outburst. He had been protecting her.

"Not everything you wrote was positive," I reminded him. "'Guffawing like a caged bird'? A mention in passing would have been a boost. The articles' utter obsession with me was marked attention. I was a target."

"I did not intend to focus so wholly on you," he said softly. I hated his soft words. I wanted anger and defense. I wanted a reason to vent my anger on him.

"So you accidentally wrote about me and nothing else?"

"You could say subconsciously. You stole my attention. I was captivated by you."

I shook my head. What a heap of rubbish.

He sighed, running a hand over his face. "I can see that you don't believe me. It took me quite some time to realize I was developing feelings for you. At first, I wrote about you because I knew your name and my man at the paper requested real stories about real socialites. I assumed mentioning one of Rosalynn's friends would be nice of me and Miss Hurst seemed off-putting. You, on the other hand, intrigued me."

"Is this an apology?" I begged. "You must see how much cause I have to be furious."

"Of course you have cause to be furious. I would be livid if I were in your shoes. When I realized how considerably you hated the articles, I tried to put a stop to it, I even refused to write for the paper at all. But all they did was assign my column to a different writer and tell him he needed to focus on you. That is when things started getting nasty."

"That was when they began harassing you, as well," I said, understanding.

He shot me a rueful smile. "That particular writer and I have never quite gotten along."

He was close now and I backed up, placing the sofa between us. "What about the book?"

"I told my publisher I was through and he would not be getting the manuscript of the sequel from me."

My eyebrow raised of its own accord. "Am I meant to simply believe you?"

"Yes," he said emphatically. "Can't you trust me? I would never purposely hurt you, Elsie."

"Do you not see that you already have? Never mind that my reputation is in shatters, you brought to light Mr. Hurst's other family, causing them unending trauma and questioning Freya's legitimacy. And you have ostracized Lord Fischer, to say nothing for countless others. That book was a horrible, horrible thing and I cannot love a man who would knowingly do that to so many people." I was crying now, my face distorting in frustration. "I am ashamed I read it, that I *enjoyed* it."

"You love me?"

"No." I said, my voice breaking on the lie. "How could I ever trust you again?"

Hurt washed over his face, and I swallowed the bile rising in my throat. I was sick to my stomach, and I wanted nothing more than for this conversation to end. It hurt too much to continue.

"I am leaving London," I said. "I don't expect to see you again."

It was a clear dismissal. But one he obviously chose to ignore.

"I refuse to leave things this way."

I shrugged. "You do not have a choice."

We faced one another. "What can I do? How can I prove I am sorry? That I love you enough to protect you always?"

I looked away, forcing myself not to falter at his pleading. "You can let me go."

My words seemed to slap him, his expression turning to one of surprise and hurt. He gathered himself together, placing his hat upon his head and making it to the door before he stopped, facing me with his hand resting on the wall. "I am sorry, Elsie."

He left, taking all the air from the room with him. I waited until the door shut before I crumpled to the floor, sobbing into my hands. I had gotten what I wanted, the chance to tell him how I felt. But somehow, again, it did not make me feel better as I had hoped it would.

"Whatever has gotten into you, Elsie?" Aunt Georgina asked. I continued to stroke Coco's fur, my eyes focusing on the chocolate brown of her coat that perfectly matched Cameron's eyes.

"Elsie," she said again, this time with more force.

"Yes?"

"What is distracting you so terribly?"

"I am sad to be leaving," I said.

Her eyes narrowed on me. "I do not doubt that, but that is not all. What has happened?"

I did not know how much to share. I could not give away Cameron's role as the writer of *The Green Door* without making him look terrible. Despite what I had said earlier, I did care for him. I only knew I could never trust him again.

"I discovered the author who wrote those horrible articles about me."

"Don't let that get you down," Aunt Georgina said with a disregarding wave of her hands. "Wendel is a pompous moron who escaped his own countrymen to be hated by ours."

"No, it wasn't Mr. Wendel, it was—"

She lifted her eyebrows and I wondered whether we were speaking of the same thing. She came out with the name so readily I could not help my growing suspicion. "How do you know that?" I asked instead.

"Because I have orchestrated gossip for the newspapers for years, darling. For payment, of course." She took a sip of tea, unbothered by the fact that she just admitted she threw her friends into the lion's den for money. "I did not do so for years without earning favors of my own. When they turned nasty, I knew Lord Cameron had ceased to write for them and I had to know who it was."

"You knew about Cameron?" And she'd known when the articles were no longer penned by his hand because of the severity of them. Aunt Georgina professed to understand his character by the gossip he would not share.

She scoffed. "Of course I knew about Lord Cameron."

"Well," I said, focusing on Coco's pouting eyes. "I did not."

The silence was thick until Aunt Georgina finally spoke. I could hear her grin through her words. "And I thought the rumors false. But you have fallen for him, haven't you?"

I was afraid to admit it aloud. "Yes. But it can never be. I could never trust him."

"Oh, pish," she said. "It has nothing to do with trust and everything to do with his intent. Did he set out to hurt you?"

"No, but—"

"Has he spread false rumors and lies about you?"

"Of course not, but—"

"Then what is there to be so angry about?"

I stared at her, smugly sitting in her golden armchair, and saw her differently. Could she really be so callous? "He *used* me. I happen to value integrity. I made a decision long ago that I couldn't marry, for it would be forcing me to give my power to a man. If I give that up now to the first man I have deep feelings for then what is it saying about my ability to stick to my ideals? How am I valuing myself if I readily disregard the ways he has hurt me?"

"It was not his idea," Aunt Georgina said. "Who do you think the busy Society matron was who entertained all of the witless victims?" She spread her arms out in indication.

So she really was so callous.

I stood to depart, forcing Coco to jump from my lap. "We are leaving in the morning, and I will miss you terribly." I stepped forward and kissed her cheek. I did not respect her anymore, but I still loved her. "I do not know when I shall return. I have many things to figure out first."

I was close to telling her that Father had lost all our money gambling but decided not to feed the gossip mill. It was a difficult thing to learn that I must guard myself in the future in what I said to Aunt Georgina.

"Come visit us the moment you return, darling. Coco and I shall miss you immensely."

I took my leave. I felt a lesser degree of hurt when I discovered Aunt Georgina knew who was behind everything than I had when learning of Cameron's role. It was evident that my feelings for him were not fleeting, for the pain only grew with time. The more I considered how I had hurt him with the things I said, the worse I felt. I would never be able to leave Town without first apologizing.

As my coachman handed me up into my carriage, I clasped my shaking hands together and said, "To Rosalynn's house, please."

CHAPTER 43

What had gotten into me? Was I sick in the head?

I waited in the Nichols' drawing room, pacing from the fireplace to the window and back fourteen times before the door opened and Cameron stepped inside.

He faced me, his brows drawn together and his hands clasped behind his back. He was distant, but I did not blame him. I would be cold, too, if the situation were reversed.

"I came to apologize," I said, my voice cracking. My cheeks bloomed and I glanced down, clearing my throat.

I looked to him again and he was still watching me from the doorway. I don't know what I expected, but I had hoped he would say something.

I took a deep breath and continued. "I have a right to be upset, but I should have extended you more grace." I glanced away, his piercing gaze causing me to rethink my being there. I had thought I would be bridging the gap and allowing us to part peacefully. This uncomfortable, tense exchange felt anything but peaceful.

I clasped my hands in front of me and then unclasped them again. "Cameron, I know it was forward of me to come here, but

I needed to apologize. I grieve for your loss, and I do not wish to add to your distress at this time. I wish to part as friends."

He seemed to be weighing something, his eyes flicking between me and the wall a few times before he said, "Wait here a moment?"

I nodded, and he left. Minutes passed and I found myself pacing again. I ran over the words I had said, trying to find what I was missing. But I could not place exactly what was bothering me. I was unsettled, and things between us were unfinished. By the time he returned carrying what looked like a stack of papers I had fully become a shaky, jittery mess.

He approached me directly, handing me the papers and stepping back.

I read the words written on the front page in his neat scrawl. "*The Liable Lady?*"

"My manuscript," he explained. "The sequel. Though it is unfinished."

I looked up to his clear brown eyes. "What am I meant to do with it?"

He shrugged. "Burn it? Read it? Toss it out the window for all I care."

I fanned the pages. "But you've worked so hard on this."

"I told you, I am done with that publisher. I refused to turn in this book and they are unwilling to work with me unless I write about society members."

"But what will you do?"

"I will figure something out."

He seemed so at ease with his decision. In fact, he seemed lighter in general. His dark hair was disheveled and bags under his eyes revealed undoubtedly sleepless nights, but he looked less haunted than he had that morning.

The manuscript was heavy in my hands, carrying the weight of our disagreement. "You did not mention that *The Green Door* was my aunt's idea."

"Does it matter where the idea originated if I was the one who put ink to paper?"

I considered his words. Yes, it mattered to me. It helped me believe that Cameron was not the orchestrator of so much painful gossip. He had written it, and by such action was not innocent. But he was merely the wordsmith to Aunt Georgina's cunning.

When he understood how deeply I hated the articles, he had tried to put a stop to it. When I revealed my anger and hurt, he took the brunt of it instead of passing the blame on to Aunt Georgina. When his publisher wanted the book he wrote about me, he refused to give it to them. Cameron was a good man.

The room was quiet, but my thoughts were loud, screaming at me that I would be an idiot to let this man walk out of my life. My aunt might not have been apologetic in the least, but Cameron had been. He did not intentionally ruin Freya's life, or anyone else's, for that matter.

My breath left me in a relaxed, smooth motion, and my shoulders released the tension they had been holding on to. Holding Cameron's gaze, I wanted nothing more than to throw the papers in my hands aside and wrap him in an embrace.

"Aunt Georgina does not have a green door," I said, an afterthought.

"Have you never noticed the daisies painted on her drawing room door?"

"Oh," I said, understanding. He had taken liberties with his use of the word "green."

I stepped toward the low burning fire. "You keep the fire lit on warm days?"

"Just today," he said, a delicious grin tilting his lips. Had he already been planning on burning the manuscript?

I dropped the papers into the flames and watched them ignite, burning quickly in a large, warm flame and then dying out rapidly. Mesmerized by the flames, I failed to notice Cameron come to stand behind me.

"I know I do not have the right to ask for your forgiveness," he said softly, his voice so close it sent shivers down my neck. "But I will work diligently for the rest of my life to prove to you I am sincere in my affection. I will devote myself to you if you let me."

I turned to him, the fire reflecting in his eyes and igniting my soul. I loved him, irrevocably, there was no denying it. I could not help but appreciate the hope displayed on his face, and stepped forward, unsure of what to say.

Words failing me, I nodded slowly.

His grin widened before his arms came around me, crushing me to him, his lips finding mine swiftly. Reason fled, and I lost myself in the warmth that engulfed me. Love and affection wrapped around my wounded heart like a bandage, healing. His kiss was earnest at first, as though he was starving and I was the manna, but slowly morphed into something achingly tender. When he pulled away, I felt the lack at once, tempered slightly by his forehead resting upon mine.

"May I call on your father?"

"You are in mourning, sir," I reminded him.

"Drat," he muttered before leaning down to kiss me slowly, the sorrow in his eyes evidence of his grief. "I suppose we must wait an appropriate amount of time. Must you go to Kent?"

"Yes," I answered, the pain in his eyes striking my heart. "I leave in the morning. But we can write." I smiled, stepping out of his arms. "And if my plan works, I shall be back in town shortly."

CHAPTER 44

SIX MONTHS LATER

The carriage pulled to a swift stop, and I did not wait for the coachman to hop down and assist me before flinging the door open and letting myself onto the street. The door of the house in front of me swung open, and I smiled at the butler before making my way to the drawing room I knew well, the smell of ginger biscuits wafting from the tea tray and filling my senses. Freya noticed me first and jumped up, clutching me in an embrace that knocked the air clean out of me.

"I've missed you," she said, stepping back and looking into my face. She looked happier, her curly, copper hair piled loosely on her head and her gown a sage green, no longer wearing the light colors that washed out her pale skin.

I stepped around her to kiss Aunt Georgina on the cheek, Coco yapping at my heels.

"All right, you mongrel." Chuckling, I leaned down to pick

up Coco, carrying her to the sofa and taking a seat. Freya came to sit beside me, reaching over to pet Coco behind the ears. I looked at her shrewdly. "You seem content."

Freya grinned, glancing to Aunt Georgina. "We are. It has been gratifying to be free of the constraints Mama placed on me. I hadn't realized how much she leaned on me to make up for my father's absence until we were separated. But she is doing well with her sister in Yorkshire, and I have planned to go out and visit them next month."

"That is good to hear. And she isn't causing you too much trouble?" I asked Aunt Georgina.

"She barks in the night at times, but we manage."

Laughing, I exchanged a look with Freya. "I wasn't talking about Coco."

"Oh, well. Yes, Freya has been a superb house guest. I had not thought before that I would enjoy a companion, but it turns out it has been quite fun having Miss Hurst around." She rearranged her shawl, looking down at the rings on her fingers. "I imagine this is what having a daughter would feel like."

Freya grinned. "Only better, because you did not have to bother with me when I was an obnoxious little munchkin." She turned to me. "Aunt Georgina's words, not mine."

I laughed and accepted a cup of tea. "Do you mind having me for a while?"

Aunt Georgina sipped her tea. "We have looked forward to it immensely."

I gave her a knowing look. "And can I be sure my secrets are safe while I am under this roof?"

It was a condition of my coming to visit. I had written it playfully, but I meant every word. I would not be fodder for gossip any longer, and she had agreed.

I came to the personal conclusion that it was not necessary for me to be unwed to stand up for myself and what I felt was right.

"Have you heard from Rosie?" I asked.

Freya nodded, chewing a bite of ginger biscuit. "She announced her engagement to Jack, and they will wed following Michaelmas. She and Lord McGregor both felt it was proper to wait the full three months out of respect for Geoffrey's death."

I eyed her but she did not seem uncomfortable. I imagined us, young girls in the attic at school planning our Sisterhood of Deserving Females, and considered how much had changed.

"Lord Cameron stopped by yesterday," Freya said.

"Oh, did he?" I tried to sound unaffected, and I was sure I had failed. I had not seen him since the day I had apologized in his home, but we spent the last six months corresponding via the post—made respectable through our engagement, of course—and I had gotten to know him on a level that went beyond childhood stories and favorite Christmas carols.

He shared his dreams with me, and I shared my storytelling with him. It was with mutual respect that we discussed the dilemma of my father losing the bulk of our money and Cameron's loss of an easy publishing relationship. If we were going to wed when he was ready to come out of mourning, then we would need to know each other well. I was not going to agree to a marriage with a man I fancied, only to realize later that it was not love.

Though, I had my suspicions this was the real thing. I was choosing to make it the real thing.

"I am exhausted," I said, rising from my seat. "By now Molly will surely be finished unpacking. Am I so very boring if I retire early?"

"Yes," Aunt Georgina said crisply. "But never mind us. I suppose we will have months to catch up with you."

I grinned. "Yes, you shall, you lucky old biddy."

The London summer was notorious for its stuffy heat, made worse by the condensed population and close buildings. That summer, however, failed to see the sun unaccompanied by clouds. Rooms were darkened due to the overcast sky and fires built up to warm against the unrelenting chill. I dressed in my warmest gown, arming myself with a shawl and thick gloves.

Making my way to the breakfast room, I stopped mid-step in the doorway when my gaze landed on Cameron, seated beside Freya and cheerfully stuffing his mouth with seared tomatoes.

He caught my eye and dropped his fork, the sound of it clattering against his plate sure to warn the room of my arrival. Freya rose at once, squeezing my hand as she left the room, the footman close behind her.

I stood rooted to the spot, the knowledge that I was going to see Cameron at some point during the day insufficient to prepare me for the handsome, dark-haired man standing before me. I could not help the grin that plastered itself to my face and refused to subside.

"You are here," he said softly.

I chuckled, dipping into a playful curtsy.

He came around the table then, sweeping me into an embrace, burying his face in my freshly arranged hair. "I have missed you," he whispered into my ear.

"Six months is entirely too long," I agreed. "Though your letters were marvelous, I find I would prefer those conversations in person."

He pulled back, grinning. "I couldn't agree more. In fact," he slid his arm around my back and led me to a chair, picking up the plate and piling it with entirely too much food from the sideboard. "I have informed my family of our engagement, and my mother insists you come and spend the holidays with us."

I scrunched up my nose. "I discussed traveling with Freya to see her mother in Yorkshire then."

"Then come after. We can have you visit for the holidays—or after—and then bring you to London for the Season."

I leaned back slightly in my chair. "You have thought this through, sir."

"I have thought of little else." His smile was boyish, and I could not restrain an answering grin.

"I had an idea," he said, turning back to his plate of food and taking a bite before continuing. I could sense his nerves were heightened. "And I took the liberty of going to a publisher with it."

"Go on."

"Well, I seem to have a knack for writing. And you have a talent for storytelling."

I felt the heat of a blush warm my cheeks, and I bit a sausage to give me something else to focus on. I had taken to writing Cameron little stories and adding them to the ends of my letters. When he professed his love for them, I had told him to not get used to it, since it was the creation of the story that I had found so entertaining and not the bother of writing them down.

"I shared a basic outline of your ongoing storytelling ability and sold him on the idea. If we choose to move forward, then we can send him our manuscript upon completion. He has promised to give it serious consideration."

"You sold my Jane and Billy story to a publisher?"

"Pending your approval, yes."

I was speechless. I had not ever considered the concept that I could create something other people would be willing to read. Well, people aside from Cameron, at least.

"Have I overstepped?" he asked suddenly, taking my hand in both of his. "I was very clear that we would be a partnership and I would need your express endorsement before moving forward."

"Do you think that will grow tiresome, Cameron?" I asked

softly, tilting my head in sympathy. "I do not want to spend a lifetime with you worrying that I am feeling properly respected. I should not be happy if you came to resent me."

"Can you not see that by caring about you it is natural for me to place your needs above my own? I am not concerned about proving to you that I will not control you, Elsie. I am simply concerned about your happiness. I don't fret about your need to feel respected; I simply respect you."

He leaned over and placed a light kiss on my lips, grinning while he pulled away. "I love you. Every part of you. From now until forever."

"Oh, very well," I sighed, contented. "I suppose I shall help you write a book."

ABOUT THE AUTHOR

Kasey Stockton is a staunch lover of all things romantic. She doesn't discriminate between genres and enjoys a wide variety of happily ever afters. Drawn to the Regency period at a young age when gifted a copy of *Sense and Sensibility* by her grandmother, Kasey initially began writing Regency romances. She has since written in a variety of genres, but all of her titles fall under clean romance. A native of northern California, she now resides in Texas with her own prince charming and their three children. When not reading, writing, or binge-watching chick flicks, she enjoys running, cutting hair, and anything chocolate.

Made in the USA
Coppell, TX
04 May 2025

49001616R00173